THE GENTLE ART OF
FORTUNE HUNTING

KJ CHARLES

Published by KJC Books
Copyright © 2021 by KJ Charles

Edited by Christopher Keeslar

Cover design by Kanaxa

ISBN: 978-1-912688-22-7

PROLOGUE

Brother and sister, pretty as a picture.

They walked through Hyde Park together, Miss Marianne Loxleigh on the arm of her brother. It was early October, before the Season had truly started, but near enough that other gentlemen and ladies were promenading. One should take advantage of the fine weather, after all.

Miss Loxleigh was taking advantage in full. Her lovely face was delightfully framed by a coquettish bonnet, and her new walking dress flattered her buxom figure, suggesting charms without displaying them too obviously. She was statuesque in build and fashionably dark; her brother stood barely an inch taller and was much lighter in colouring, with hazel eyes to her deep brown, and honey-coloured hair to her mahogany. Mr. Robin Loxleigh was as smart as his sister, in close-fitting pantaloons and a waistcoat of sober pattern but cheerful hue, and like her, blessed with striking good looks.

Two attractive, elegant, well-turned-out young people walking in Hyde Park: what could be more pleasant? As such, they received a number of glances, though no greetings. They were strangers to London, but if they felt isolated in the great metropolis there was no sign of it in their bearing. Robin walked with a confident gait; Marianne looked around with unaffected pleasure. She seemed content in her brother's company, and quite unaware of the many admiring masculine looks that came her way.

Brother and sister, pretty as a picture.

Marianne smiled at Robin, and murmured, "There's a man following us."

"You or me?"

"Me, you fool. If I talk to him, you could try for his pocketbook."

Robin prodded the rounded arm that lay through his in a playful manner. "Don't tempt me."

"We've got exactly three pounds and sevenpence left. And he's annoying me."

"Doing what?"

"Existing."

"The bastard. Look, there's no need to rush. We've got plenty of clothes, some of them paid for, and rent's not due for six days. I'll play tonight."

Marianne heaved a pretty sigh. "You'd better win."

They exchanged looks of glowing mutual affection for the benefit of watchers, and strolled on.

"What do you think?" Marianne asked after a few moments' contemplation of the duck pond. "Group of women over there."

Robin followed her gaze and saw three well-dressed young ladies, with an older companion walking behind. "They'll do. Drop an earring?"

"Teach your grandmother to suck eggs."

Brother and sister made their casual way along a loop of path that would bring them up to the young ladies, where Marianne gasped and clutched her earlobe.

"Oh! My earring! Robin, I think it fell!—Oh, how very

kind you are, thank you—I was so afraid I had lost it, it was Robin's birthday gift to me. My brother, Robin Loxleigh, and I am Marianne. —Delighted to meet you. No, we are quite new in London..."

Robin stood back, smiling, as Marianne struck up the acquaintance, bowing to their guardian companion and looking on the young ladies with a respectful admiration that was sufficiently modest as to be flattering yet give no offence.

They'd been preparing the ground for two days already and would be doing it again and again for the next weeks, in haberdashers' and bookshops and tailors, at theatres and at Tattersall's, assemblies and coffee-houses. By the time the Season began, plenty of people would recognise the well-mannered Loxleighs—friendly but not encroaching, up from the country, modest but so charming! They would have dinner invitations. They would find their way into parties. They would slide into the notice of the lower Upper Ten Thousand without anyone quite knowing how they'd got there.

And then the hunt would begin.

CHAPTER 1

Sir John Hartlebury surveyed the ballroom with a jaundiced eye and wondered how soon he could leave.

"There," Mrs. Edwina Blaine said through a fixed smile. "There he is with Alice now. By the negus. *Look*, Hart."

He looked. Despite their vantage point at the top of the steps, which was severely incommoding the flow of people in and out, it took him several seconds to locate his sister's stepdaughter. After all, she wasn't very notable.

Miss Alice Fenwick had not been blessed with Nature's charms. She was short, undistinguished in build, and plain in looks, with a mass of freckles and mousy brown hair, and there was nothing in her birth to make up for it. Her father, a provincial brewer, had lost his first wife in childbirth and persuaded Edwina Hartlebury, just twenty-three but firmly on the shelf, to replace her. The marriage had not borne fruit, but they had been surprisingly happy for five years, until the brewer's untimely death.

Edwina had loved Alice from the start and regarded her as her own daughter. Unfortunately the world didn't share that view. The Hartleburys could trace their lineage back to the fourteenth century but plain Alice Fenwick had no claim on that distinguished heritage.

The joint lack of birth and beauty was enough to disqualify her from the notice of high society, which confirmed Hart's view that high society was witless. Alice was a delight, a studious and strikingly intelligent girl, shy in company but amusing in private, sharp-witted but never unkind. She was a loving companion to Edwina, and she was also, thanks to her father's will, a substantial heiress, with twenty thousand pounds to come to her on her marriage under no restrictions at all.

Society might change its mind about her if that fact was widely known, but the family had agreed to keep quiet about Alice's wealth for her first Season. Granted the portion was her best chance for a good match, it was also all too likely to bring her a bad one. That kind of money without strings was bound to attract fortune-hunters, and both Hart and Edwina were all too aware of the dangers of being swept off one's feet by a handsome face.

The siblings had agreed that Alice needed a little town-bronze, which was to say a little knowledge of humanity's infinite capacity to disappoint, before it became common talk that the plain girl came with a very attractive dowry. And here was their chance to learn if their strategy had been right, because Alice was being squired by a handsome man.

Hart folded his arms and watched.

The suitor was *very* handsome, if not in a classical way. He was of no more than medium stature, and boasted neither an athletic Corinthian build, nor a graceful and willowy form. Rather, he was solid and compact in a way that brought the word 'yeoman' to mind. He was in his early twenties, with honey-brown hair, an open, honest face, and a well-shaped mouth, full-lipped and promising pleasures. He looked like the kind of country youth they wrote ballads about, whether proclaiming his steadfastness as a faithful lover, or his enjoyment of a roll in the hay. Alice might count herself fortunate in such a suitor if his character and finances were as appealing as his exterior. Hart put a lot of mental emphasis on that 'if'.

"Who is he?"

"A Loxleigh, of Nottinghamshire," Edwina said. "Do you know the name?"

"It seems familiar, but I can't place it."

"That's what everyone says. They aren't anyone in particular, they're quite clear about that. No presumption at all, pleasantly modest, and pretty-mannered. I find them both delightful."

They. Yes. Hart looked away from the pretty-mannered pretty man with Alice. "Where's the sister?"

"Dancing, I expect. Look, there she is with Giles Verney."

Hart scanned the ballroom floor, found his best friend, noted his partner, and was forced to say, "Good God."

"Isn't she?"

Mr. Loxleigh was handsome, but Miss Loxleigh was extraordinary. Hart had a fair aesthetic appreciation of female beauty and she was easily in the top five he'd seen in his life. Dark hair, dark eyes, perhaps an overly sun-kissed complexion when milk-white skin was held up as a virtue, but that was countrywomen for you, and by God it suited her. Her gown wasn't immodest by any standards, but still made the watcher aware of the lush curves it covered. She didn't wear lavish jewels or plumes; she didn't need them. She was quite simply lovely.

Giles Verney spun her round on the dancefloor. She said something to him, they both laughed, and Hart revised his opinion to top three. Maybe two.

"Good *God*," he said. "Spanish blood?"

"Their grandmother, I think."

Hart looked back at Alice and her squire. "They're an exceedingly handsome pair."

"Miss Loxleigh is the belle of the Season, even if they are nobody. I hear Tachbrook is taken with her."

"How unfortunate."

"He's a marquess," Edwina pointed out unnecessarily.

"He is a self-regarding, vindictive, pompous fool, and if she is encouraging him, I think worse of her. Do we know anything at all about these people?"

"They've been in London since autumn, I think. Several months. Invited everywhere. Florence Jocelyn and Miss Loxleigh have become great friends, I believe, and Mr. Loxleigh seems to be on terms with everyone."

"Almack's?"

Edwina had not attempted to claim those dizzy social heights for Alice. "I really don't know. If Tachbrook is interested, one must assume they're acceptable."

"That doesn't follow. He's a fool."

Hart contemplated the lovely Miss Loxleigh in his friend's arms, then the not-quite-as-lovely but still damned appealing brother bowing over Alice's hand. Alice had gone a murky red: she didn't have the gift of charming blushes, and she'd never had a desirable piece of man-flesh casting lures before.

Loxleigh was too handsome for her. That wasn't a flattering thought to have of his niece, or one he'd ever express in his sister's hearing, but it was the way of things. Beauty was a valuable commodity, a fact that Hart, an ugly man, knew all too well; beautiful people made use of their advantages just as much as the wealthy or the titled.

Perhaps Loxleigh was wiser than that. Perhaps his pretty face hid a noble nature that prized character above appearance. Hart wouldn't have put money on it.

"I don't know," he said. "Don't rush into this, will you?"

Edwina tutted. "I'm not going to. That's why I wanted you to see for yourself."

"Let me ask around. Don't encourage him too much yet. And I want to talk to Alice."

He headed down to the floor as the waltz came to an end, walking up to Giles and his stunning partner.

"Giles. I insist you introduce me, or I shall call you out."

Giles gave him an affectionate grin. "Miss Loxleigh, this is Sir John Hartlebury. Hart, Miss Marianne Loxleigh, of Nottinghamshire. Hart and I come from the same part of the world, and have been friends all our lives."

She greeted him with charm, and he kissed her hand, as the only possible tribute. He did it awkwardly enough, not being a man made for flourishes, but Miss Loxleigh gave him a melting smile and assured him she was delighted.

"Sir John Hartlebury? Am I right in thinking you're Miss Fenwick's...?" She hesitated.

"Uncle by marriage. My sister is Miss Fenwick's stepmother."

"You're Mrs. Blaine's brother. Of course. I've had the honour of visiting Mrs. Blaine at her home. She is wonderfully kind, and so welcoming: I feel I have known her for years." Miss Loxleigh's smile illuminated the room better than the crystal chandeliers above. "And Alice is delightful. You are very fortunate in your family."

It sounded so sincere that he couldn't help but warm to her. He could see why she was making such a hit. "You're new to London, I think?"

"Yes, this is our first visit. I am here with my brother."

"Making your come-out?"

"Making new friends, I hope. We were told London would be unwelcoming, but we've been blessed with nothing but kindness."

The back of a head presented itself to Hart's face as a man

shouldered his way into their little group. "Miss Loxleigh?" The pompous voice belonged to Lord Tachbrook. "You are to dance with me, I think." He gave Giles a look down his nose, cut Hart entirely, and extended his arm. Miss Loxleigh bade Hart and Giles a smiling farewell, and went off with her aristocratic suitor.

Giles stared after the disappearing pair. Hart snorted. "His manners don't improve. Probably doesn't want her to talk to other men in case she realises what a prating fool he is. Walk with me?"

It was too cold to go outside, despite the heat in here, so they snagged a couple of glasses of champagne and headed for the library. This had been plentifully set up with card-tables, since their hostess, Lady Beaumont, was a notorious gambler. Lord Tachbrook must be keen: Hart doubted he would normally have attended one of her events. It was crowded, and sufficiently noisy that they could lean against the mantelpiece and chat in low voices.

"Have you met the lady before?" Hart asked.

"Miss Loxleigh? A few times over the last weeks."

"Know anything of her?"

"What sort of thing?"

"Background. Parents. Brother's antecedents. Means of support."

"Ah," Giles said. "Are you thinking about Alice?"

Hart grimaced. "Is young Loxleigh's pursuit common talk?"

"Hardly that. Alice isn't particularly interesting—to the gossips, I mean—and Loxleigh isn't notable except for his sister. He seems to be paying her a great deal of attention, though. Is there something in the offing?"

"My sister believes so."

"And you're here to be the watchful uncle?" Giles's eyes

brimmed with mirth. "Marvellous. Will we see you acting the heavy moralist? I cannot wait."

Hart glared. Giles smirked. Hart returned a quelling scowl, and Giles pulled a grotesque face in reply, the sort of expression one might find on a schoolboy rather than a sensible Foreign Office man. A passing dowager looked at him with shocked hauteur. Giles said, "I do beg your pardon," with a deep bow, and they both hid shamefaced grins behind their champagne as she moved on.

Face-pulling aside, Giles was quite right that Hart would look absurd playing the moralist. He wasn't a rakehell, or anything like, but his lack of social graces, some loud complaints of mortal offence from a few people of rank, and a single, highly notorious affair had added up to a rather blemished reputation.

It was, for the most part, undeserved. He spent the majority of his time blamelessly at home in Aston Clinton, managing his lands and running the brewery Fenwick had left to Edwina. But his second life as a provincial brewer did nothing to improve his standing in London society, and on the rare occasions he attended social events, he didn't help himself by his refusal to dance or flirt with young ladies. Society mothers found his misanthropic nature offensive, since he had a baronetcy and a reasonable income; the young ladies themselves seemed generally relieved by his lack of interest.

Hart didn't care. His friends were mostly businessmen and Cits who knew the value of money and did something to earn it. He preferred gaming hells to social clubs; he had no interest in putting himself up on the Marriage Mart, no need to beget an heir since the baronetcy could descend to his sister's son, and no family who took it upon themselves to interfere. In fact, at the age of thirty-two, Hart was very satisfied by his industrious country life, and increasingly uninterested in the goings-on of the Upper Ten Thousand.

But Edwina had demanded he assess the young man who was interested in Alice, and that cast him in the role of guardian, for which he had little inclination and no actual authority.

"Who *are* these people?" he demanded.

"The Loxleighs? Just people, Hart. Not encroaching or offensive. Modest, and very pretty-mannered."

"So everyone keeps telling me. What do they have other than manners?"

"Charm," Giles said. "Something you could do with cultivating. Loxleigh's a decent fellow from what I can see. Plays, but not too high. Never quarrels, knows how to hold his drink."

"That sounds like faint praise."

"Does it? Perhaps. I couldn't claim to know him."

"You don't like him." Hart spoke with the certainty of a lifetime's friendship.

Giles gave him a look. "You're too severe, Hart. I don't *dis*like him. I just... Well, if you will have it, there's something a little...I don't know. 'Calculating' is too harsh. As if he's watching the room rather than being in it."

"Acting a part?"

"You say that with such disapproval. Most of us act a part in society, you know, for everyone's benefit. It's polite to make the effort."

Hart snorted. Giles went on, "Anyway, I wouldn't even go that far. He's probably self-conscious, and one can't blame the fellow. They're provincials who came on holiday to London and now Miss Loxleigh is being courted by a marquess. I'd watch my words too, in his position. In fact, considering all that, I'd say he's remarkably unaffected."

"You have talked yourself round to the very opposite of your first statement."

"It's amazing how a little empathy can change one's mind

about someone," Giles retorted. "Again, you should try it. The only conclusion I can offer is that I don't know him. But I have met Miss Loxleigh several times and she's wonderfully open. Delightful. Unaffected. She has such a frank enjoyment of everything, so unlike the tedious cynicism of all the world-weary folk in this room."

"Am I to take that remark personally?" Hart enquired.

"Yes. Whereas unlike you, Miss Loxleigh is full of joy. Thoughtful, amusing but not frivolous. She lifts one's heart."

Hart lifted his brow instead. Giles gave him an embarrassed smile. "Am I raving?"

"You are, yes."

"She has that effect. I could only secure one dance with her tonight. There's a host of admirers, Tachbrook at their head."

"Are you in the running?"

"Don't be absurd."

Giles was a third son—admittedly of an archbishop, of excellent family and holding a good post at the Foreign Office, but still a mere salaried man. Miss Loxleigh might be a wonder among women, but Hart would still put ten pounds that she'd plump for wealth and title, given the choice. She wasn't fresh from the schoolroom and could clearly have her pick of men; she had doubtless come to London to secure a prize. Good luck to her. Hart just hoped Giles's enthusiasm wasn't too serious.

"Has she a portion?" he asked.

"I've no idea."

"Do they have any estate back in Nottinghamshire?"

"I really don't know. Why don't you ask the brother?" Giles nodded to the door. Hart turned and saw that young Loxleigh had come into the gaming room.

He took a moment to assess the man closer up. He might be perhaps twenty-five, a little older than he'd looked from a distance, a year or two his sister's senior. There was no fault to be found with his tailoring, or his cravat, or his demeanour as he accepted a seat at the whist table, waved there by a man named Kinnard who was hail-fellow-well-met with anyone who'd play with him.

Loxleigh's eyes were hazel. Hart had rather expected them to be blue, like his own, and found himself oddly put out by that.

He leaned back against the wall to watch. Loxleigh smiled and chatted to the people around him, and his expression remained relaxed and pleasant as he took up his cards, but Hart thought his eyes sharpened slightly.

They played a few hands. Hart watched, ignoring Giles's efforts to make conversation until his friend muttered a rude remark and went off to find someone more entertaining. He watched the young man's face, and the casual set of his shoulders. He watched the ebb and flow of the game. He watched Loxleigh's hands—well-used ones, not as smooth and pale as a gentleman's hands were supposed to be, a little older-looking than his face—and then he pushed himself upright and sloped out of the room. He wanted to think.

When he returned to the ballroom, Alice was sitting by the wall. He went to sit with her. "Enjoying the evening?"

"Not really."

"Nor am I," he assured her. "I loathe this sort of thing."

"I can't decide if everyone is noticing me and I hate it, or nobody is noticing me and I hate it."

Hart threw back his head and laughed. "You've my entire sympathy."

"Well, thank you." She made a face. "It's not terrible. I have danced twice."

"I hope the gentleman was suitably appreciative."

"He was very pleasant." Hart couldn't tell if Alice was blushing: her colour was high anyway, given the oppressive heat of the crowded room. "A gentleman up from the country. I've made friends with his sister—"

"The beautiful Miss Loxleigh? I met her."

"She *is* beautiful, isn't she?"

"Outstanding."

"And she's lovely, too," Alice said earnestly. "In character, I mean. We met in the park, and started chatting—they hardly knew anyone in London either—and we get on delightfully. So many people aren't interested unless one is pretty or wealthy or well-born, and many of the belles are simply too busy to be kind. Marianne is always kind, *and* the best-looking woman of the Season, which just goes to show."

Hart nodded. There was quite a lot underpinning that speech, none of which made him happy. "And the brother is a gentleman?"

"Oh yes. He has escorted us—Marianne and me—several times now. I know she is older than me but she doesn't assume I'm a silly girl because of it. And Mr. Loxleigh is very respectful and pleasant."

"That is flattering attention."

Alice scuffed her shoe on the floor, the little movement making her seem terribly young. "I know he's just being polite, but he does seem interested in what I say. It's quite unusual to have someone interested in what I say."

Hart felt a stab of guilt. "I'm interested."

"Well, you aren't really," Alice pointed out without reproach. "We have different concerns in life. And I wasn't complaining. It's just—well, do you know when someone is truly listening to you, properly, not just exchanging remarks? And it feels like you're talking to a friend, even if you haven't known the person long at all?"

"That's good."

"It is," Alice said. "Because to be quite honest, Uncle Hart, I didn't in the slightest want a Season, and I haven't liked it very much, and it's costing Mama a great deal of money to do this for me. Making friends means I can honestly say I'm enjoying myself so she doesn't feel she's done the wrong thing. You aren't to tell her that, of course."

Hart turned to look at her. "I hope Edwina realises how lucky she is in you."

"I'm very lucky in her, but I do wish she'd stop fretting about me. Look, it's Giles."

Giles Verney was indeed approaching. He exchanged a few mild insults with Hart, and gave Alice his hand with the ease of long acquaintance. "Can I beg the next dance?"

"If you like. I'm not in great demand. But I'm a terrible dancer."

"So am I," Giles assured her. "To say I have two left feet is to understate things considerably. I have as many left feet as a centipede."

That was arrant nonsense since he was a superb dancer, but it made Alice giggle and she stood with a smile. Hart left them to it. Giles would give Alice a couple of dances, bring her an ice, and enliven her evening. It was the sort of thing he was very good at, having a bevy of sisters, cousins, and nieces, and he'd always extended that kindness to Alice as well. Hart, hopelessly lacking in grace, had long given up trying to imitate Giles's charming manners. The effort had made him feel, and probably look, like a dancing bear.

So he didn't attempt to uproot any wallflowers, but merely strolled around the ballroom for a little while, chatting to acquaintances. He watched young Loxleigh return to the ballroom in company with a couple of other men, and saw him drift casually over towards Alice, then he returned to the card-room.

Kinnard was still there, the seat next to him empty. Hart took it. "Evening. How are the cards running?"

"Shocking," Kinnard assured him. He had the look of a

man caught in gambling fever, eyes bright but hollow. "I've just lost sixty pounds to a sprig from the country with the best luck I've ever seen. Want to let me make it up at your expense?"

"No, but I'll happily make things worse," Hart assured him, and settled down to play, thinking hard.

CHAPTER 2

As an unmarried man who preferred the country, Hart didn't trouble to maintain an establishment in London. He kept a set of rooms in Cursitor Street instead, unfashionably far east and thus both larger and more economical than gentlemen's lodgings within a stone's throw of St. James's. He had his own entrance and three good-sized rooms; the married couple who lived upstairs cooked, cleaned, and valeted as required. What he lacked in convenience by not having a servant at shouting distance, he gained in privacy, and as a deeply private man he found that very much worthwhile.

He spent the day on his own business, sent his sister a brief note telling her he would report back in due course, ate a simple meal at home, and set out that evening to visit as many gaming hells as he could.

The third he tried was Lady Wintour's house in Rupert Street, a place which teetered on the far edge of acceptability. Sir George Wintour had married a hostess from a faro den—some said while drunk, but that state had covered most of his adult life—and when his passing left his widow in dire straits, she had returned to her old profession. It was a very reputable place, in that the rooms were better lit and aired than those of the average hell, and the drinks less likely to leave you with a painful head. There was still a big man with a cudgel who watched out for the law and made sure you paid up, but at Lady Wintour's he wore livery.

Hart nodded to the big man in question as he was admitted. "Evening, Ned."

"Evening, Sir John. Herself is upstairs, she'll be glad to see you."

Herself, or Lady Wintour, appeared at that moment. "Hey there, Ned— Why, John Hartlebury, as I live and breathe! Hello, Hart!"

She came down the stairs in a rush and flung herself at him in a cloud of perfume, powder, and skirts. Hart caught her and lifted her off her feet, feeling corsets creak in his grip. She was his notorious affair—three months of self-delusion that she'd ended with some stinging home truths—but they'd parted on good terms for all that, and proved far better friends than lovers.

"Evangeline." Hart kissed her rouged cheek. She squeezed his arse, which she had always and loudly admired. "You're looking well."

"I'm a haggard old woman. A wreck. More ruined than the Parthenon."

"The house is losing, I take it?"

"I'm going to retire to the country and keep chickens."

"Before you do that, I could use your help," Hart said. "I'm looking for a young man."

"Are you, now?"

He glowered at her. "Yellow-brown hair. Handsome face. Goes by the name of Loxleigh."

Evangeline raised a plucked brow. "Him? He's upstairs."

That was a stroke of luck; he'd been resigned to trying a dozen places. "Do you know anything about him?"

She jerked her head and escorted him into a side room, to speak in private. "What are you after?"

"I want to know more about him." Her expression conveyed without words that information was to be exchanged, not merely given. Hart sighed. "He's courting my niece."

"I didn't know you had a niece."

"My sister's stepdaughter."

"Did I know you had a sister?"

"They live in Aylesbury. She's here for the Season, making her come-out."

She nodded. "And why shouldn't he court her?"

"Perhaps he should. That's what I want to find out."

Evangeline narrowed her eyes. "Has she got money?"

"She'll have a portion on her marriage."

"And you've come round the gaming houses to find out about him."

Hart grimaced. Evangeline nodded as though he'd spoken. "You've got a feeling about him, haven't you? I know what you mean."

"You think there's something wrong?"

"He's very pleasant," she said. "Very modest, polite, never takes offence or crows about his winnings. He's been here four times, and came out to the good all of them. Wins fifty or sixty pounds a night."

"That's not huge." It was vast amounts by normal standards, of course, entire sections of the annual accounts to John Hartlebury the prudent brewer, but mere tokens to a gaming baronet.

"It's not breaking the bank, no. It's the kind of money you can win at a gaming hell without attracting too much attention. The question is how many gaming hells he's winning sixty pounds a night at, and how often."

"You think he's a sharp?"

"I've never caught him at it and I've no grounds for saying it, which is why I haven't had Ned throw him into the street and stamp on his fingers yet. I just have a feeling, that's all. And my feeling is, he looks like a pigeon but he plays like a hawk, and I don't like him."

That wasn't a long way from Hart's own feelings. "So why haven't you warned him off?"

"His sister's hooked Tachbrook, that's why. I've had enough trouble from that quarter. So have you."

The Marquess of Tachbrook had honoured Lady Wintour with his attentions after her widowing, although honour hadn't been involved at any point. He'd pursued her solely as a matter of conquest, since she was too vulgar to become his acknowledged mistress. Evangeline had chosen to take offence at that, declined his approaches in a loud and public manner, and plunged into the affair with Hart instead: a mere baronet, tainted by trade, and a man with whom Tachbrook had a long-standing quarrel. It had caused a great deal of amusement in raffish circles. Tachbrook had not come out of the affair well, and he had not forgiven it.

That was six or seven years ago. Evangeline was older, wiser, and drinking a lot less these days, and Hart could well understand why she had no interest in reigniting an old feud with a man so powerful, wealthy, and vindictive. "Very fair. Thank you, Evangeline. That's helpful."

"You can pay me back by losing some money."

"I'll do my best," Hart said. "Or I might see if Mr. Loxleigh wants a game."

"Make sure you win."

Hart went up to the card room, which was busy but not crowded, with a hubbub of talk going on above the serious players. It smelled of tallow, tobacco, spilled drink, and the aggressive scent of men en masse. He had no trouble spotting Loxleigh's dark honey hair in the crowd.

His quarry was at a whist table with a few others, wearing an easy smile. The litter of coins and scraps of paper by his elbow showed his run of luck was continuing.

Hart watched for a few moments. The play wasn't fast and furious. Loxleigh wagered sensibly, and took his time as if he were thinking about his choices. He gave every impression of being a sensible gamester, just as he had when Hart had watched him before, except for the eyes.

Loxleigh looked up then, as if he'd felt the observation. His gaze met Hart's with a direct look of recognition. A practised smile curved his full lips, and he stood with a word of apology to the other players. "Sir John Hartlebury, I think."

"I am he."

"My name is Loxleigh. I have the honour of being acquainted with your sister, and with Miss Fenwick."

Hart bowed. "My sister has mentioned you, I think. I was introduced to Miss Loxleigh at Lady Beaumont's ball. Are you playing?" He indicated the table.

"We have just finished a game."

"Which you won, again," grunted Tallant, one of the other players. "You want to watch this one, Hartlebury, he'll have the coat off your back."

"Perhaps you'll give me a hand or two," Hart suggested.

Loxleigh hesitated. "I live with my sister, who is at a soiree, and we have a pact to be home by midnight. I dare say that is a dreadful admission in masculine company." He smiled. It was a wide, charming smile lit with rueful laughter at his own expense, and Hart couldn't help thinking, *Damn*.

"You sound henpecked," Tallant said brutally.

Loxleigh's smile didn't falter one whit. "I am domestic. There is only Marianne and myself, and responsibility comes before pleasure. That said, I have half an hour before I need leave, Sir John, so if you'd care to play…?"

They took a table in the corner. "Whist?" Hart suggested.

He played that only adequately, but no matter: he didn't plan to put any significant money on the table.

They set very low stakes. Hart handed Loxleigh the pack, watched him shuffle and deal, watched his capable, fluent hands.

"You're from Nottingham, I believe?"

"Nottinghamshire. A village some way from the city—do you know the area?"

"Not at all."

"Then I shan't bore you with specifics. It is a charming place. Quiet and safe, with kind neighbours and a slow rhythm of life. Very different to London, though we have found a great deal of kindness here too."

Hart picked up his cards. "Your sister said this was your first visit to Town."

"It is. We have been planning the trip for some time, and it's been a remarkable experience. To see such monuments as St. Paul's, and the Tower…" He expanded on the glories of London like a human guide-book while they played out the hand. He came across as earnest, honest, perhaps not very dashing, but a sturdy and reliable young man. He played like one too, considering his cards carefully, not taking a risk when one might have won him the hand.

A slow and steady winner? Or a man making a particular effort to present himself as good husband material?

"Do you play much in your village?" Hart asked abruptly.

Loxleigh's gaze flicked up. The smile followed a second later, and didn't touch his eyes. Hart was beginning to dislike that smile. "Not like this, I assure you. We have a little group where we play for entertainment. The local squire, the landlord of our inn, the parson." Another smile. "Who, I may add, has often warned me of the evils of gaming to excess, but he will like to hear of my adventures in London all the same."

"That seems very cosy."

"It's a small society, but a friendly one."

It sounded delightful, just right for a woman like Alice, whose friendships were deep rather than wide. Hart didn't believe a word of it. It was too pat, too much an unasked-for explanation of why a man who was so keen to show himself as steady and domestic spent so much time in gaming dens.

"But despite the provincial bliss, you felt the urge for a change of scene?" he suggested.

"Don't we all feel that now and again?" Loxleigh returned, dealing the next hand. "Mrs. Blaine said you divide your time between town and country."

"I run her brewery," Hart said bluntly. "Alice's father left everything to my sister, and now I am in charge of the business." Which was to hint, heavily, that Alice had no money of her own.

"Then you are an excellent brother and uncle to work for your family's benefit," Loxleigh returned.

"I am paid a salary." In fact he took a cut of the profits, which could be described as dividends rather than something as lowly as a salary, but he wanted to see what bland platitude Loxleigh would come up with.

He wasn't disappointed. "The labourer is worthy of his hire. I believe a man does well to have an occupation."

"What's yours?"

"We have a very little land. Nothing grand. The area is beautiful."

"A country soul," Hart said, spinning a card onto the table. "Do you intend to live out your life in this rustic haven?"

Loxleigh's face showed nothing but the smile. "That was always my expectation. I have wondered recently— Well, we shall see what fate brings."

"Such as a wife?"

"Perhaps, if I am so fortunate. Or a husband for my sister. That would change things."

"She's very lovely."

"She is."

"You seem a devoted pair."

Loxleigh looked up from his hand. "I dare say domesticity is mocked in sophisticated company, but in truth, I don't care. It has been the two of us for a long time. Marianne deserves everything London has to give her, and she will have it if I have anything to say to the matter."

His hazel eyes were different when he said that. Alive, but not smiling, not smiling in the least. Hart watched him as he looked down at his cards again, and thought, *So that's what you look like when you're telling the truth.*

He nudged a bit further. "I suppose you will be very lonely if she makes a match in London."

"I should be a poor brother if I let my selfish concerns stand in her way. But I hope we will always be close, and she will be a sister to my wife too. If that should come to pass, of course."

"Of course."

They played the hand out with little more talk and Hart emerged the winner by a few pounds. He couldn't fault Loxleigh's play, any more than he could fault the man's words. There was barely a chink in his facade of steady humble decency.

And every instinct Hart had screamed he was a liar.

CHAPTER 3

Robin Loxleigh was in a mixed frame of mind.

The Beaumont ball had gone well. He'd got a good few blushes out of Alice, the kind that came with proper smiles, and when he'd enquired if she might be at home to receive a caller the next day, she'd said her stepmother would be pleased to see him. She wasn't precisely falling into his arms, but that was for the best: if she had a habit of flinging herself at any man who showed interest, all but the most negligent parent would raise doubts about a swift marriage.

Robin had initially hoped that Alice's family would be negligent, or that Mrs. Blaine would want to push out the cuckoo in her nest, but nothing could be further from the case. The older woman obviously adored her stepdaughter, who called her Mama. They were a happy and a loving pair. It gave Robin a feeling in his stomach that he preferred not to have.

Still, if an affectionate home made Alice less vulnerable to a lover's blandishments, it offered Robin a different advantage: Mrs. Blaine would not want to deny her anything that made her happy. He just needed to persuade them both that that included himself as a husband.

In fairness, he had every intention of making her happy. She was not a pretty girl, but he didn't care about that, and she was pleasant company, very amusing when she got over her shyness. They'd rub along well and he'd make her a good husband by the world's standards. He had no intention of squandering her money: he'd live happily on the interest of twenty thousand, well invested. He'd respect her, present a face of affection and mutual kindness to the world, make her a matron to be envied by prettier misses, and plough her if she wanted, albeit while thinking about other people. That surely made him better than most husbands he'd heard of. Robin might be a fortune hunter, but he'd treat his prize well once he'd won her.

And he would win her. He had a handsome face and taking ways, plus Marianne to attest to what a good, kind brother he was, and standing ready to embrace the lonely orphan Alice as her sister. What girl could resist?

The only fly in the ointment was Hartlebury.

Robin had an uncomfortable feeling about him. He'd seemed aggressive when they'd played at Lady Wintour's hell, and Robin couldn't quite put that down to his notorious brusqueness. He'd been pushing, Robin was sure, and he'd watched too closely.

Doubtless some of the awkwardness had sprung from Robin's own thoughts. He'd felt extremely self-conscious at being found by the man in a hell. Gambling was a common recreation for all classes, and there was no reason he shouldn't play, but it was undeniably a poor match for his parade of domestic virtue.

What else was he to do? They needed the money. Marianne was spending it like water on bonnets and dresses while insisting they build up a substantial reserve in case the fortunes they hunted got away. She didn't intend to flee the city with nothing but the clothes they stood up in, not again.

Robin had all the incidental expenses of a gentleman to meet, including making sure he could cover his occasional losses. Those were inevitable, no matter how good he was with the cards, and if he ever failed to pay a debt of honour they'd be sunk.

No, he had no choice but to play. And Hartlebury was a gamester too; he would be a hypocrite to hold another man's play against him. That probably wouldn't stop him—hypocrisy was the defining feature of the upper classes in Robin's view—but who knew; perhaps a man who actually worked rather than simply waiting for money to be handed to him might be a little more tolerant.

Except, he had watched Robin. At the Beaumont ball, at Lady Wintour's, and again just last night at the Laodicean Club.

Robin had joined the Laodicean at vast expense, sponsored by an unimportant but rich young man named Mowbray whose fiancée had become bosom friends with Marianne. It was an investment. Playing at informal events in the houses of the rich was safest, but he had to be restrained or the upper-class sheep would start to count up how many of them he'd shorn. Gaming hells had big unfriendly men who kept a weather eye out for sharps. A gentleman's club was the perfect compromise. Large winnings and losses were entirely expected in the Laodicean, where the play was frighteningly high, with hundreds wagered on the turn of a card. Robin had had to learn not to count it as money, only a means of keeping score, because throwing away those sums terrified him. He'd had to excuse himself from the table his first time in a deep hell, because his stomach had rebelled, and he'd feared disgracing himself in public.

He was hardened now, or in too deep to turn back. One of the two. He was ready to play anywhere he could find a game, and take whatever money he could wring out of the wealthy.

But he hadn't been ready for Hartlebury's looming presence in the corner of his eye.

'Hart', the man's friends called him. It was bizarre he had friends at all, the intimidating bastard. Sir John Hartlebury was an imposing, heavy-set man, looking forty for all Alice claimed he was a mere thirty-two, inelegant and powerful, with a gruff voice, thick thighs, strong shoulders, and absurdly heavy eyebrows that gave him a permanent scowl. A bruiser, except for those striking, clear blue eyes set over a prominent Roman nose.

And he'd stood behind Robin, watching for some unspecified length of time without him noticing. That was not good, because last night Robin had been forced to play by Vincent's law. The cards had run against him; a series of risks hadn't paid off. He'd found himself eight hundred pounds down at one point, a sum that didn't bear thinking about when a jeweller's bill had eaten into their cash reserves that very morning. He'd had no choice but to even the odds. Improve his chances. Cheat.

Another man might have panicked in the face of that mounting debt. Robin had stayed calm, enhanced his hands with a few judicious aces, and come out of the night only seventy pounds down. It would have been a relief except that Sir John Hartlebury had been there. Not playing. Watching.

It would be nice to think he'd been observing his niece's suitor with a view to giving his blessing, but Robin wasn't holding his breath for that. Hartlebury was notoriously rag-mannered, with his brusque unwillingness to trouble with social niceties, but even given that, he'd radiated hostility. Robin had done his best to charm, but everything he'd tried had bounced off the man's armour. He just hoped that was because Hartlebury was protective of Alice, rather than what he really feared, which was that he'd spotted Robin fuzzing the cards.

He didn't want to consider that possibility. He hadn't even mentioned it to Marianne, in the hope that if he didn't voice it, it wouldn't be true. Not talking about things was almost the same as them not having happened, a principle that had served Robin well for years. And surely if Hartlebury had seen he'd have spoken up at the time, exposed Robin in the act. Surely.

It couldn't be that, Robin assured himself, but he felt a pulse of nerves at what awaited them at Mrs. Blaine's house, where he and Marianne were heading for tea.

"You look like you're off to your own execution," Marianne remarked. "Cheer up. You need to approach this in the right spirit. Are you going to make a declaration?"

"Too soon, but I'll make sure she's amenable, get her hopes up. You could drop a hint I've spoken to you about it."

"Of course, my best of brothers."

Marianne's presence on visits to Alice was window dressing: making sure his interest wasn't too blatant, and showing himself a loving brother who could be trusted with a woman's well-being. It helped Marianne too, since she made a point of treating other women as friends rather than rivals. Her behaviour proclaimed that she was not one of those beauties focused on the hunt for a husband, but rather a delightful woman who would make a very amiable daughter-in-law. That ought to undermine the competition nicely.

They arrived at Mrs. Blaine's house a little chilly but refreshed by the walk. Robin gave his hat, coat, and stick to a fatherly and smiling butler—that was a good sign, since the staff seemed fond of Alice—and they were admitted to the drawing room, where Robin got an unwelcome shock because Hartlebury was there.

He stood in the corner of the room, a looming figure of disapproval. His clothing was almost aggressively drab, and though well-enough cut showed no great care in the dressing. If Robin had had thighs like that, he'd have made sure his pantaloons showed them to full advantage, but this was a man who dressed for functionality alone. The dun-coloured coat emphasised his breadth of shoulder in an intimidating sort of way, not helped by that beaky nose and of course the eyebrows. They were thick, dark, and set in a perpetual scowl over enviably blue eyes. Robin would have liked blue eyes himself. He'd also have liked Hartlebury not to be here.

"Ah, Mr. Loxleigh, Miss Loxleigh. My brother, Sir John Hartlebury," Mrs. Blaine said. "Have you met?"

Robin said they had, and produced a sincere and charming smile as he bowed. Hartlebury simply nodded in response.

Tea proceeded rather awkwardly, given his grim and silent presence. Robin tried asking about the man's business, hoping to draw him out, and received monosyllabic replies. He switched his attentions to Mrs. Blaine, who seemed rather conscious of her ungracious brother. Marianne did her best, always smiling, speaking to Hartlebury without a hint of flirtation, and suggesting various ideas for excursions to Alice.

"And would your brother accompany you as escort?" Hartlebury asked, finally breaking his silence when Marianne proposed a shopping trip to Clark and Debenham on Wigmore Street.

"If Alice wishes it," Marianne replied calmly. "Robin is the best of brothers, always ready to give up his own pleasures to squire me around."

"I thought you had plenty of squires."

That could have been a poorly phrased compliment. Robin was pretty sure it wasn't. Marianne inclined her head as modestly as if it were blatant flattery. "We've been fortunate to make a wide acquaintance in our short time here, but I prefer my brother's company to any other. We were orphaned quite young and it has always been the two of us. That is very important to me."

"Aren't you looking to change your state?" Hartlebury's blue eyes flicked to Robin. "Either of you?"

Marianne smiled. "To marry? I don't feel any great urgency."

"Not at your age?"

"Hart!" Mrs. Blaine almost shrieked. "Good heavens!"

"I'm twenty-one," Marianne lied, smile pinned on her face. "Perhaps that is on the shelf by London standards, but not, I assure you, as a countrywoman. Marry in haste, repent at leisure, we say back home. Well, I believe you are a bachelor, Sir John, so I assume you agree."

Hartlebury's cold eyes flicked to Robin. "Do you always let your sister do the talking?"

Mrs. Blaine interjected forcefully at this point, with an account of the respective lengths of her two courtships that carried them through the rest of the teapot. Hartlebury sat silently, his eyes on Robin's face.

It was staggeringly uncomfortable. The hostility was a palpable thing, and Robin could feel his cheeks heating. He set himself to ignore it and speak pleasantly to Alice, trying to ease her evident discomfort. It was almost a relief when Hartlebury said, "A word in private with you, Loxleigh."

They went into a study, the desk littered with papers. Hartlebury took the chair without offering Robin one, leaving him standing in front of the desk like a boy in the headmaster's presence. The devil with that. He spotted a chair against a wall and carried it over, putting it at the side of the desk rather than in front of it. "May I sit?"

Hartlebury looked like he wanted to say no, but waved his hand irritably. Robin seated himself, crossing his legs. "You seem concerned, Sir John. Perhaps you'd tell me what your concern is."

"What are your intentions toward my niece?"

That was to the point. Robin put on a little frown. "Miss

Fenwick is a delightful young lady. I enjoy her company, and she and my sister have struck up a close friendship—"

"I didn't ask for an assessment. I asked your intentions."

"My intentions are to pursue the acquaintance of one of the pleasantest women I have ever been privileged to know. Let me be quite honest—"

"If you would."

Prick. "I have wondered if my suit would be acceptable to her, and of course Mrs. Blaine, but I am well aware she hasn't known me long, and I have to consider my and my sister's situation, and my responsibilities. If I were a wealthy man, able to indulge my wishes—"

"You would sweep Alice away on a white charger?" Hartlebury said drily. "I suppose you received a leveller at the sight of her? Bowled off your feet?"

Robin clenched his fist, in full view, and let a little of his annoyance leak into his voice. "I suppose I understand your implication. It is an unworthy one from a man who ought to be her protector."

Hartlebury's heavy eyebrows went up. It was more sarcasm than surprise, but it still made those vivid blue eyes stand out. "Are you telling me how I should speak of my niece?"

"You should speak of her as she deserves. Miss Fenwick has good sense, a good heart, and a good wit," Robin said swiftly and angrily, the picture of an outraged defender. "Those are the qualities for which I love Marianne and which I want in my own wife."

"Good heart, good sense, good wit, and twenty thousand pounds."

Robin widened his eyes and went still with shock. He had a knack for that. "I beg your pardon?"

"You were not aware of the extent of her fortune?"

"I knew she had an inheritance from her father. She didn't say— I had no idea."

"Did you not." Hartlebury spoke with clear contempt.

"That explains your concern. I understand." Robin frowned, to show he was thinking it through. "As I told you, I'm not a wealthy man. I can't offer anything to match such a portion—"

"Except a loving heart and a gentle hand to guide her in life, and so forth? Spare me."

That was exactly what Robin had been working up to. How absolutely typical that the best pair of thighs he'd seen in years should be parcelled up with such a damned inflexible, unaccommodating, sceptical personality. "Sir, I resent your tone. I may not be rich, but I have done nothing to deserve your implications."

"You have arrived from nowhere—"

"Nottinghamshire!"

"—nowhere, and wheedled yourselves into the ton very successfully. Your sister is encouraging the attentions of Lord Tachbrook, a pompous fool whose only recommendation is his title. You have set yourself at my niece, whose qualities I know a great deal better than you. You cheat at cards."

Robin stood explosively, shoving the chair away. "What? How dare you!"

"Very easily. I saw you do it."

"You did not, because I did not. You will take those words back. You may insult me if you wish, but you may not make implications about my sister, and you will not accuse me of dishonouring my name. Take it back!"

"Or what?"

That was a good question. He was substantially the bigger and looked like a boxer, and Robin had no intention of starting a fight that he was bound to lose. Hartlebury was also rich, well born, and well connected: he'd doubtless be believed if he chose to spread the story that Robin was a leg, especially since it was true. Robin had absolutely no weapons against him, except that the bastard was a gentleman.

Fine. He'd use that.

He set his teeth, the picture of a man trying to keep his patience. "This is unjust. You rely on the fact that I have no desire to argue with the relative of a lady I admire and respect. You use your power and station to insult me with impunity. Well, I may be a mere countryman of limited means, sir, but I will not be bullied by you, and I would scorn to mete out abuse to anyone with whom my station had a similar disparity." He'd got the grammar of that mixed up somewhere, but it sounded well enough. "Perhaps you think honest birth, a modest home, and a true heart are not sufficient for the niece you have sneered at. Perhaps you hope this dowry from her father will come to your family if she doesn't marry." That brought the blood into Hartlebury's face in a very satisfactory way, also a dangerous look to his eyes. Robin pressed on. "But you could at least conduct yourself with more decency and dignity than to invent scurrilous and damaging accusations about a man who has never done you harm. And if you speak one more disrespectful word about my sister, sir, by God I will give you the thrashing you deserve, and I only wish I had the right to offer the same protection to Miss Fenwick!"

He let his voice rise on that last part, since he'd heard a rustle of movement in the hall. Mrs. Blaine was Alice Fenwick's guardian, and Hartlebury had, legally speaking, no authority over her. He might denounce Robin, but he couldn't forbid the match. If Robin drove a wedge between him and the women, he might outflank him.

"Enough speechifying," Hartlebury snapped. "I know what I saw, and I know what you are."

"You know nothing. You have invented an untruth because you believe I am a fortune hunter. I don't know how I can persuade you that I am nothing of the kind; I can only tell you that Miss Fenwick's wealth may be common knowledge in London, but I am not from here and nobody mentioned it to me. And I'll tell you something else—"

"Is it possible to stop you? You should be on the stage, with this gift for the dramatic monologue."

Utter prick. Robin spoke very clearly, so his voice carried. "You believe I am a fortune hunter because you cannot see any other reason a man might wish to marry your niece. You don't think she's worthy of love. That says a great deal more about your character than mine."

"You little turd," Hartlebury said savagely, and rose with real fury in his eyes.

Robin scooted behind the chair, and backed rapidly to the door. "That's the last insult I will tolerate from you. You must be quite mad, sir. Good day." He let himself out of the room in a hurry, and encountered Mrs. Blaine in the hall, very high coloured. He'd hoped she'd been listening.

"Mr. Loxleigh!"

"Excuse me, madam. I'm very sorry, but I have had some words with your brother, and I think it is best if I take my leave. Might I say goodbye to Miss Fenwick?"

"You will get out of here now," said Hartlebury, from too close behind him.

"Excuse me," Mrs. Blaine told him furiously. "It is my house and I decide who stays or goes. I want a *word* with you, John Hartlebury. —The girls are in the sitting room, Mr. Loxleigh. I think it would be best if perhaps—"

"We'll go at once. I am deeply grateful for your hospitality." Robin executed a graceful bow, and cleared out in a hurry.

Alice and Marianne were sitting together in the drawing room. Alice's eyes were wide with alarm as he came in. "What on earth has happened, Mr. Loxleigh? Have you had an argument with my uncle?"

"He had one with me." Robin put on a shaky smile that said, *I am trying to keep countenance for your sake.* "He said some very unkind things, about— Well, some very unkind things, and made certain accusations that make it impossible for me to remain under the same roof."

"What? *Why?*"

"I thought at first he was protecting you. I could respect that, however wrong he might be about the need. But then— I must ask, is he unkind to you? Violent?"

Her jaw sagged. "Uncle Hart? Of course not. What on earth did he say?"

Robin raised his hands. "I'd rather not repeat it. The way he spoke to me was intolerable, and I had to tell him he lied. I don't know why, but I believe Mrs. Blaine is with him now. Perhaps she will have an answer for you. But I promised her we would leave, so come, Marianne." He stepped forward and extended his hand. Alice touched hers to it with some awkwardness. "You will of course need to speak to your stepmother but I hope—I very much hope—that this falling-out can be resolved. If I can mend matters, I will." He paused, then said, in a rush, "I shan't be driven off by anyone but you, Miss Fenwick. I feel too greatly for that." He brought his lips to her fingertips in a swift movement. Alice snatched her hand back, cheeks scarlet.

It wasn't a bad exit, under the circumstances. Robin and Marianne returned in silence to their rooms, where Marianne snatched off her shawl and threw it on the settle. "What the fuck, Rob?"

"Fucking Hartlebury is what. He called me a card cheat."

"Why?"

"Because I am one, I expect!" Robin paced up and down. "I think he caught me at it last night. He's been watching me."

"Nobody's supposed to see you do it! That's the point!"

"I'm aware of that!" Robin snarled back. "I can't help it if he decided to stare at my hands all evening!"

"Well, why did you cheat when you were being watched?"

"How was I to know? Did you want me to lose?"

They glared at each other. Marianne stalked to the mirror and jerked out hairpins in a testy manner. "What did he say?"

Robin flopped into a chair. "Asked my intentions, made it clear he didn't believe me. He asked if Alice had given me a leveller. Sarcastically."

"Oh, that's charming," Marianne said, with vitriol. "Is she not *beautiful*"—she made wiggling finger-motions around her own lovely face—"enough for his high standards, when he has a mug like that? Arsehole. What did you say?"

"I asked if he was insulting her looks, and suggested he wanted to get his hands on her money."

Marianne's mouth dropped open. "Oh, wonderful. I'm glad you said that, it'll definitely help."

"I had to say something! Anyway, he isn't her guardian so he can't forbid the banns. And mostly, if he was sure he'd caught me he'd have made a fuss last night. He was guessing. I don't think this is a disaster yet."

"It's not far from one," Marianne said grimly. "You've set your cap at her clearly enough that if you switch to another heiress, it'll be obvious."

Robin scrubbed at his face with the heels of his hands. Fortune hunting was not proving the smooth path to riches he might have hoped. "We shouldn't risk it. Tachbrook is the bigger prize."

"If I can land him." Marianne lifted one shoulder irritably. "Did I tell you, the fathead must have his mother's approval?"

"What? Why? He's forty-five if he's a day."

"He doesn't need her permission, but she is the chief trumpeter of his greatness, and he lives only to be told how marvellously important he is."

"Therefore he doesn't dare lower himself in her eyes? Got it." Robin exhaled. "What are our chances?"

"They were better before you got caught cheating at cards."

"I didn't get caught. I can deny it."

"You do that. As to our chances, that depends. If it's a matter of being sufficiently awed by my unworthiness, I can give her the perfect meek daughter-in-law. But I have to meet the old trout first, and Tachbrook's dragging his heels."

Robin sighed. "If we go through this whole palaver and the only people who end up rich are the modistes and tailors…"

"Then at least we tried. Come on, Rob. I could be a marchioness yet, and Alice might decide she wants you in the teeth of her uncle's disapproval. Do you know what, you should make your declaration."

"Now?"

"Why not? The prospect of being parted from her focused your mind, et cetera. Bring it to a head. If she refuses you, you can be pale and interesting at other women before the end of the Season, and spend a lot more time in hells."

"Unlucky in love, lucky at cards," Robin agreed. The maxim had always held true for him, although he wasn't so much lucky as manipulative when it came to cards. Mind you, he could say the same about love.

"We'll win this," Marianne said. "I'll marry *someone*."

She could unquestionably find a husband to give her a life of security, with clothes on her back and food on the table. It was less likely she could switch from the marquess to another man with the sort of wealth that would let her fund her brother too. Robin didn't say anything, but Marianne put out a swift hand. "We're in this together, Rob. I'm not looking after myself at your expense."

"You should if you have to."

"I don't have to. This is a mild setback, that's all. We'll get you your heiress. Should I charm Hartlebury, do you think? Or seduce him. Shall I put him on his knees?"

She was joking, Robin knew, but it brought up an unexpected mental image of doing that himself. He took a second to picture Hartlebury begging for his touch, all that scowling temper and physical power reduced to pleading. It was a satisfying thought.

"Best not," he said. "Or at least, not unless Tachbrook drops out of the running. Then again, Hartlebury's not poor. Why don't you take him and I'll have Alice? We could have a double wedding."

"Oh, that would be lovely, with you panting after the other groom."

"What? I am not panting for anyone, especially him."

"Please. You're a fool for legs like that."

Robin was easily swayed by thighs, no denying it, but he preferred them when they weren't standing between him and twenty thousand pounds. Sir John Hartlebury was an obstacle to his future prosperity, and a threat to his current solvency if he chose to spread accusations about card-sharping around. Robin would need to play his hand very carefully indeed. And if that meant playing foul, so be it.

CHAPTER 4

The Loxleigh siblings had left Mrs. Blaine's house in haste, but in harmony with one another. The same could not be said for the brother and sister who remained behind.

"What on *earth*?" Edwina demanded in a voice that tried to be at once a whisper and a screech. "What have you done?"

"What you wanted. You asked me to look into the man—"

"Look into! Not drive off!"

"Yes, and I looked, and I don't like what I see. I don't trust him. I don't like him."

"You aren't being asked to marry him," Edwina said through her teeth. "That is up to Alice, for heaven's sake. If you had something to say about him why didn't you say it to me first?"

"I think he cheated at cards last night."

It ought to have been a clincher. Unfortunately, that would require his opponent to care about the codes governing gentlemanly behaviour. Edwina threw up her hands. "And?"

"That matters!"

"Of all the male nonsense. *Games.* I'm talking about marriage!"

"It's a matter of honour. Doesn't that count in a marriage?"

She rolled her eyes. "So men who play cards the right way are always good, honourable husbands?"

That was not an argument he could make, given her unlamented second husband. Nobody could have accused Blaine of cheating at cards, given how much money he'd lost at them. "Men who don't probably aren't."

"Do you know, Hart, it's quite hard to find a good man without making some compromise," Edwina said. "Perhaps he has a temper, and one hopes its violence is not turned against oneself. Perhaps he has a wandering eye that one must ignore. Fenwick was twenty years my senior and a widower, not to mention that I married beneath myself in the world's eyes."

"Yes, but—"

"But what? Card games! As if that matters! And you only said you 'think' he cheated. Did you accuse him without being sure?"

Hart cursed internally. In truth, he couldn't be certain. But he'd had Evangeline Wintour's suspicions in his mind, and he'd thought he'd seen Loxleigh's nimble hands do something odd, and then the man had started winning.

He hadn't meant to mention the cards. He'd intended to hold that in reserve, but something about Loxleigh irritated him like a splinter in his thumb. The man was so false, with his flowery speeches and his smiling good looks and that full, inviting mouth spouting cant and false virtue. A mouth shouldn't be at once so detestable and so desirable. It made him think of a fairy tale about an unkind princess cursed to have toads drop from her lips when she spoke. And Loxleigh intended to take Alice's money, doing God knows what to her in the process. At best he'd abandon her, at worst—well, there was little bottom to 'worst' for a woman in a bad marriage.

Or, at least, Hart was fairly sure that was what Loxleigh

intended. Unfortunately, he had no proof but instinct, and Edwina had her arms folded and a martial light in her eye.

"Do you believe he loves Alice?" he tried.

"I believe that he likes and respects her and thinks she would make him a good wife. Is that so implausible?"

"Yes!" Hart said, saw her swell, and added hastily, "For him. Not Alice. Of course anyone might love her."

"So why did he say you didn't believe she was worthy of love?"

"He twisted my words!" Hart protested. "I don't think someone like *him* would love her."

"Why not?"

He didn't want to spell it out. Of course a glossy young Adonis like Loxleigh wouldn't court plain Alice for her delightful character, even if he wasn't a prating liar. That was not the way of the world. But he didn't feel like embarking on that conversation, and he had plenty of other objections to raise. "He's false all the way through. Can you not see? Smooth-tongued and calculating and manipulative. He's a fortune hunter, I'm sure of it."

"What fortune do you think he's hunting?" Edwina demanded. "We kept her portion secret!"

"But the world knows her father was a successful man. Anyone might guess he left her something. Will you believe me if I can prove he knew about her money?"

"Is it unreasonable to ask about a girl's portion?"

"If he found it out before he made her acquaintance—"

"How will you possibly prove that? You've decided you don't like him and you're looking for reasons to justify it. If you have anything concrete to say of Mr. Loxleigh, tell me. But if you've just taken against him because he's handsome, that's not fair."

Hart felt himself redden. He did mistrust beautiful people as a general rule; he hadn't realised that was obvious to others.

"I don't have anything concrete," he said, jaw set so hard it hurt. "But I do not believe he's honest. Everything about him is wrong. And I love Alice a great deal too much to see her made miserable by a fraud."

"I want her to be happy too." The self-control was audible in Edwina's voice. "I want her to enjoy herself. To experience a London Season and meet new people and realise there is more to life than her books. And I don't want you to spoil it by frightening off every new friend she might make!"

"He isn't a friend if he's after her money. And anyway she doesn't *like* new people. She's much happier doing algebra with Dr. Trelawney at home."

Angry colour flared in Edwina's cheeks. "That is exactly the problem! She will never pay attention to the wider world if I don't make her. It's not that I want her thinking of marriage now: it's that if she buries herself in her studies to the exclusion of all else, she won't be fit to find a husband by the time she *does* want to. You ought to understand that, Hart. Alice needs to acquire polish. She needs to learn to be comfortable in society, and how to talk to people. She can't simply sit with her studies and then expect to find a good husband—which does not simply *happen*, you know, she will have to meet new people and show herself to advantage, not just depend on her fortune to bring the right man along. Goodness me, do you want her to be as awkward as you?"

That was a low blow. Hart was well aware he'd never acquired the social poise Edwina described. He'd never gone to university, attended rural festivities to prepare him for London ones, or even had a dancing-master. He hadn't learned to make elegant conversation or to look as if he belonged in the society to which his birth entitled him. Probably he would never have been a graceful man since he lacked any natural gifts in that direction, but he could, undeniably, have been a more polished, confident one.

"I'm doing perfectly well," he said, rather defensively.

"You are a man, a Hartlebury, and a baronet. You will always command *some* respect for those things, no matter how gracelessly you conduct yourself. Alice is none of them, so she needs to make the most of what she is. I'm not a fool, Hart; I know she isn't greatly enjoying this. But she is my daughter and I have to think of her future. I could not bear to have her ask me in later years why I didn't guide her better. I'd rather she sat through a few parties now and was relieved to go home than that she should ever believe I didn't consider her well-being. She suffered too much of that." Her voice shook.

Hart passed her a handkerchief. "I do understand."

"I want her to be happy," Edwina said, muffled. "And she truly likes Miss Loxleigh. She had started enjoying London. Why did you have to spoil it?"

That felt unjustly accurate. "If I'm wrong about Loxleigh I'll apologise," he made himself say. "If I'm right, it isn't I who will have spoiled anything."

"And if you've insulted him so grossly he doesn't return and Miss Loxleigh takes offence, and she marries Tachbrook, and all *that* starts up again—"

"Let's not borrow trouble. And don't you find that odd, Edwina? Two siblings, unknowns, both setting themselves at wealthy possible spouses?"

"It's what people do!" Edwina almost shouted. "That is the entire *purpose* of the Marriage Mart, to exchange wealth for beauty! Why shouldn't Miss Loxleigh set her sights at a marquess, if one is willing to marry her? Why should Alice not use her riches to find a husband when she's ready for one? My goodness, Hart, do you think Blaine married me for my looks?"

Even when young, Edwina had been far too much a Hartlebury to be called beautiful, with the family's heavy build

45

and strong features. Hart said, "There is a difference between a practical marriage and a fortune hunter."

"What difference?"

He opened his mouth and realised that was in fact a very good question. "What the other party has to offer," he tried.

"Beauty is a commodity. The Misses Gunning had nothing but beauty, and one married an earl and the other married two dukes."

"All right, then: frankness about one's position."

"The Loxleighs have made it clear they have very humble means."

"They dress damned well on it."

"Don't swear. I dare say they saved for this opportunity. Why should they not?"

And why should Loxleigh not gamble to fund it, Hart supposed. "What about the future? Would a man who only wanted her money make a kind husband?"

Edwina shook her head, almost pityingly. "Do you believe love-matches are safer? I made a business arrangement with Fenwick and I was very happy. Whereas when I married Blaine, I thought I loved him, and I believed he cared for me. You would not have called him a fortune hunter when we married, would you?"

His sister's second husband had come from a good family: it had been his only worthwhile feature. "Granted, any man might mistreat a wife."

"Or perhaps a poor man might be more appreciative of a rich wife, and try to please her," Edwina countered. "Or maybe not. Perhaps you're quite right and Loxleigh is a cruel man who sees easy prey, and perhaps his sister is part of his cruel lie when she takes long walks with Alice and they laugh like children, or go to the theatre together. I don't know. But I don't want to tell Alice that a gentleman who respects her and a lady who is her friend are deceiving her if I don't know it for a fact. Prove it and I'll listen."

Hart shoved both hands through his hair. He'd felt entirely justified in his defence of Alice before, and he was sure—almost sure—he was right about Loxleigh, but as ever, the backwash of losing his temper took ground from under his feet. He had overstepped, and he knew it. "All right. But give me a little more time, and don't let Alice accept him if things come to that. If he is honest, he'll understand her family's caution."

"Alice is her own mistress, as you well know. She doesn't require my consent."

"But she listens to you because you are her mother," Hart said. "Give me time, please. I wouldn't forgive myself if she was trapped by a cozener, and nor would you."

"I will give time if you give tolerance," Edwina returned. "Which is to say, you will be civil to Loxleigh. If you need to apologise to him—"

"The devil I will!"

"—then you must do that, and if you cannot behave you must stay out of the way. I won't have Alice sitting alone because you prowl around snarling at her friends."

"I do not snarl."

"Of course you do." Edwina gathered herself and rose. "I shall go to Alice. Can I assure her that you will not spoil her best acquaintance in London?"

"Edwina—"

"Can I, Hart?"

"I'm damned if I'm apologising."

"Don't swear. Can I assure Alice that you have not ruined her friendships?" Her tone was militant.

Hart pinched the bridge of his nose. It looked like this round would go to Loxleigh.

CHAPTER 5

Three days later, Hart was elegantly dressed, and in an extremely bad mood.

The aftermath of that disastrous afternoon rolled on. He had sought a quiet word with Alice, sitting miserably alone in the drawing room after all the shouting, and asked her point-blank if she inclined to Loxleigh. After all, this would be a lot of fuss about nothing if she were simply enjoying a flirtation.

Unfortunately, Alice had blushed hotly and mumbled that he was very pleasant and his sister was delightful. Hart had to take that as a yes, because Edwina had chased him out of the house at that point.

He had gritted his teeth and sent Loxleigh a curt note saying that his temper had driven him into unwary expression. He could not bring himself to apologise properly, and he didn't want to phrase it in any way the man could wave around as proof of vindication. Loxleigh had returned an entire paragraph of waffle in a neat if schoolboyish hand, indicating that he respected Hart's concern for Miss Fenwick and was prepared to overlook his unwarranted implications as expressed in private. The implication of 'don't say it in public' was very clear. Hart threw the paper on the fire with a curse.

He spent the next couple of days working on the problem. He had no idea where the Loxleighs were from, and Alice couldn't remember the name of their village if she'd ever been told, so that line of enquiry would likely take some while to pursue. He started it anyway, asked Evangeline Wintour to keep a very close eye on the man at her tables, and wrote to his lawyer and his brewery manager in Aston Clinton to discover if anyone had been asking questions.

Maybe he was wrong. It had to be faced. Maybe the Loxleighs were just what they seemed—charming, remarkably attractive people who wanted to make good marriages. If they were of adequate birth, one could hardly hold limited means against them, still less ambition to improve their circumstances.

That didn't make him like Loxleigh's practised smile any better. A clever, ambitious man could do as he pleased with an impressionable girl, and he was determined Loxleigh would not have that chance. And therefore when the fellow invited Alice to make one of a party at Astley's Amphitheatre, Hart had said he'd escort her.

Hence his bad mood, and his attention to his dress. He didn't generally make an effort with his appearance—there was little point—but Loxleigh had made him feel conscious of his carelessly tied cravat and crumpled coat. So he had summoned Spenlow, the man of the house who valeted for him in London, had a close shave, ensured his clothes were freshly pressed and his shirt-points starched, and put more effort into his cravat than he could recall doing in years. He still looked like a scowling brute at the end of it, but at least a smart one.

The performance began at half past six. He joined Alice and Edwina for a small collation at five o'clock to keep the wolf from the door and took Alice to Westminster Bridge in a carriage.

She was glowing with excitement, eyes bright. Hart hoped

to hell that wasn't about seeing Loxleigh. "Looking forward to tonight?"

"Oh, yes." She beamed at him. "Everyone says it's a marvellous performance. There are equestrian exercises and a Lapland scene and magical tricks and a harlequinade and a minuet danced by horses!"

"Good God."

"How do you think they teach horses the minuet? Because I find it awfully difficult and I have a dancing master. And only two legs."

"It could be worse," Hart offered. "It could be a Scotch reel."

That set Alice off laughing, and they arrived at Astley's in good spirits and great charity with one another.

The party was made up of Giles Verney, escorting Miss Jennifer Verney, his niece; Mr. and Miss Loxleigh; the feather-headed Miss Florence Jocelyn; and Miss Jocelyn's fiancé, a pointless young man named Mowbray. Miss Loxleigh welcomed Alice with great warmth. Hart bowed civilly, including to Loxleigh, who bowed back, face neutral.

The box held eight, in two rows of four. The four ladies sat together at the front. Hart, who had no interest in dancing horses, sat at the end of the back row with Giles.

"What are you doing here?" he asked, without preamble.

"Escorting Jenny, of course. I have squired her to several events this Season, as you'd know if you ever took Alice anywhere."

"I'm here now," Hart protested.

"I'm glad to see it. If you're looking to come out more often, I will cheerfully give you a list of my movements in the hope of your company. These things are a great deal less trying with someone to talk to."

That was a lure. Giles, as Hart knew well, had no need of

support on these occasions; he was trying to draw Hart out into society, for his own sake as well as Alice's. If only his gregarious friend would grasp that Hart found social drawing-out only slightly less unpleasant than the same process applied to teeth.

The equestrian exercises took place to much cheering and applause. They were followed by two musical pieces, which lost Hart's attention entirely, though Alice and Jennifer seemed delighted by them. The rest of the party shifted around a little. Miss Jocelyn rose to talk to her fiancé, and Giles hastily excused himself and took her place next to Miss Loxleigh. She turned with a smile that painters would have wept to see, and Giles leaned in, speaking to her in a low voice. Miss Jocelyn and Mowbray then disappeared to obtain drinks, or possibly privacy, which left Loxleigh and Hart together in the back row.

Hart stretched out his legs as best he could and leaned back, unwilling to betray his awkwardness. He didn't look at Loxleigh and Loxleigh didn't—so far as he could tell—look at him. They sat for some time in silence as the idiocies in the amphitheatre continued.

Not speaking to him, not acknowledging him, simply seemed to make Hart more aware of him. He was vividly conscious of Loxleigh's presence, the compact form, the thighs encased in tight kerseymere cloth which were all he could see out of the corner of his eye, the soft sound of his breathing despite the noise and chatter around him. He became irrationally aware of his own breath, which seemed to be in time with Loxleigh's, and tried to change the pattern by breathing slower, then felt short of air and had to restrain himself from gasping.

This was absurd. But he couldn't stop noticing Loxleigh, and he was sure, absolutely sure, the man knew it.

The musical interlude ended, and another began, this time

a pastoral comedy dance announced as 'Who Stole the Sheep?' Hart gave an involuntary grunt of distress.

Loxleigh leaned over. He didn't touch, nothing like it, but Hart thought he could feel the heat of his body all the same. "Are you enjoying the performance?"

"Frankly?"

"I don't expect you to sugar-coat your words."

"Then, no."

"What a shame. I'm sure you'll love the dancing dogs," Loxleigh said, and sat back.

Hart had to look at him then. He was watching the stage with an expression of absorbed innocence, yet Hart could swear the bastard was laughing at him. He leaned over in return. "I suppose you're enjoying this? The sheep, I mean."

Loxleigh's brows went up. "Why?"

"You made a point of being a country boy. I'd expect you to be particularly fond of sheep."

He intended that vulgarity to provoke offence. Instead, Loxleigh gave an involuntary, explosive choke of laughter, which he attempted to stifle with a cough so noisy that Alice looked round in some alarm. He took a moment to recover his composure. "I fear you have greater knowledge of countryside practises than I, Sir John."

"Weak," Hart said, quietly enough that it could be meant for himself, just loudly enough to be heard. Loxleigh didn't reply but his lips tightened. He was clearly trying not to smile, and Hart had to bite the inside of his own lip. They were not supposed to be entertaining one another.

The sheep people went off. The dancing dogs came on. Hart watched the younger girls shrieking and cooing in the front row while Miss Loxleigh and Giles talked quietly, heads together. Loxleigh sat in silence, his presence throbbing in Hart's awareness.

The dogs went off. The magician came on. It was possible

the evening might last forever. What was he doing here? He'd come to ensure Loxleigh didn't spend the evening flirting with Alice, but they'd barely exchanged a word, and she was entirely absorbed by the entertainment. That was a relief—a young lady in the throes of calf-love wouldn't apply all her attention to dancing dogs. Perhaps they'd made a great to-do over this for no reason. Perhaps Loxleigh had made no impact on her at all.

But he glanced over at Loxleigh—at his generous mouth made for kissing, at his clever, fluent hands and the shifting light in his eyes—and he couldn't quite see how that was possible.

CHAPTER 6

Days after the trip to Astley's, Robin was still thinking about it.

Bloody Hartlebury. As if it wasn't enough to be mannerless and inconvenient and intimidating, with those ridiculous eyebrows and that magnificent, unapologetic nose, he was so *obtrusive*. He'd sat in the corner of Robin's vision the whole endless evening. It hadn't even occurred to him that he'd put all his attention into his intended prey's uncle and none into the prey herself until Marianne had asked him, somewhat tartly, which one he was trying to seduce.

Hence he was walking with Alice in the park now, well wrapped up against the cold. She was a sturdy walker, who probably tramped tireless miles in the countryside for pleasure. Robin had tramped a lot of miles himself out of necessity. It was why he intended to become sufficiently rich to take carriages for the rest of his life.

"I'm glad you enjoyed Astley's," he said.

"Oh, it was marvellous! Thank you so much. Did Marianne have a good time?"

"Very much so."

"She seems to be good friends with Giles—Mr. Verney.

You know he is Uncle Hart's best friend, and the families are very close, so I have known him all my life."

Robin filed that away as a warning for Marianne. He had not failed to notice her black head next to Verney's fair one, deep in laughing conversation all evening. It was ill-judged when she should be concentrating on a marquess. Verney seemed adequate from the little attention Robin had paid to him, but they had bigger fish to fry.

"I wondered if you would care to see Grimaldi's Pantomime," he offered.

"Oh, I am to go with Jennifer Verney tonight. I'm sorry. It was very kind of you to invite me. I hope you will go anyway?"

He smiled down at her, making it a little amused and very tender. "Not without you. The pleasure you take in theatre is better than the piece for me."

Alice blushed. "I do enjoy it awfully. I suppose I should be more restrained."

"Why? It's there to be enjoyed. That's its purpose."

"I suppose so. It's just, most people are used to it here, whereas we have very little chance to see these things at home. There is some theatre, tours and so on, but not the grand spectacles. So I do like being able to see them, and I can't pretend to be sophisticated and jaded about it."

"I'm glad you don't. Would you prefer to live in London, and have these things to hand?"

Alice considered that for a couple of steps. "Would it be terribly boring if I said, not really? London is awfully large and very dirty and there are so many people. And I can't be myself. At home I have my friends and my studies, and people know I'm a bluestocking but they consider it an oddity, rather than a terrible ailment to be concealed."

Robin laughed. "Are you that much a bluestocking?"

"I study mathematics," she said in a rush, as if admitting to stealing the spoons. "With a tutor, Dr. Trelawney. He has a doctorate from Oxford and went to the university at Heidelberg too."

"Good heavens."

She searched his face. "Do you think that's unseemly? My interest, I mean."

"Not at all. If you enjoy it, why should you not pursue it?"

"It's not what most young ladies do."

"But you are not most young ladies," Robin said, a practised line that he hoped would evoke another blush.

It got a scowl instead. "Well, nor are any other young ladies, by definition."

"I meant, there is nothing wrong with having unusual interests."

"Or usual ones, either. I think it must be very nice to be interested in the things one is expected to be interested in, as well as a great deal easier."

"Lord, that's true," Robin said with deep feeling. He'd have been saved a lot of trouble in life if he were interested in women, for a start.

"Of course I don't think there's anything wrong with parties, or wanting to be married," she pressed on, rather giving the impression she was arguing with someone in her head. "I just think there ought to be space for mathematics *as well*."

"I'll take your word for it. I'm afraid my own studies of the subject were limited by my capacity. Don't despise me."

"I don't despise anyone but—well, really? Surely you are a mathematician?"

"Er…no?"

"But Uncle Hart said you play at the gaming tables."

"Occasionally, as do most men," Robin said, poised for defence or denial.

"Yes, but isn't that mathematics in action? Or do you play dice, or roulette?"

"Cards. I prefer a contest of skill." More to the point, he couldn't cheat at the others.

"Good. Roulette is absurd. Are you familiar with d'Alembert's system?"

"Who?"

"A French mathematician. He has a betting system for roulette which is based on mathematical principles—but I'm sorry, I'm running on."

"No, no, I do want to hear it, very much," Robin assured her. "Does it work?"

"*Well*," Alice said, and was off in explanation. It sounded, as far as he could gather, like a martingale system for betting, in which one increased stakes after losing and decreased them after winning, though with some refinements.

"I've seen people play martingale," he said. "Most of them swear by it, but quite a few of them lose."

"Of course they do! Over the long run it might even out, but to follow his system properly would require infinite funds, which most people do not have—"

"I certainly don't."

"And it makes no sense at all in terms of probability, because the fall of the ball, or the dice, is not affected by what came before."

Robin blinked. "You might have to explain that."

"Say you roll a die six times, and the first five times it comes up one. Do you think it's more likely to come up a six on the next throw?"

"It's probably Greeked. I'd ask for new dice."

She gave him a look. "All right, say it has been rolled ten times and everything *except* a six has come up. Would you wager on it being a six on the next roll?"

Robin thought about it. "Ten times? Probably. A six is due."

"But it *isn't* due. The die has no memory of what was

rolled before, any more than a pack of cards remembers the last deal. Perhaps a six hasn't been rolled in ten tries or even a hundred, but the odds of a six remain what they always were: one in six."

"After a hundred?"

"Or a thousand. I grant you, if a die didn't roll a six in a thousand rolls it might be—what did you say?"

"Greeked."

"Greeked," she repeated, with relish. "Assuming a fair die, though, it's just a long string of chances."

"But surely—"

They walked and talked for the next hour, Alice as animated as he'd ever seen her, eyes bright, not resting until she had persuaded him of d'Alembert's fallacy, and then delving into the mathematics of other games of chance. Robin had good card sense and a long practical acquaintance with what he might expect in a game: he would not have expected an eighteen-year-old girl to dismiss his experience so confidently, but he found himself forced to listen as she chided him for superstition.

"But it doesn't feel right," he protested at one point. "Surely if the cards have been running badly for me, my luck—"

"Does not exist." Alice had spoken strongly on the subject of luck.

"My *chances* will improve. A series of bad hands is bound to be followed by a good one."

"Over time, of course. Over time, a fair die will come up on each side equally. But 'over time' is—oh, years, not an evening. Runs of cards, or dice, are inevitable, but a winning or losing streak is an illusion."

"Then I've won a lot of money on things that don't exist."

"I expect you have. I'm not saying you *can't* roll a six ten times in a row. I'm saying that when you do it's simply a series of individual one in six chances."

"But ten sixes isn't a one in six chance, is it?" Robin said, attempting to work that in his head. "It can't be."

"No, of course not. It's one-sixth multiplied by one-sixth multiplied by one-sixth and so on, ten times."

"Wouldn't that be very large?"

Alice gave him a kindly smile. "No, it would be very small. Fractions multiplied by other fractions become smaller. So it would be a very small chance indeed, but what you have to remember is that *any* specific outcome is just as unlikely. Suppose you rolled a die ten times and it came up three, one, four, one, five, nine, two, six, five, three. Would you see that as a streak?"

"How would I roll a nine?"

Alice waved a hand. "You're using a ten-sided die. It's an illustration. Answer the question."

"I have never seen such a thing. And of course it isn't a streak. It's random numbers."

"Actually, it's pi."

"It's what?"

"Pi. Archimedes' constant? The ratio of a circle's circumference to its diameter? Surely you studied geometry at school."

She looked genuinely puzzled, as if Robin ought to know who Archimedes was or why he was constant. "I didn't always pay my tutor his due attention, I fear," he lied smoothly. "What have circles to do with dice?"

"Nothing. All I meant to say is, as a matter of probability, it is exactly as likely, or as unlikely, that you should roll three, one, four, one, five, nine, two, six, five, three in that order as it is that you should roll ten sixes. Each combination is as unique and surprising and impossible to predict as the other."

Robin attempted to grasp her point. "So Archimedes' constant is as rare as ten sixes—"

"And so is *any* ten numbers in a specific order. Whatever combination of results you get is unique, and absurdly improbable once you consider all the other possibilities. It's just that people don't notice if they aren't showy."

Her voice was passionate, as though she truly cared about the injustice to a string of numbers. Robin turned to examine her face. She gave a little shrug.

"I'm going to be thinking about this for days," he said. "I had no idea you were so clever."

Alice blushed, this time seeming pleased rather than embarrassed. "Please don't mention it to Mama. I'm not really supposed to talk about mathematics to—as part of my Season."

To men, she probably meant. The devil with that. Robin had a sudden fantastical vision of them as husband and wife, she developing foolproof mathematics to give him the edge at the card table, he turning her dowry into hundreds of thousands. He cleared his throat, wondering if it was time to put his luck—his *chances*—to the test.

"Oh, there's Florence waving at me," Alice said. "Goodness, is it noon already? I had no idea we'd talked so long, I'm probably late. I'm so sorry for running on."

"I'll walk you over." Robin steered her in Miss Jocelyn's direction. "And that was without question the most interesting conversation I've had since we arrived in London."

Alice stopped to look at him. "Really?"

"Really."

She smiled. It was a smile full of happiness and relief and even joy, exactly the sort of smile he ought to be eliciting from a girl with twenty thousand pounds, and it hit him like a punch to the heart.

He left her with her friends and walked back through the

park in an aimless sort of way. Marianne was out for a carriage-ride with the Marquess of Tachbrook and would, with luck, not be back for some time. That was a shame. If he told her that Alice had confided in him against her mother's wishes, that her eyes had lit and she'd blushed and smiled, Marianne would have cheered, and encouraged him to strike while the iron was hot, and he wouldn't have dared say anything such as *I think she likes me, and I truly like her, and I feel like a swine.*

Wouldn't it be better for Alice to marry a man who enjoyed her company, rather than some other and entirely heartless fortune hunter? Might they not be as happy as any married pair might reasonably hope? Admittedly she might be expecting a love-match, because he might have led her to significantly overestimate his feelings for her; but if he had *some* feelings—affection and respect and every intention of maintaining amicable relations—was that really so bad?

There were worse men than himself. The Upper Ten Thousand sold women into marriages with cruel, greedy, brutal men every day for social or financial advantage, and that was acceptable because they had birth and upbringing. Robin was sure Alice would rather have a good friend.

He told himself that over again, glowering at the grey water of the Round Pond and the red brick of Kensington Palace, until his hands were so cold he had to go home, but he still didn't feel any better.

CHAPTER 7

They were to attend Mrs. Verney's soirée that evening. She was Giles Verney's brother's wife, and though the invitation had come from her, Robin had little doubt who had asked for it. He'd seen the way Verney looked at Marianne.

"Why are we going?" he asked her as they dressed. Marianne wore a very simple gown that showed off her magnificent figure, with a plain string of pearls that had cost Robin an entire evening's winnings and her hair dressed au naturel. She looked stunning, more than she did in the most elaborate toilettes. Robin suspected it was because she was happier.

"Why would we not? Mrs. Verney is wonderfully respectable." Marianne held a pearl drop to her ear, considering. "This or the little string of seed pearls?"

"The drop. It looks much more artless."

Marianne smiled into the mirror. "You've no idea how hard I work to be artless."

"Is Tachbrook going?"

"I hope not."

Robin was mid-cravat and, not having a stack of fresh linens to hand, he couldn't afford to get this wrong. He lowered his chin carefully to press the creases into place, squinted in the mirror, decided he was satisfied, and said, "Really?"

"Christ, Rob, do you want to listen to him? Neither do I."

"You'll have to listen to him if you marry him."

"If I marry him I'll be paid to listen to him." The light had gone from her face. "Meanwhile, I shall take every opportunity I have not to."

"And you don't want to look like you're living in his pocket," Robin said, in lieu of asking if she was going to listen to Giles Verney instead.

"No indeed. In fact, I intend to be busy for several days. Absence might concentrate Tachbrook's mind."

"Might he not take offence?"

"If he takes offence I won't get him anyway." Marianne inserted the ear-bob's wire. "He needs to court me, chase me, win me. He won't be satisfied else."

She was sitting with her back to him as he spoke, but he could see her face in the mirror. Her eyes met his in the glass, a long, silent look, then she went on to the other earring. "Is Alice coming?"

"No. She's going to Grimaldi's pantomime."

"You should have taken her to that."

"I walked with her in the park for two hours, talking," Robin said. "She told me about…her interests." He felt as though Alice's mathematics might be private, somehow. "We got on wonderfully."

"Excellent. Are you going to propose soon?"

Robin searched for a reply, but there was only one, really. They'd left too many angry people and unpaid debts behind them; they'd invested too much money and effort into their targets here. They were in too deep to stop.

"I'll do it tomorrow."

"I wish you would." Marianne tweaked a ringlet. "You will be good to her, won't you, Rob?"

"Of course I will."

"I like her. She's clever."

"I've noticed."

"And she's kind. She deserves a good husband."

"Then why do you want to saddle her with me?"

That came out of his mouth unplanned. Marianne's eyes widened. She rose swiftly and turned to take his hand. "What's that about? You won't hurt her, will you?"

"I won't love her either. You know I don't feel that way."

"You can love someone without tupping them. You can be kind and patient and friendly—"

"Is that what you want out of a marriage? Kind and patient and friendly?"

Marianne dropped his hand and stepped back. Her voice was several degrees chillier when she said, "What I want out of a marriage is the title of marchioness and eighteen thousand a year. Kindness and patience won't come into it. Still less whatever romantic notions you may be harbouring which, if I may say so, are absurd for a man of your tastes. How much kindness do you find on your knees in a dark alley?"

"Maybe I'd like a little more kindness than that."

"Maybe we all would." Marianne returned to her mirror. "The world isn't kind. Are you ready?"

They barely spoke on the way to the party. Marianne was silent in the way that usually suggested simmering rage. Since her rage was aimed at, or at least near, Robin, he felt it best to keep his mouth shut. He'd spoiled her pleasure quite enough for one evening.

As if things weren't sufficiently dismal, the first person he saw as he entered was Sir John Hartlebury.

He couldn't help noticing the man. It wasn't his size—he was broadly built, but not particularly tall—or even his severe appearance, with the eyebrows and the plain clothing. It was just his solid, bristling presence, like a mastiff in a room of bright birds.

Hartlebury was part of a crowd that included Giles Verney and two men who were clearly his brothers, plus an older man in the purple plumage of an archbishop who resembled them all. They were talking with noise and animation, Hartlebury among them, laughing unguardedly. He seemed comfortable and at home, and the unaccustomed expression made him look completely different. Robin had never seen the man look relaxed before.

"Stop staring," said Marianne under her breath, and swept forwards to greet Verney.

Robin greeted people, exchanged frostily civil bows with Hartlebury, and made himself scarce. The least he could do for Marianne was to not start a fight.

He probably wouldn't have played cards anyway, as potentially provocative, but there was no card table. Of course not. The Verneys were far too high sticklers for cards, with their patriarch the archbishop and his bevy of well-married, well-behaved children, and their impeccable respectability. You could choke on the gentility round here.

Instead, the entertainment on offer was a chamber orchestra. Wonderful. Robin sat and listened to music for several hours, and was disappointed to learn that only forty minutes had passed on the clock. He found a drink, and made pleasant conversation with highly respectable people in a modest, friendly, charming way; he sat for supper at which he was pleasant and modest and did some more friendly charming, and finally he went out into the garden with a vague idea of finding a fishpond and drowning himself, because if he had one more vapid interaction in the name of society, he might scream.

It was dark outside, and very cold, but that was welcome

after the heat of a crowded house. He smelled smoke as he went down the garden and saw a dark form that could have been a statue except for the glowing end of his cigar. Robin swallowed down his justified annoyance at bloody people everywhere and said, "Good evening."

The figure turned, his profile catching the light spilling from the house, and Robin bit back a groan. Of course it was him. Of course.

"After fresh air?" Hartlebury enquired.

"And a little cool." And some silence, and an absence of people, and not seeing Marianne's bright eyes as she laughed with Giles Verney.

"I'll finish my cigar and leave you to your solitude."

Evidently Hartlebury no more wanted to be in the garden with Robin than vice versa. That thought made him respond, perversely, "Not on my account."

Hartlebury didn't reply to that. He simply stood, smoking. Robin looked away to let his eyes adjust to the darkness, and saw there was indeed a fishpond, and a stone bench near it. He tested the bench with his hand for dampness, sat down, and inhaled sharply.

"Cold?" Hartlebury enquired.

"A little bracing, yes."

Pause.

"Alice told me she walked in the park with you today."

"She did. We had a very interesting conversation."

"She has more than once said she has interesting conversations with you, yet I have rarely had anything but pleasantries, platitudes, and speeches," Hartlebury said. "I wonder, why is that?"

Robin shrugged in the dark. "I find it equally improbable when she tells me she has enjoyable conversations with you."

There was a brief silence, then a snort. "That was plain speaking."

"Is that not what you wanted?"

"Indeed it is; I just didn't think I'd get it. I'd be very pleased to learn your inmost thoughts."

"Bet you wouldn't," Robin said, instantly and with feeling.

"Do you know, that's the third honest thing you've said to me? You should be careful. It might become a habit."

Robin sighed. "Whereas I have lost count of the offensive things you've said to me."

"But at least I mean what I say."

"I can't imagine why you pride yourself on that. Any fool can say what he means and mean what he says. That's why we invented manners, as a way to stop society descending into a brawl."

Hartlebury tossed the stub of his cigar into the pond. It fell like a star and hissed as the water extinguished its brief brightness. "Where are you from?"

"Nottinghamshire."

"What village?"

"Are you hunting for information on me?"

"Yes."

"Then why should I help you?"

"I'd think you'd want to establish your name, if you had one."

"To be good enough for you?"

"For Alice."

Robin folded his arms to stuff his achingly cold fingertips under his armpits. He was *not* going to leave the garden first. "If Alice wants to know anything of me, she is welcome to ask."

"Mouthy under cover of darkness, aren't you?"

"You complain about me being courteous, you complain about me being frank. Do you ever stop complaining?"

Hartlebury chuckled, a ghost of a sound. They both fell

silent for a moment, as the music and chatter floated out from the Verneys' house.

"What do you want?" he asked at last.

"A cushion."

"What?"

"This seat is very hard, and extremely cold."

"That was surely predictable when you sat on it," Hartlebury pointed out. "I didn't mean at this moment."

"I know what you meant. Why do you ask?"

"I want to know."

"I want what everyone wants," Robin said. "I want to be happy. I want the people for whom I care to be happy. I want to be reasonably secure in that happiness."

"Secure?" Hartlebury repeated, and the fact it sounded like a real question took Robin's breath away.

"Secure. Yes. You know the word? Or have you never lacked for it, that you ask why someone might want it?"

"My sister was happily married to a loving husband," Hartlebury said. "A blood vessel burst in his brain and he dropped dead without warning. There's no security against fate."

"I'm not talking about fate. We all die, you won't win betting against that. I want—"

He wanted to wake up in the certainty that there was enough food in the house for the week, every single day of the rest of his life. He wanted to have enough money that he never again had to pawn his clothes and sit wrapped in a blanket. He wanted to be so used to having a roof over his head that he never, ever thought about it, and not to have arguments over the spending of sixpence. He wanted to be able to fuck on a bed, in his own home, without the constant fear of discovery. He wanted something better and brighter and, yes, kinder than damp knees in a dark alley with one ear cocked for the avenging law.

Marriage wouldn't win him those last, or at least not with anyone he wanted to fuck. Everything else was achievable, if he could just get his hands on some real money. Gambling money slid through the fingers like water. You won it and staked it and spent it on the trappings you needed to keep playing with the people who had money for you to win, who could lose five hundred or a thousand pounds in a night but only wanted to lose it to men like themselves, because it would be degrading for their money to go to someone poor.

"I want the privilege of not worrying more than I have to," he said. "I'm sure you worry about Alice. Do you worry about anything else, ever? Do you fear for your sister's future, or wonder if you will be cold-shouldered from society for an ill-judged remark, Sir John?"

There was quite a long pause.

"Not really," Hartlebury said at last, quietly, even reflectively. "Not any more. The brewery does well. I don't concern myself with society's judgements. I wish that Alice and my sister will be happy and, as you say, secure. I had not worried about that recently. Until your arrival."

I will make her happy. I will take care of her. Those were the obvious things to say, with Hartlebury in this oddly gentle mood. Robin wasn't sure he could make them sound convincing.

"Perhaps Alice should decide what makes her happy," he said instead.

Like everything else this evening, that was a mistake. He could feel Hartlebury stiffen. "And your sister? Tell me, does Tachbrook make her happy? Is it his witty conversation, his kindly nature, or his modesty that she finds most appealing?"

"As I understand it, the marquess has considered marriage several times. Would you ask the same questions of those other ladies?"

"Yes."

"Oh. Well, you shouldn't."

"Why not? Tachbrook is selfish, consequential, and a bore. The fact that he comes with wealth and a title should hardly be a consideration for a decent woman."

"You were born with wealth and a title," Robin said. "You're condemning other people for wanting things you were handed when you came out squalling from your mother's belly, because you had the double fortune of the right parents and the right parts. Who are you to judge someone else for wanting what you never had to earn?"

"If I didn't have a title, I wouldn't stoop to acquire one."

"Aren't you grand. It must be wonderful to stand apart and judge the rest of us from the superior height of your moral high ground. I fear those of us not born to the peerage cannot aspire to your nobility in claiming not to want what you've already got."

"Careful, Loxleigh." It was a rumble. "Your envy is showing."

"Envy," Robin said. "I heard a sermon about that once. The poor shouldn't envy the rich, it said. They should accept their lot in life and not want to possess just a fraction of what others have. I wonder who paid the first priest to declare *that* from the pulpit."

Hartlebury started to speak, then stopped himself. Robin shifted in the silence, aware he'd been indiscreet. Well, what the hell. Hartlebury already suspected him. He could win Alice's hand and fortune with or without the man.

"You're *very* frank in the darkness," Hartlebury said at last. "I prefer your night-time persona, you know. What it lacks in charm, it more than makes up in interest."

Interest. Hartlebury found him interesting. That was probably bad. The tingles down Robin's skin were probably the first signs of frostbite. "If we can't be honest in the dark, where can we?"

He heard Hartlebury's sharp intake of breath, and his own chest constricted. His words hadn't had an explicit meaning, they could have gone past without notice, but Hartlebury had read something into them, and now the icy air between them was alive.

"We find—show—our true selves in the dark?" Hartlebury's deep voice was almost a rumble. "Is that what you mean?"

"Don't you?"

Silence again. Robin's pulse was thumping.

When Hartlebury spoke again, though, there was nothing of that deep note in his voice. He sounded crisp, almost contemptuous. "That suggests you have something to hide."

Hell's teeth. "There is a difference between hiding and not putting one's entire self on display to the world at all times," Robin said with equal crispness. "I doubt you do that either. And on that note, I'm going in. This has been delightful, but I think I'm freezing to death."

He rose as he spoke, buttocks painfully cold from the stone. Hartlebury didn't speak, but as Robin moved stiffly past, he caught his arm.

Robin stopped dead. Hartlebury had a big hand, a strong grip. He stood very close, his cigar-scented breath curling in plumes in the frosty air, and Robin had the sudden thought that Hartlebury would jerk him even closer, that he would feel a mouth, a hand, a hard body pressed against his own, that Hartlebury would pull him into the bushes—

Not in this weather.

"Sir John?" Robin managed, in a voice that wasn't quite outraged enough.

Hartlebury didn't say anything at all for a second longer, just breathed. Finally he rasped, "Don't try to marry my niece," and let him go. It was almost a push.

CHAPTER 8

"Great heavens, man, will you cheer up?"

Hart shot an unpleasant look at his best friend. He and Giles had been sparring at the Fives Court, under the genial supervision of Bill Richmond, an elder statesman of the pugilistic art who many considered the best boxing instructor in England. He was still a handsome fellow in his fifties, trim and lithe, his dark skin betraying enviably little sign of advancing age. Hart had twice had the privilege of watching Richmond beat men two decades his junior in the ring, and thought him a superior fighter to Jackson and Cribb, not to mention far better company.

Richmond's speech had traces of both America, where he had been born a slave, and York, where he had lived for years. It made Hart wonder again why Loxleigh didn't sound like he came from a Nottinghamshire village.

And there he went again, thinking of Loxleigh. He had not wanted to do that here. He'd wanted to work up a sweat, to give his body so much to do that his mind couldn't keep bringing up that bloody evening by the fishpond. He'd had only limited success.

"You've been like a bear with a sore head for two days,"

Giles added, throwing a towel at him and mopping his own face. "Is something wrong?"

On almost any other subject Hart would have shared his concerns without further thought. But he'd seen the way his friend looked at Marianne Loxleigh, and there was nothing at all he could say about that encounter in the garden. Giles was his friend, but there were some truths that he could never dare disclose.

He said things. Just things. I held his arm and I can still feel the touch of it in my hand.

"Nothing," he said.

Giles leaned in. "It is to do with Alice?"

Hart jerked his head and they strolled over to the empty far corner of the saloon, where a window was open, as if to cool down. "Meaning what?"

"Don't be an oaf, Hart. Loxleigh's pursuit is clear enough, as is your attitude to him."

"Would you want him marrying your sister?" Hart retorted without thought.

Giles paused for a moment. When he spoke, it was carefully. "I find him perfectly pleasant."

"I don't. I find him false."

"You find most people false. It isn't dishonesty to choose one's words carefully. It's *society*."

"That's what Loxleigh said."

"Well, he's right. I know you'd rather have plain truth plainly presented, but you aren't in the majority."

"Leaving that aside, they've appeared from nowhere. All their friends have been made since arriving in London."

"It's not an offence to come from the provinces, or to lack fashionable acquaintance."

"That's not what I mean. It's one thing if they're gentlefolk of limited means and no particular birth. Goodness knows

Miss Loxleigh's beauty is enough to earn her a place in the first rank by itself—"

"Yes, it is," Giles interrupted. "She is lovely, and she is intelligent. She asks me to tell her of the European political situation—"

"Oh, come on."

Giles stiffened. "She listens, and understands, and I know she does because she makes observations of remarkable acuity. Or do you believe a woman can't grasp these matters?"

"On the contrary. I'll take your word for it that she's born to be a political hostess."

"She is. She's beautiful, clever, quick, and charming. Exceptional."

"I grant all that."

"Then what's your problem?" Giles sounded positively hostile.

Hart wondered how he could possibly be tactful. "A man might choose to elevate Miss Loxleigh to his station, and consider it a well-struck bargain. My concern is the brother. He has made stringent efforts to hide his background; he has come to London without a name or a family and set himself to court a girl barely out of the schoolroom for the sake of her portion—"

"I didn't think you'd told anyone about Alice's wealth."

"We didn't. I'm trying to find out how he knew. I am sure he knew. He's a clever man, a sharp one, under the platitudes. A schemer."

"I can't agree," Giles said. "If he is a schemer, so must she be, and I would stake my life she is not."

This was beginning to sound worrying. "Nonsense," Hart said, rather than get into a fight over Miss Loxleigh's character. "Good women have had unworthy brothers since the beginning of time. Half the novels Edwina reads feature good women with unworthy brothers. Some people might take that personally."

Giles gave a reluctant smile. "True, I suppose. But are you sure the brother means ill?"

"I cannot be: that is the devil of it. But we can't take the risk. Alice is too young. If she makes a mistake now it will affect her whole life. I picture her used, left, her portion spent, and—no."

"Have you spoken to her?"

"To Edwina. I don't want to make Alice feel I'm against her."

"Not to offend you, but Alice isn't a Hartlebury. Does it truly matter if a suitor is of no great distinction, if he treats her well?"

"It wouldn't if I were sure he would, and if she made an informed choice. I don't believe deceit is a good start."

Giles made a face. "No. Curse it. I do see your worry, Hart, but… You know Marianne—Miss Loxleigh—is devoted to him."

First names. Hart had an increasingly bad feeling about this. "All those good women with unworthy brothers probably love them too."

"Who are you, and where is my friend Hart?" Giles demanded. "You know very well you are itching to call her a fortune-hunter and rain disapproval on her head."

"I don't give a curse for her. Or, to put it better—"

"If you would."

"Miss Loxleigh is not my concern. That's up to her future husband. My only care is for Alice."

"I suppose that's fair. Have you found out anything to support your suspicions?"

"Not yet. I've written to the family lawyer in Aylesbury and my solicitor in Aston Clinton to see if there have been any enquiries about Alice's circumstances. And I've hired a man to track down the Loxleighs in Nottinghamshire. I will catch the little swine if he has put a single foot wrong."

"You seem to be taking this very personally, Hart." Giles hesitated. "I had not meant to press you on this, but, well, you aren't terribly good at speaking of these matters and I think it has to be said. Is it—do you care for Alice yourself?"

"Of course I do."

Giles made an irritated noise. "Not like that. I meant, you have never been greatly interested in women, other women, and you aren't related to Alice, and now she's grown to womanhood—"

"Good Lord, stop!" said Hart, appalled. "She's my niece in every way but blood. I have no interest in marrying her, stealing her fortune by keeping her unmarried, or anything else. All I want is not to watch a rascal ruin her life."

"I can't argue with that." Giles sighed. "Never mind, it was only an idea. Though I think you would do well with a woman to look after."

The last thing Hart needed now was a discussion of his unmarried state. "I have quite enough to look after, thank you."

"You thrive on taking care of others. Perhaps a woman in need of protection, of shelter—"

Hart cut him off with a grimace. "That's the most revolting sentiment I have ever heard. Ought you not to consider your own marital prospects before advising me on mine?"

He wouldn't have said that last if he'd thought, but the words slipped out. Giles twitched as if stung. "I wish I could. Alas, I have little to offer but my name and person."

Which weren't enough for Miss Loxleigh, Hart inferred. "Don't do yourself down. Your name and person are perfectly adequate. I'm sure any woman of reasonable standards would agree."

"Thank you, dear friend," Giles said, much moved. "Come on, let's dress unless you feel the urge to hit anything else. Have you plans for the evening?"

"Nothing. You?"

"The Tauntons are holding a salon."

Lord Taunton was a crony of Tachbrook so Miss Loxleigh would doubtless be attending. Hart wished to hell he could offer some useful advice, but he could think of nothing Giles would want to hear. His friend would soon see behind her lovely face to the heartless, grasping soul Hart suspected lurked there, based mostly on his dislike of her brother. And if he didn't, her marriage to Tachbrook should give him the hint.

He went home feeling far better in body for the exercise, and a little calmer in mind. It had been a relief to express his suspicions to someone who listened, whose vision wasn't obscured by hope that Loxleigh might after all be the man he pretended.

Not that Hart's vision was much clearer after that moment by the fishpond. He'd barely been able to control his voice as his smouldering awareness of Loxleigh had flared into scorching life. Christ, he could not have the man marry Alice. To have him so close, part of the family, within reach, *smiling*—

He'd lain awake a whole night interrogating himself, his motives, whether his desires had clouded his judgement. He'd sworn to himself that if Loxleigh turned out to be a decent man after all, he would accept the marriage, choke his own urges back down to the secret place they belonged, and pray that nobody ever saw.

He didn't think it likely. The little bastard was as crooked as they came.

Good God, he wanted to go home. Back to Aston Clinton, where life was filled with useful work and his garden would need attention, and there were no smiling, charming, dishonest men in his way. He would leave this damned city as soon as he was no longer needed.

When he returned to his rooms, there was a letter waiting for him, with an unmistakable legal hand. He broke the seal, wondering if any of his investigations had borne fruit.

They had.

CHAPTER 9

Hart marched up and down his sister's drawing room. Edwina sat with her head in one hand and the letter in the other.

"It doesn't prove anything."

"Of course it does!" Hart said for the third time. "A man made enquiries about Fenwick's will in September and learned that Alice has twenty thousand coming to her on her marriage. A young, handsome, fair-haired man. What more do you need?"

"Mr. Loxleigh isn't precisely *fair*. He has golden-brown—"

"Lawyers don't care."

"I care, and so will Alice if you are going to accuse her suitor of being a fortune hunter. Think, Hart. If you're right he will use any loophole. If you're wrong—"

"I'm not wrong."

"You're prejudiced against him. You have been from the start."

"It's not prejudice if I'm right. He looked into her affairs, he knew about her fortune before he set foot in London, and he deliberately set out to entrap her!"

"To engage her interest. He hasn't compromised her."

She paused on that, eyes widening. Hart almost shouted, "*What?*"

"She was glowing after that walk in the park with him the other day. I have never seen her look so well. Contented. As if she had a secret."

"I'll break his bloody neck!"

"Don't swear, and you will do no such thing, and don't be absurd. She is not in that line yet. I dare say he kissed her."

Hart fumed. Edwina sighed pointedly. "She is a girl with a handsome suitor. Do be reasonable. My poor Alice, she won't want to hear this." She looked up to meet his eyes. "And you won't tell her."

"Are you serious?"

"*I* will tell her. She's my daughter. This will hurt her, and you will kindly keep your loud voice and great trampling feet away from her sensitivities."

His own sensitivities must have shown themselves on his face at that because she went on, a little less harshly, "I know I asked you to do this but you can hardly expect me to be happy with an outcome that will make her sad. She considers them friends."

"Any hurt to her is Loxleigh's fault, not mine."

"I doubt Alice will see it that way, and her feelings are the ones that matter. She has a party tonight. I'll tell her tomorrow, rather than spoil her evening."

"What if she doesn't believe you?"

"Then it will be a very unpleasant conversation, and she will be all the more determined to have her way," Edwina said wearily. "Please heaven she doesn't feel driven to elope."

"You don't imagine she will. Do you?"

"I hope I have brought her up better than that but…" Edwina smiled without any happiness at all. "I married a handsome face when I was old enough to know better. And Alice is very young, and Loxleigh is very handsome."

Hart rubbed the bridge of his nose. Edwina sighed. "Or perhaps she will be terribly sensible and cry in her bedroom. Either way, it is my responsibility. What I need from you now is calm. Don't talk to her about it—unless she wishes you to, of course—and do not confront Loxleigh, especially not in public. Leave it all to me."

Hart was boiling with fury as he left the house, at his sister's misery and the prospect of Alice's. Loxleigh's calculating perfidy was disgusting, and the fact he'd targeted Alice's innocence and vulnerability made Hart want to pummel his handsome face to a ruin.

He went to Lady Wintour's hell that evening for lack of anything better to do. Perhaps Evangeline might have some further thoughts on Loxleigh. Perhaps he could work his way through his anger via a few glasses of brandy.

The hell was bustling and Evangeline was busy presiding over the hazard table in an extremely low-cut dress. Hart exchanged a few words with a couple of people, found a game of whist to join, and ordered a bottle.

He played for about an hour and a half, losing himself in the game, the smells of wax candles and tobacco, male sweat and scent, the riffle of pasteboard and the taste of brandy that wasn't worth what Evangeline charged for it. He'd lost thirty pounds or so when he felt a hand on his shoulder.

He looked round and up into a large amount of bare bosom.

"Hart, my dear," Evangeline said. "How lovely to see you. We are blessed with our visitors tonight."

Her eyes flicked sideways, meaningfully. Hart looked past her and to another table. He wouldn't have recognised the back presented to him, but by God he recognised the dark honey hair.

"Thank you," he said.

She leaned down with a flirtatious smile and murmured in

his ear, "He's losing. If you want to join the game, I'll arrange it. We'll keep an eye on his hand."

Did he want to? Edwina had told him not to confront Loxleigh, but that was about his wretched scheming. This was an entirely different matter. If he could prove Loxleigh was a cheat, perhaps he could use the threat of exposure to make the man stay away.

He needed a weapon. It had occurred to him, not pleasantly, that the conversation by the fishpond might well have betrayed a chink in his armour to Loxleigh, a place where pressure could be applied, and he did not like to consider that someone so manipulative might hold that knowledge against him. Not that there was anything for him to cite, and Hart hadn't indulged his desires in a year or more, but even a baseless accusation was a frightening prospect. The thought of being named, humiliated, publicly shamed was enough to make him feel hot and sick even before considering the savage penalties of the law.

Loxleigh was a threat and he had to act. He would play. And he would win, or catch the man cheating. Either would suffice.

"Please do," he told Evangeline, and she smiled back.

She arranged matters with a swift and ruthless efficiency. Within a very few minutes, he was seated opposite Loxleigh. The fellow looked a little strained—no doubt because he had ended his game over a hundred pounds down—but wore a little quizzical smile, almost a smirk, all the same. It faded as he took in Hart's expression.

"You look grim, Sir John."

"I'm here to play. I think it's time you and I took each other on directly. Don't you?"

Loxleigh's brows flickered—surprise, amusement, something else that tightened Hart's groin. "An excellent idea.

I should very much like to take you on." His lips curved. "Shall we start with whist?"

He wasn't sure what this was—Loxleigh toying with him? —but it did not bode well. Or perhaps it did. Perhaps if Loxleigh thought they were playing a different game, it might give Hart an edge.

Not whist, though. He was at best an indifferent player, which was doubtless why Loxleigh had suggested it. "How about piquet?"

"If you prefer."

"Five shillings a point, to begin?"

Piquet was a fiendishly complicated game, requiring a good memory and endless calculation of odds. They started slowly, taking the measure of one another as players. Loxleigh was obviously good, discarding with skill, playing with an appearance of smiling carelessness that Hart didn't trust for a second. He took his own time, considering discards longer than he needed, made a couple of defensive moves when he could have been bolder, and saw Loxleigh notice.

They played out the first partie cautiously. Hart won three hands, but not showily, never declaring more than a septieme. He lost the partie by a reasonable margin while still scoring over a hundred points, which kept his losses minimal. In the second partie, he played just a little better, and Loxleigh played a little worse, leaving Hart the victor. The third went to eight hands and was a draw.

"We seem evenly matched," Loxleigh said, a smile on his inviting mouth. "Perhaps we should raise the stakes?"

Hart had expected that, much as he expected Loxleigh's play to improve steadily in the next parties. "Certainly. A pound a point?"

The smile fell off his opponent's face, as well it might. That was high play: if either of them failed to score a hundred on a partie, he might find himself owing several hundred pounds.

"That's going it," Loxleigh said lightly.

"I thought you liked to take chances." Hart let his voice drop just a little.

Loxleigh's eyes snapped to his, wary, alert, alive. Hart clenched his hand under the table against the tension in the air. "A pound a point, then."

The man had reason to be confident: he was a good player. One would be a fool to take him on at those stakes unless one had an unlimited budget. Or a secret weapon.

Hart had taken charge of Alice aged eleven for three months, as Edwina dealt with her second widowhood while approaching what proved to be a difficult confinement. He'd been twenty-five, awkward, and utterly baffled as to what he should do with a sad-eyed, shy child. With no idea what to talk about in the evenings, he'd taught her piquet, thinking it might pass the time. It was his first inkling of her capabilities: she had mastered the game in a couple of days, and was trouncing him nightly within a week.

There was only so much of that a man could take at the hands of an eleven-year-old girl, and he had set himself to sharpen his skills. Piquet had consumed their every night for months and brought them to a strong mutual affection without the difficulty of conversation; they still played vicious tournaments, which Alice almost always won. It was a shame she was no dashing young matron who could play without reproach: she'd clean out the hells.

Hart wasn't Alice, but he was prepared to back himself against anyone else in London, and very much against Loxleigh now.

Loxleigh was good, no question, and he was lucky too. The cards ran his way in the earlier hands, but Hart had the advantage of funds. He could afford to lose, so he didn't have fear undermining his decisions, and that allowed him to push on till the current of play turned. He declared a septieme, a huitieme, put together a quatorze of aces that made Loxleigh hiss. He played with a single-minded savageness that felt like obsession, each loss spurring him on, each win a triumph, watching the running total of points on each side. Watching, too, the way Loxleigh's face and posture changed from relaxed amusement to something paler, tenser.

He knew he'd been trapped. He knew it, and his nostrils flared, and Evangeline drifted over to stand behind him, watching the game, while Ned stood casually behind Hart.

Now cheat, you little bastard. Just try.

They weren't talking any more, except the terse exchanges of gamesters. "Not good." "Carte blanche." "Hand of four." No more flirtatious looks or knowing smiles. This was a duel: Loxleigh was fighting for his life, and panicking with it. His tongue darted out to lick his full lips more than once, and Hart didn't even find it distracting. He was occupied.

"Repique and capot," he said at last. "Your ninety-eight points to my hundred and sixty."

"Oh, well played," Evangeline murmured.

"Three hundred and forty pounds." Loxleigh smiled, or at least made his lips move over his set teeth. "I fear I must call a halt. This is too deep for me."

"Of course. Let's see." Hart scanned the scrawled list. "Four thousand, two hundred and twenty pounds, fourteen shillings, I make it."

"I'm sure you're right." Loxleigh's skin had a clammy, unpleasant look. "I shall call on you tomorrow, if I may."

Hart gave him the direction. "I shall see you then."

"Uh—the evening," Loxleigh added. "I am engaged in the morning. I hope that will be satisfactory."

"Of course."

"Thank you. Thank you for a pleasant evening, Lady Wintour." He made his way out, walking straight-backed.

Evangeline took his abandoned chair and swung it round

close to Hart's. "That was brutal. Never play like that against my house."

"I intended to ruin him. I'm sorry he called a halt."

"I'm surprised he went on so long. Think he'll pay?"

"I doubt he has the funds."

"Think he'll run?"

"And embarrass his sister in front of Tachbrook? I doubt it."

"Then he'll ask you for time to pay," Evangeline said. "What will you respond?"

Hart's face felt flushed. He realised he had a headache, and his hands were trembling a little. He knocked back a mouthful of brandy. It tasted sour. "I'll let him make me an offer."

CHAPTER 10

Robin managed to get a good twenty yards from Lady Wintour's hell and round a corner before he vomited.

He doubled over, retching uncontrollably until he'd puked up the night's brandy, and at least some of the stewed horror that had coagulated in his stomach. Christ, he was doomed. Marianne would kill him. And if she didn't, Hartlebury would ruin him, and if *he* didn't...

Robin ran through his litany of enemies. Then he threw up again.

He would have walked the streets alone in the darkness as a ruined man should, hoping to be knocked on the head by a bravo and shanghaied for foreign climes or perhaps just thrown in the Thames, but it was too bloody cold for that, so he went home. It was only one o'clock in the morning and Marianne wasn't back.

He stared at himself in the spotty glass. *Through a glass, darkly*, he thought, and *This is what a condemned man looks like.* He had an idea he ought to drink an entire bottle of brandy in rakish fashion, but he would probably be sick again and anyway they only had gin. He went to bed instead, so that he could pretend to be asleep when Marianne finally came home.

He told her about it the next morning.

"*How much?*"

"Four thousand, two hundred and twenty."

"And we have set aside…"

"Nearly three hundred pounds." That had seemed a good sum yesterday.

"Christ Jesus fuck," Marianne said. "And you lost it to Hartlebury. Was he cheating?"

"No. He's just bloody good."

"Were you cheating?"

"I couldn't. That bitch Lady Wintour and her brute stood over me to 'watch' the game once I was in deep."

"Why didn't you just stop?" She waved a hand almost before she'd finished speaking. "I know, I know. But what now?"

"I don't know. I told him I'd call on him to settle up today."

"We have to think of something, Rob. Tachbrook has assured me he does not require a portion in his bride, but there's a wide gap between no portion and a brother with four thousand in gambling debts."

"We could go," Robin said. "Vanish. We have three hundred pounds. We could go to, uh—"

"No, do go on. List all the wonderful places we could go. Manchester? Oh, no, that might be a problem, mightn't it. Salisbury, can you think of any reason we shouldn't go there?"

That was hitting below the belt. Robin returned the favour. "We could go somewhere new. To Paris."

Yearning flared in her eyes, but she shook her head. "Don't be stupid. We don't speak French."

"We could learn. It can't be that hard. Children can speak French."

"*French* children."

"Are they cleverer than English children?"

"Shut up. And we're not going to Paris."

"Why not?"

"Because I am this close to eighteen thousand a year and a title," Marianne said savagely. "We've earned this, Christ knows we've worked for it, and I will not give it up now. We are going to be rich and safe, Rob. We swore it and I'm not running away when the prize is finally in my grasp. We will fix this. *You* will fix it."

Robin knew that note in her voice: it conveyed non-negotiable decisions that other people would be unhappy about. He poured himself a third cup of tea. "I suppose we have to assume Hartlebury did it deliberately."

"Because of Alice?"

Because of Alice, and that quivering moment by the pond, and the fact that Robin—idiot, idiot—had thought he'd meant something quite different when he sat down to play. He'd thought—well, be honest, he hadn't thought at all. He'd just reacted in the belief that Hartlebury was approaching him.

No: Hartlebury *had* approached him. Or, at least, had very much let him think that was what he was doing. Had responded, even. Robin had seen the look in his eyes.

He snarled into his tea. "Because he's a bullying swine. Right. I'm taking Alice for a walk in the park today."

"It's raining."

"It would be. I'm taking her anyway."

"Are you going to propose?"

"I'll have to. If I marry her, he can hardly dun me for debt."

"If you marry her quickly enough, you can pay him with her money." Marianne's lovely mouth twisted on the words, as if they were spoiled and sour. "Confess all before he does it for you. Play the wronged and noble youth."

"There's not much else I can do."

"We're nearly there, Rob. Tachbrook has asked me to visit his mother."

"Marnie!"

"Don't call me that. Yes, I know. Triumph. I just have to charm the old hag and we'll have our eighteen thousand a year, if you don't bitch it up now."

"You'll make a lovely marchioness. I won't spoil it for you, I swear. I'll fix this."

I know you will." She frowned. "I don't suppose we can get the money anywhere else?"

"Such as?"

"Can we borrow from anyone? If you could win it back—"

"I can't play if nobody thinks I'll pay. And Lady Wintour was watching for me to fuzz the cards. She might tell the other hells."

"No. Ugh. I can't ask Tachbrook, Rob, it's too risky."

"Lord, don't do that. I'll make it work with Alice."

"Be kind to her," Marianne said. "Oh, damn it. I wish—"

"What?"

"Nothing."

"Do you not want me to do it?"

She grimaced. "What's the alternative? It's this or throw yourself on Hartlebury's mercy without a single bargaining chip."

"In other words, no choice at all. I'd better shave."

❧

The rain had slowed to a faint prickle of damp in the air by eleven. Robin strode along to Mrs. Blaine's house, where he was startled to see Alice hovering outside the railings, muffled in a huge coat and hat, with an unhappy-looking maid at her heels.

"Miss Fenwick?"

"Thank goodness. Do hurry." Alice slipped her arm through his and tugged him along. "I didn't want you to come in. Can we speak? Oh, I'm doing this backwards. Good morning."

"Good morning," Robin said warily. "Is everything all right?"

"Yes and no. Can we go somewhere we can talk, like the Pavilion in the park?"

Robin took her there, wondering what could possibly be going on. The Pavilion was empty on this grey and dismal day, with very few walkers to watch them. They seated themselves, shaking the rain off hats and shoulders, while the maid huddled under a tree.

"You wanted to talk," Robin said. "And I have something —two things, indeed—to say to you."

"I dare say, and I think I know what one of them is, and I think you ought to let me go first. It might be embarrassing otherwise. Well, it might be embarrassing anyway but I will try not to make it worse."

She was bright red, but ploughing ahead with determination. Robin wondered what the devil this was. Surely, if he was to be given his marching orders, she wouldn't have made him walk so far, so damply. "As you think best."

"All right," Alice said. "The thing is, my mother told me yesterday that—well. That you had investigated my financial situation and ascertained I have a fortune of my own before you ever spoke to me. That probably you were making up to me for my money. I do understand, you know. I didn't really believe you liked me for myself."

"I do like you." Robin's face felt stiff. "Miss Fenwick— Alice—I care for you enormously—"

"Yes, never mind that, but you are a fortune hunter, aren't you? Please don't mind me mentioning it: I assure you I don't object. But I do need to be certain, otherwise this won't work."

Robin attempted to parse that speech a few times. The words all made sense individually: it was just the meaning that escaped him. "What won't work?"

"Are—you—a—fortune—hunter?" Alice repeated, with the sort of enunciation used by kind-hearted people to deaf uncles. "Because the thing is, if you *are* hoping to win my fortune, we might be able to come to an agreement."

Robin's jaw was hanging open. He shut it so hard his teeth clicked. "I… uh… Yes. Yes, I am, since you ask. Sorry. Agreement about what?"

"You see, all I have is my portion," Alice explained. "My father left me a huge sum tied up for my marriage, and everything else to Mama outright. I was only a baby and I dare say it was the right thing to do, but it does mean I have nothing of my own until I marry. Don't think she's ungenerous! She's wonderful. But she has given me so much, and there is Georgey to think of—her son by Mr. Blaine, you know, who is at school and must be paid for, which is rather hard because Mr. Blaine left her nothing. In fact, he spent most of what she had, and Uncle Hart has worked immensely hard to restore her fortunes. So I don't want to ask for more, for something I know she will not like. Whereas if I were to marry, I could have my twenty thousand pounds and spend it as I chose, and not ask Mama for anything or make her worry about Georgey's future. That would be much better for everyone."

Robin rubbed the bridge of his nose. "What do you want that she won't give you?"

"I want to go to the University of Heidelberg and study mathematics."

Robin's brain took several seconds to catch up with his

ears. "You want to *what?*" He seemed to be saying 'what' a lot. There was really no other word.

Alice clutched her hands together. "Mathematics. My tutor Dr. Trelawney studied in Heidelberg for two years and has been teaching me the language. He wrote to Professor von Lehman, a great friend of his, who has agreed to tutor me personally. Me! I want it more than I can say. But when I told Mama, she said it was out of the question, which is why I'm here having a Season to make me think about dresses and parties, but I don't *want* to. I know she wants me to be happy but her idea of that doesn't appeal to me at all, and I know she thinks that's because I haven't learned to enjoy parties yet, but we've been here months and I haven't liked most of it in the slightest, whereas I want to study mathematics so badly it hurts. I read the journals. I could do it, I know I could. What do you think?"

Robin had no idea what to think. "Can you really do that?"

"As a private student. But it will cost money, of course—to go, to live there, the fees and the travel. And if I had my twenty thousand, I could pay for it myself. Dr. Trelawney wants to go back as well, now the wars are over. He could escort me, if I had a companion."

"Without your mother's permission?"

Alice sagged. "He said I must have it. He doesn't want to be accused of running away with me, which is a nonsense because he's terribly old, and anyway I don't want her to be upset. But it would be even worse if she reluctantly agreed and offered to pay when there is Georgey and her own comfort to consider. She has given me so much all my life, and it simply isn't fair to demand more. This seems a far more practical solution. If I were married I'd be mistress of my own money and it would be up to me where I travelled, and she wouldn't have to fret in the slightest, would she?"

Robin looked at her, wondering if he'd ever been that young. "So what is your proposition for me?"

"Well, if you don't want to marry me for my, uh, person, and I really would prefer not, I wondered if we could simply marry for money?" Alice said in a rush. "If you took, say, fifteen per cent, and agreed not to—well—because if the marriage wasn't consummated, it could be annulled, couldn't it? So we wouldn't be tied to one another. It might be a little embarrassing, of course, but I'm not at all important so I dare say nobody would care, and you could marry someone else rich in due course because you're very good at being charming and handsome, and I could do what I want with my money. What do you think?"

"Heidelberg," Robin said, stalling for time. He didn't even know where that was. "Marianne and I have often spoken of travel."

Fifteen per cent. Three thousand pounds. He could probably argue her up to twenty per cent. Take her money and hand it to Hartlebury and be back where he started, while she went off to follow her dreams, being careful not to inconvenience another soul on her way. And all it would cost was the knowledge that he'd used her innocence, her trust, for profit.

He put his face in his hands.

"Mr. Loxleigh?" Alice sounded alarmed.

"It's a good plan." His voice was muffled by his hands. He lifted his head. "A plan with some excellent features, and some less favourable ones. You do understand that if we married without you protecting your fortune, it would all be mine to spend?"

"Yes, but—well, I don't think you'd do that," Alice said simply. "You have nice eyes, and you've always been very kind to me."

"I really have not."

"There are other ways men make heiresses marry them." He looked at her, startled. She shrugged. "I've learned a dreadful lot in London. Anyway, I don't think you would cheat me, but we could draw up an agreement to be sure."

"I've a better idea," Robin said. "I think that first of all, you should tell your mother that you have given her opinion serious consideration and tried your hand at the Polite World as best you could, but that you are still determined on studying, and want her support. I think you should let her decide how to spend her money, and not put yourself last before anyone has done that for you. If she refuses to consider the idea, you should point out that you can have your money by marrying, and see what that does to her opinion. And if she *still* doesn't change her mind, then I will marry you, but I really don't think she'll refuse if you talk to her properly. She loves you dearly, and it's not her fault she doesn't entirely understand, because she's a quite ordinary person—I mean that in the best way—whereas you are very special."

Alice was beetroot. Robin gave her a rueful grin. "And if you have to marry me, I'll do it for five hundred. I'd say nothing, but to be honest I'm in rather a hole."

"Oh, that's not fair!"

"Five hundred," he said firmly. "Not a penny more, or the deal's off. But I truly don't believe you'll need to. And it would make her dreadfully sad if she couldn't attend your wedding, wouldn't it? You don't want to do that."

That hit home, he could tell. He pressed on. "Promise me you'll talk to her properly, and give her a chance, yes? If she says no after that, I'll be your husband for long enough to get the money and no longer. So you can go into this discussion knowing you have a position to fall back on. All right?"

"All right, I promise. You *are* nice," Alice said.

"I'm not, and don't *ever* ask another man to do this. The next one might not be so soft. Um. This conversation—"

"Between us," Alice assured him. "Quite private."

"That would be best all round." He gave it a moment's consideration. "Actually— Do you know, if your mother was under the impression that you were seriously considering my suit and didn't believe the calumnies heaped upon me, or thought I was redeemable or some such, she might become a little more receptive to the idea of sending you out of the country."

"Oh!" Alice clapped a hand to her mouth, eyes sparkling. "That's wicked."

"Tactical. Suppose you let that idea sink in for a few days until she's good and worried, and only then speak to her about your Heidelberg plan?"

She paused then narrowed her eyes. "Do you get something out of that?"

God, she was sharp. Robin considered lying, but what on earth was the point? "Your uncle took an exceedingly large sum of money off me at cards last night."

"Uncle Hart? You didn't play piquet with him, did you?"

"I see I should have been warned."

"But—was it money you can pay?"

"No." There was something rather liberating about telling the truth. "Not even slightly. Which he knew, of course. I don't think he likes me."

"No," she admitted. "He found out that you asked the lawyers about my fortune. He's very protective."

"So I have discovered."

"Do you want me to speak to him?"

"Good God, no! I just need a little leeway to avoid any consequences to—uh, anyone else."

"To Marianne. I have thought of that. She is so beautiful, and she quite deserves to be a marchioness."

"She does, yes."

"But do you think she'll be happy with Tachbrook?" Alice

said in a rush. "Because he isn't very nice at all. Really, he is not."

Robin shut his eyes. Alice made a distressed noise. "I'm sorry, I shouldn't have said that. I hope she gets whatever she wants. She was always very kind to me."

"No she wasn't, and stop calling people kind. People aren't friendly to you because they're kind-hearted; it's because you're clever and funny and they like you. Marianne likes you." He was counting on that fact to save his skin when she found out he'd thrown away their best advantage. He decided not to think about that quite yet. "That reminds me. Are you going to develop a foolproof gaming system?"

"One that means you won't lose money? I have. Don't play."

"If you can do any better than that, I want it first. Three months before you publish your discovery, something like that. Then, if you haven't spent everything on education, you can lend me money and I'll travel around the spa towns of Europe, breaking banks. We'll make a fortune."

That piece of shocking nonsense drove the hint of moisture from Alice's eyes. She gave a startled yelp of laughter, and they expanded on the idea together, Alice giggling, Robin with a feeling of light-hearted freedom that he enjoyed while it lasted. He doubted it would long survive his next contact with reality.

☙❧

Unexpectedly, Marianne didn't throw a chamber pot at his head when he told her what he'd done. She sat still, eyes searching his face, and made him repeat a few times that he had turned down their sole chance to get the money, and then she shook her glossy hair like a horse shrugging off flies and said, "Well."

"What does that mean?"

"It means, Well. What would you like me to say?"

"I couldn't do it, Marnie. She trusted us, she likes us. She wouldn't betray us if she had the chance."

"Are you sure of that?" Marianne flashed back.

"I am. Or, at least, I didn't want to be the one who'd teach her to do it."

"Fine. She's a good soul and you did a good thing. You didn't take money from a girl who's never done any harm to a fly and who definitely deserves to have twenty thousand pounds because she was born. You're positively glowing with human decency. Is it warm and comforting?"

"It felt better when I did it."

"And now?"

"We're fucked."

"I'm glad you've noticed."

Robin sighed. "We were probably fucked anyway, in fairness."

"We're still more fucked than we could have been."

Inarguable. "She wished you well. Alice, I mean. She hopes you get what you want."

Marianne's mouth turned down sharply at the corners, almost as if she might cry, though she never cried any more, then settled back into a hard line that made her look older. "How sweet. I want eighteen thousand a year and a title, and I don't want to lose my chance at them because you've made a pig's ear of this."

"Alice was the wrong target," Robin said. "That's what it comes down to. Hartlebury's too protective, she's too young, and to be honest I don't think I'd have stood a chance anyway because she's got better things to do. It was never going to come off. Sorry, Marnie. I've let you down all the way."

"Then fix it," Marianne said savagely. "Stall Hartlebury however you can, for long enough that I can secure

Tachbrook's proposal. A month should do it. If he hasn't come up to scratch by then, I doubt he ever will. Get me a month, Rob." There was a martial light in her eyes. "Whatever it takes. Grovel. Tell him he's won. Beg for time or to pay in instalments. Use the savings and sell some clothes."

"If we do that and Tachbrook doesn't come through—"

"I thought you were a gambler. Pay to play."

Robin wanted to suggest again that they just didn't. They had three hundred pounds, enough to survive for a good while, plus whatever they could get for selling their accumulated wardrobes. They could flee to the Continent and see the world as Marianne had dreamed, run away from all their mistakes and start afresh. And spend their money and have to find more, and do it all over again...

He looked at his sister's militant expression, ran through the likely course of that conversation in his head, and said, "All right, I'll do my best. I dare say I can beg."

"You do that. Let's have supper before you go. You can't squirm on your belly on an empty stomach."

"You're all heart."

"I'm not the idiot who lost four thousand pounds and turned down another three," she retorted, and Robin had no answer to that.

CHAPTER 11

Hart sat in his study, reading a book, or at least holding one. He hadn't turned the page in a while, and would have had to check the frontispiece to find out what the title was.

He didn't feel as triumphant as he should have. It was one thing to celebrate a victory, another to grind a man in the dirt. Loxleigh had faced catastrophe last night and Hart had recognised the fear in his eyes, that terror as your world span out of control under someone else's direction and you felt the foundations crumbling.

Loxleigh deserved it, and he did not merit pity. He'd needed to be dealt with like any venomous pest, and it was absurd to feel guilty at putting that sick, terrified look on a man's face when he'd brought it entirely on himself.

Hart glared at his book. It was aesthetic, that was all. Loxleigh was a handsome piece, appealing to the eye, but when he'd realised the scale of his losses he'd looked stark, and older. Hart probably wouldn't have thought twice if the contrast had been less striking. A man didn't deserve more consideration for good looks. Hart had struck a blow for ugly men like himself in teaching a pretty one his place.

Edwina had written a note that morning saying Alice had taken the news about her suitor very calmly, like a good sensible girl. This was followed by another note, two hours later and a great deal less placid in tone, to report with frantic punctuation that Alice had *gone for a walk with Loxleigh!!!* and had afterwards said only that she had much to consider but *felt he was maligned!!*

He hadn't heard anything more, which might or might not be good.

Anyway, it was not his concern. Alice was in safe hands; he had done his duty in exposing her fraudulent suitor, and would now put an end to the man's remaining pretensions before retreating to Aston Clinton and the life he liked.

Perhaps he would forgive the debt. The thought had come to his mind a few times; now he considered it more carefully. After all, he didn't want the fellow's money, still less to drive him to desperation. He simply wanted him not to batten on Alice or pose a threat to Hart himself.

Suppose he gave Loxleigh a few bad moments then offered a truce—no, not a truce, but a deal. He wouldn't enforce the debt if Loxleigh stayed away from him and his family for good. Or would that lead Loxleigh to think he had a bargaining position?

He would judge it on the man's demeanour, Hart decided. Loxleigh would be here soon. If he seemed humbled, Hart would be magnanimous in victory. If he was defiant, he could take the consequences.

That decision made him feel somewhat better and he managed to read a good three pages before Spenlow knocked on his door and informed him Mr. Loxleigh was here to see him.

Hart stood as he was ushered in. "Thank you, Spenlow, that will be all for the night. Good evening, Loxleigh."

"Sir John." Loxleigh was well turned out, but with a little

tension in his eyes. Perhaps he was paler than normal; it was hard to tell in the candlelight.

Hart gestured to the armchair opposite his. "Drink?"

"Thank you."

Hart poured two brandies. It was important to be civilised. Loxleigh didn't precisely sit on the edge of the seat, but his posture was undeniably tense.

"Well," he said, handing over the glass. "Let us not beat about the bush. I suppose you have my money?"

"I'm sure you know I don't."

Hart hadn't expected it so bluntly. "That's frank."

"There isn't a way of phrasing it that will make the money appear. I don't have four thousand pounds, or the rest. Would you be willing to give me time?"

"How will you find the money, given that time?"

"I would think that is my affair."

"It is mine if you propose to pay me from my niece's dowry."

Their eyes met. Loxleigh spoke slowly. "I said before that you underestimate Miss Fenwick. I still think that." His lips curled in a tiny smile that looked, to Hart's surprise, quite genuine. "She's a remarkable young lady. I'm privileged to have made her acquaintance."

"Let us be clear. Do you intend to pursue my niece?"

"I have asked her to marry me, and she is giving my request consideration."

"And if she says yes, you will promptly hand me four thousand pounds of her money?" He didn't bother to hide the contempt and anger in his voice. This bloody man, trading on his pretty face, as though he were entitled to exploit Alice and leave her with nothing. It was despicable. "How exactly has she wronged you that you feel this is suitable vengeance? Or do you simply not understand that she is a woman with a heart and soul, not a cow to be milked of her wealth? Good

God, how can you resolve to treat another human in such a way, as if she counts for nothing more than what you can take from her?"

Loxleigh's face twitched, almost like a flinch. He looked at Hart for a long moment, then put down his glass with a click.

"All right, Sir John, no more games. As it happens, I have a great deal more respect for Miss Fenwick than you imagine, but more to the point, I'm in no position to bargain with her money. I'm not fool enough to try, she wouldn't be fool enough to let me, and I don't think you're fool enough for me to persuade you otherwise. Which is tiresome, but here we are."

That was frank, almost disarmingly so. Hart wasn't quite sure where it left them. "So you owe a debt of honour that you can't pay," he said, returning to the main point.

"Indeed."

"You understand the consequences of that."

"Of course I do. I would prefer to avoid disgrace as far as possible, to avoid embarrassing others."

"Is that a threat to Alice?"

"What? No, of course not." Loxleigh sounded slightly testy. "I mean my sister."

"Your..." Hart hadn't given a thought to Miss Loxleigh, or her campaign to snare Tachbrook, but if Loxleigh were drummed out of his club for non-payment of a debt of honour, that would inevitably sway the self-important marquess. "Yes. Miss Loxleigh's aspirations will suffer along with your reputation."

"And she has done you no wrong, so she should not pay the price for my folly. You've won, Sir John. You hold my and my sister's fates in your hand, and there is very little I can do about it because I cannot pay that debt. Hence, I'm hoping we can come to an agreement."

An agreement was exactly what Hart wanted, and if

Loxleigh proposed it, so much the better. He might renounce his pretensions to Alice more willingly if it was his idea to do so. Hart leaned back in his chair, and gave the man a long look. "So if you don't have the money, what do you propose to offer me instead?"

Loxleigh's eyes snapped to his, widening sharply. Hart didn't understand why for a second, and then realisation dawned with a dizzying rush of blood to the head. He opened his mouth to say, *Christ, no, I didn't mean that!* but somehow the words wouldn't come as he stared at Loxleigh's wide hazel eyes, his parted lips.

Neither spoke, and every second that ticked by made it more impossible to recant, carved the meaning deeper into stone. Hart's pulse was thudding. The air felt thick.

After a very long moment, Loxleigh broke the silence. "You suggest I pay my debt another way. Well. That *is* an idea, Sir John. A fascinating idea."

"I am making no sort of demand on you." Hart's lips felt oddly stiff.

"Oh, naturally not," Loxleigh said. "Not a *demand*, that wouldn't be fair. Shall we say, a gentleman's agreement? A matter of business, entirely between you and me."

His lips were curving. Hart couldn't stop looking at his mouth. He couldn't think for the blood roaring in his ears.

Loxleigh cocked his head. "Well? Are we negotiating a… private arrangement?"

No. Say no, tell him you want the money. Say no now.

Even better, make Loxleigh be the one to voice it. Let him make an offer that Hart could refuse with outrage, or of course accept if he'd misread the situation entirely and Loxleigh had something entirely different in mind. He swallowed. "What do you suggest?"

"I think we should probably specify the terms first," Loxleigh said. "For avoidance of doubt."

"Go on." The words came out roughly.

"The forgiveness of the whole debt, all four thousand two hundred and whatever. Easy come, easy go. And I want your word that you will not impede my sister, directly or through me, by act, word, or complication."

"I don't give a damn for your sister. For her aspirations, I mean. She can marry a dozen marquesses for all I care."

"One will do," Loxleigh said. "If you ask me, Tachbrook is more than enough. Are my terms acceptable?"

"As far as they go. And you will break things off with Alice. Leave her alone."

"I should rather let her break things off with me, as a matter of courtesy. And she may wish to remain on civil terms, since she likes my sister. I'll promise you I won't marry her, or cause her any form of harm: will that suffice?"

It would avoid a fuss and please Edwina, Hart thought through the haze in his brain. "I don't want you embarrassing her in any way."

"I won't. I really wouldn't want to."

"Then those are the terms. What's your offer?"

"Why, whatever you want," Loxleigh said softly. "Exactly as you want it."

"You—"

"Me." He breathed the word. It tingled through Hart's skin. "Myself. Entirely at your disposal for…shall we say a month?"

Oh Christ, he did mean it. Hart hadn't misread things; the flaring heat between them that he'd felt at the fishpond hadn't just been his imagination. He could actually truly have this.

It had been more than a year since his last furtive encounter, four since he'd been with a man whose name he knew. Loneliness and lust ignited together, like brandy thrown onto flame, and sucked all the air from his lungs.

He was still a tradesman, though. "You rate your charms highly. A thousand a week?"

"It is, isn't it. A thousand a week." Loxleigh's eyes glittered in the candlelight. "Might that make me the most expensive fuck in London?"

Hart nearly swallowed his tongue. He had to clear his throat before he could say, "If not, you wouldn't be far off."

"But worth it. Anything you want. Whenever and wherever and especially however. At your pleasure. Starting now."

Christ. This was unconscionable and outrageous, and his cockstand was pushing painfully against his breeches. He wanted it more than he'd ever wanted anything in his life. It had been so long, and Loxleigh was beautiful, and he'd desired him from the first moment he'd seen him.

He ought not do this. Obviously he ought not. But it was Loxleigh's idea, and four thousand pounds was no negligible sum to forgive, and mostly words like 'wrong' and 'stupid' held a lot less power in this moment than 'anything' and 'now'. Still, there was something he could not ignore. "You spoke of my pleasure," he managed. "What about yours?"

Loxleigh raised a quizzical brow. Hart glared at him. "I've no interest in a partner who finds me repulsive."

"Repulsive?" Loxleigh echoed, sounding somewhat startled.

"Unappealing, then, or what you will. I don't want an unwilling man, does that make it clearer?"

"Entirely. You needn't worry about that."

"I want a proper answer. Not fine words."

Loxleigh's brows tilted to a frown. "Did I offer any?" His gaze flickered over Hart's face, then slid down his chest and lower, the kind of blatant assessment Hart had never been subjected to in his life. It had to be a performance, but it was a bloody good one. "Are you really asking if I want those thighs of yours wrapped round me? I'm quite sure we settled that question last night, just before you took me for four thousand pounds like a hopeless flat. You could have taken me over the table instead, and saved us both a lot of effort."

Christ almighty, he sounded—truly sounded—like he meant it. Hart wanted to believe him so much it ached. He gathered the shreds of his composure together. "If that's the case, shouldn't you pay me?"

Loxleigh snorted with real amusement. "I would, but for some reason I find myself financially embarrassed at the moment. Quite seriously, Sir John, I assure you I don't grudge this. I'll enjoy making sure you get your money's worth."

"You seem very certain of that."

"Of course I am. Modesty aside." Loxleigh's lips curved. "But naturally you don't care to buy a pig in a poke. Why don't I demonstrate?"

Hart couldn't find words. Loxleigh clicked his tongue. "Come on, you pride yourself on being a plain-spoken man. Tell me what you want and let's see if I can give it to you."

He swallowed. "Show me that you're willing."

"How?"

"You choose."

Loxleigh paused for a couple of seconds, head cocked in thought, then he leaned back in the armchair. "We're alone, yes? Won't be interrupted?"

"Yes."

"Good." He settled himself, legs sprawled, and ran his hand—that clever card-sharp hand—over the front of his pantaloons, where there was a notable bulge. "You want to know I'm willing. Willing to get on my knees and suck your prick, for example. Would you like me to do that at some point?"

"Get on," Hart rasped.

"I talk, you listen? All right. Where were we? Me,

swallowing you down. Maybe at some society event, a ball, perhaps, you might give me the nod—not in the ballroom, of course, though could you imagine? If I dropped to my knees there and then? Because I would, you know, given the choice; I'd let them all see your cock between my lips with pleasure. But, things being as they are, you'd tell me to meet you upstairs. Me, in my best clothes—not paid for, but you know that, don't you?—sliding down in front of you. You'd already be hard, I think. Excuse me."

He flicked the buttons that secured the front fall of his breeches. Hart watched, barely able to breathe, as he pushed cloth aside and bared the thick flesh of his stand, leaving it untouched, entirely visible to Hart's gaze.

"You wanted to see willing," he murmured. "Is this willing enough? Because I'll be this willing as I suck you, with the music and chatter below us hiding the noises I make as you hold my hair and fuck my mouth. Driving it in, bringing tears to my eyes." He wrapped his fingers round his erection, moving them up and down. "And you can tell I'm fumbling for my own prick, tossing myself off as I suck you, and you say, 'Stop.'"

"What? Why?"

"Because you want me to go downstairs with your taste in my mouth and an unslaked prick of my own, so hard I can barely do my breeches up and it hurts to move. You want to make me spend the rest of the evening thinking of nothing but the ache between my legs." Loxleigh's hand slid up and down his prick, caressing it faster. "So when you tell me to come back here, you'll know I'm in a fever for release. And that way you can take your pleasure with me squirming and begging for it—"

"Stop."

Loxleigh snatched his hand away. The sense of power was overwhelming, sending a shock to Hart's groin.

The moment stretched out—Loxleigh bared, shamelessly aroused, prick glistening at the tip, red with friction; Hart stiff in his armchair in every way.

"Come here." His voice didn't sound like his own.

Loxleigh rose, and walked over, standing before him, apparently unconcerned by his jutting erection.

"Turn round."

He turned.

"Sit."

"On you?" He didn't say it as a question, more confirming the order.

"Yes."

Loxleigh sat, putting his considerable weight on Hart's lap. Hart's erection pressed against his buttocks. Hart put one arm round his waist, holding him still, and got his other hand to that jutting prick.

Loxleigh inhaled. "Oh."

"Now go on." Hart began to stroke him, rejoicing in the sensation of firm flesh. It had been far too long since he'd felt one not his own, and Loxleigh's was sized just right for a big hand, fitting to Hart as if made for him.

"Where was I? Here, of course, with my cock aching with need, and you tell me, 'Over the desk.' No niceties, I wouldn't expect that. And you take your time, making me tell you how much I want it, making me plead for your prick until you're deep in me—*Christ*."

"Keep talking." Hart's fingers were slick with moisture now, with Loxleigh aroused and leaking. He moved his hand faster.

"Oh God. And I say, fuck me, please, and you ask me, what are you, and I tell you I'm your thousand-a-week whore, and you drive into me till I cry out, and you do it again and again, and *fuck*—"

He convulsed on Hart's lap, thrusting into his hand, hips

lifting, tensed stomach muscles straining against Hart's encircling arms.

Hart tightened his grip and firmed his fingers, until he felt a last dribble of hot wetness against them, and Loxleigh moaned and slumped back against his chest.

Hart's blood was thumping, and he felt almost dizzy with the unreality of it. Loxleigh had talked more in that one fantastical encounter than the sum total of words Hart had had from every partner of his life. He'd had no idea anyone could be so exuberantly, vocally unashamed. He wanted more.

"Thousand-a-week whore?" he said in Loxleigh's ear.

"The thought occurred to me." Loxleigh sounded rather breathless. "I have a vivid imagination." He resettled himself on Hart's lap, a deliberate movement that made it impossible to ignore his own insistent need. "Talking of which, what might you be imagining now?"

"Wait," Hart said. "The terms. My niece and your sister to both go about their respective businesses unmolested by action, word, or implication. The debt fulfilled after one month. Or four weeks?"

"A calendar month is fair. This day next month."

"And—" He had to clear his throat. "You, uh, at my disposal until then."

"Entirely."

This didn't feel so much like a primrose path to destruction as an open gate clearly signed 'Calamity This Way'. But it was too late now. It might have been too late for a long time, and there was no point pretending he would refuse. "We have a bargain."

"I'd offer to shake your hand," Loxleigh said. "Unless you'd prefer me to seal the agreement another way?"

Hart let go the softening prick he held. "My hand is a little sticky."

"Let me help with that." Loxleigh leaned forward, taking

the fingers in his mouth, tongue and lips sliding up and down. Licking off his own spend. Hart felt his balls clench at the thought, while his fingers tingled at the ministrations. He wanted—

And he could have it, whatever it was, for the asking. Those were the terms, and at a thousand a week, he was entitled to make full use of them. As if he had the first idea how.

"How do you—we—proceed?" he found himself asking.

"However you please. Talk to me. The more you tell me what you like, the better I can fulfil it."

"And if you don't care for it?"

Loxleigh gave a tiny shrug, as if that were irrelevant. Hart scowled, fruitlessly since he could see only the back of Loxleigh's head. "Well?"

"Do you want me to tell you that?"

"Of course I do."

"If you like."

"I mean it, curse you. I don't wish to be constantly wondering if you're wishing you were elsewhere."

Loxleigh twisted round to look at his face, then shrugged. "All right, you have my word I will tell you if anything is not to my liking. Though don't expect it, honestly: I have extremely catholic tastes. That's with a small c. Not, you know, the Pope. I'd object to that."

Hart spluttered. Loxleigh resettled his seat on Hart's lap to ease the strain on his neck. It brought their faces so close they could have kissed. "I can see you mean it, and your consideration is appreciated, but really, you needn't fear you're forcing anything on me. I like to fuck, and you must have noticed I wanted you. To be quite honest, I think I've got the best of this bargain."

Hart stared at him, the bright eyes, the curved, full lips. "Are you *enjoying* this situation?"

"Shouldn't I be? I mean that," he added. "If you'd prefer reluctant submission, or a struggle—"

"No!"

Loxleigh lifted his thumb to brush Hart's jawbone. "You don't play much, do you?"

"I play piquet."

"Don't remind me." His thumb moved up, stroking Hart's heavy scowling brows. "Very, very serious."

Hart caught his hand. They stared each other. Loxleigh's brow lifted in a question. "You don't want to be touched?"

Oh God, he wanted it, painfully, as a marooned man wanted water. "I—"

He shut his eyes. This was ludicrous. He'd bought, or at least rented, this man for a month: he ought to feel strong and in control, rather than exposed and afraid. It was absurd to be trembling at a tender touch; that was not what this was. He wanted another taste of the power he'd felt when Loxleigh had responded to his words.

"You're here for my pleasure," he said, voice rattling in his throat. "So pleasure me."

He still had his eyes shut so he didn't see Loxleigh's expression, but he felt the swift, sinuous movement as the man slid off his lap. The hands that ran up the insides of his thighs, the fingers that ran over his arousal, still covered by cloth, then nimbly unfastened his breeches.

He had to look when Loxleigh's fingers curled round his prick. He didn't know what he'd see on his face, and couldn't help but fear, for all Loxleigh's fine words. If it was reluctance, resignation, disgust, he ought to know it.

He opened his eyes. Loxleigh was examining his member with both brows up. The hazel eyes flicked to his, and all Hart saw in them was a wicked, laughing glint that set off a bubble of lightness in his chest.

"Maybe I *should* be paying you," Loxleigh said. "Good heavens." He leaned forward to take Hart in his mouth.

It was superb. He hadn't had this in far too long, and Loxleigh was good at it, using lips and tongue, the very edges of teeth, even the roof of his mouth to bring Hart to a toe-curling ecstasy of sensation. His hands were on Hart's thighs, holding the meat of them, so he used only his lips, slowly sliding up and down, warm and wet. He pleasured Hart till his muscles were rigid with anticipation, slowly bringing him close to the edge and keeping him there till he could have begged or bellowed for the torture to end, and never wanted it to stop. And then finally he moved faster, the slide of Hart's prick through tight wet lips creating a delicious friction, and Hart shouted aloud as he spent, jerking and thrusting into Loxleigh's mouth.

He let his head flop back against the chair for a moment as he recovered himself, then looked down.

Loxleigh was still on his knees, arms resting on Hart's thighs, apparently quite comfortable. He caught Hart's eye, winked, and swallowed, then drew a pink tongue slowly over his reddened lips.

Christ.

They stayed that way in silence for a few moments, only the crackle of the fire and the sound of breathing in the room. Finally Hart said, "What's your name?"

"Sorry?"

"Your first name. I can hardly do this for a month without knowing your name."

"Oh. Robin."

"Well, Robin, I— Wait, what? Robin Loxleigh?"

"That's me."

"The devil it is. You and your sister are Robin and Marianne Loxleigh, of Nottingham?"

Loxleigh's mouth curved. "Ah, you noticed."

"I'm surprised everyone hasn't. Are those your real names?"

"Oh, what's in a name? What do I call you?"

"Hart."

"Do you mind Sir John? Appropriately used, of course."

"Call me what you want." Hart was still reeling from the absurdity of it. He'd grown up on tales of Robin of Locksley, Maid Marion, and the Sheriff of Nottingham. "Stealing from the rich and giving to the poor?"

"I wouldn't say stealing. But Marianne and I are definitely the poor, so…"

"Good God." He started laughing. "Good God, you've a nerve. Are you always like this?"

Loxleigh—Robin—shrugged, grinning. Hart shook his head.

This was absurd, and wildly outwith his experience. He really didn't want to consider what he was doing, still less ask himself how he, a plain-spoken sort of man, found himself in this situation with a rogue of a very different stamp than he'd realised.

It was too late for quibbling. He was launched now and the tide would carry him where it pleased.

CHAPTER 12

One of Miss Marianne Loxleigh's most admired features, at least by the kind of people who catalogued beauty rather than reacting to it, was her noble and lofty forehead. She usually emphasised it in the way she dressed her hair. Currently she was emphasising it by banging it on the breakfast table.

"Yes, all *right*," Robin said.

Marianne lifted her head, glared incredulously at him, then thumped it again, making the cups jump.

"Look, you told me to grovel."

Bang. Rattle.

"Well, I couldn't pay him! What else was I supposed to do?"

"What else?" Marianne repeated. "Well, yes, true, what else could you possibly do but offer to fuck him for a month? I'm sure you'd tried all the other options!" She thumped her head so hard that milk splashed from the jug.

"You'll bruise yourself," Robin said.

"Shut up."

She did, he was forced to concede, have a point. It might not have been the most considered move of his erratic career, but—well, it had worked, hadn't it?

"Suppose he makes a complaint," Marianne added.

"He'll be hard put to do that without incriminating himself."

"Suppose he becomes afraid you'll make a complaint."

Robin lifted his hands. "That's how it always is. Can't be helped."

"Which is why you should be careful who you fuck!"

"Easy for you to say. I really don't think you need worry. If the poor bastard's ever had a decent tupping, it isn't recently. I'm going to fuck him till he doesn't know which way's up, he'll love it, spit spot."

Marianne put her elbows on the table, and her noble and lofty forehead in her hands. "Let me try to make this clear to you, Rob. Granted, I didn't want Hartlebury telling people you don't pay your debts. Granted, you have dealt with that issue with remarkable expediency. But—and I dare say I should have spelled this out—I didn't mean that he should be able to tell people you molly for money instead."

"There's no need to be rude."

Marianne gave a strangled scream. She was definitely taking this with less than her usual aplomb.

"You wanted a month," Robin told her. "You have one, and more, because I think Hartlebury will play fair. He doesn't give a damn for Tachbrook; he only cares about Alice."

"And about getting his hands on your arse."

"Well, I do have a fine arse."

"Rob." She looked up. "I can't ask you to do this. Not for me, not for a month."

"You didn't ask me. He didn't ask me. Nobody had to ask me because it was *my idea*. God's sake, why wouldn't I want to?" He recalled the way Hart had said, *Shouldn't you pay me?*, the sudden humour that lit his grim-set features and told Robin that his gamble had paid off. "Really, those thighs, I'm sure I've mentioned them. And we agreed I can't possibly pursue another heiress this Season, so I need something to do that isn't drifting around endless tedious events."

"Something to do," she repeated. "Have you not heard of watercolours?"

Robin sighed. "Marnie, it's not hostile. He didn't force me into this. It's more like—we wanted to fuck, and now we can, do you see? It was already there. The money is just his excuse."

"What's yours?"

Robin fluttered his eyelashes. "Brotherly love, of course."

"God damn you, Rob." She slumped back in her chair. "Just be careful. If he hurts you, I'll never forgive you."

Robin awaited the evening with a certain trepidation. Hart had told him, brusquely, to come to dinner. That seemed a civility the situation didn't merit. Maybe he needed to pretend this was something other than it was. Robin didn't mind that, but he spent much of the day wondering if a note would arrive revoking the invitation, or the agreement. He imagined Hart was having quite a lot of second thoughts.

Second thoughts would be perfectly acceptable—if accompanied by an assurance that he didn't need to pay the money and Hart would not meddle with Marianne's ambitions, of course. But Robin would unquestionably be a little disappointed.

For one thing, he hadn't had a good bout in months. For another, he rather thought he could like Hart. The glimpses he'd had of the inner man were appealing: the humour, the kindness, the protectiveness of his loved ones. Robin had often prayed for someone to protect himself and Marianne; he was a grown man now and looked after himself, but it was still a trait that struck a chord somewhere deep within him, at least now it wasn't standing directly in his way.

He saw no reason this shouldn't be a mutually satisfactory arrangement. There had been a spark between them from the start, and that didn't happen often enough to go around wasting it. Perhaps it was a *little* bit depraved, but that was all part of the fun. Or at least it was for Robin, who liked to play. Hart gave every impression of never having played in his life, and it occurred to Robin that he might be able to do the fellow some good. Leave him better than he found him. That would make a nice change.

Hart didn't look like a man anticipating fun when Robin arrived, dressed to the nines and with a flask of oil in his pocket. He was remarkably severe, mouth tense, brows knotted and dark, standing stiffly by the window as the manservant showed Robin in.

"Thank you, Spenlow, that will do for the night," Hart said. "We will serve ourselves. I wish to be undisturbed, so you may clear the plates in the morning."

"Certainly, Sir John."

Robin waited for the door to shut. "You have a good arrangement here."

"Spenlow lives upstairs with his wife. It's more convenient than maintaining a second staff or moving my household from Aston Clinton. Sherry?"

"Thank you."

Hart poured them both drinks. His fingers were tense on the cut crystal glass, enough that Robin wanted to warn him not to smash it. "There is a dinner laid out but— Curse it. Last night, you were in a vulnerable position, albeit entirely of your own making. I did not intend—"

"I haven't changed my mind," Robin said.

"I hadn't finished."

"I realise that, but you have remarked on the tiresome

nature of rehearsed pompous speeches and now I see you were quite right."

Hart's lips parted. "Cockish bastard, aren't you?"

"Am I wrong? Were you not going to ask that?"

"No. That is, no, you aren't wrong, and I was going to ask that."

"Then we've saved some valuable time. Very valuable, if you consider what mine is worth to you."

"Kindly allow me to speak," Hart said, with a strong suggestion of gritted teeth. "I don't choose to force you—anyone—into a position which—"

"Speechifying," Robin told him.

"Will you shut up and let me finish!"

Robin folded his arms, looking Hart in the eyes. "I haven't changed my mind. You are not forcing anything on me. If you don't want to fuck, nothing obliges you to do so, but I made a proposition which you accepted, so kindly don't treat me like a helpless victim of your wiles. There is only one person in this room with wiles, as we both know."

Hart stood a moment, mouth moving slightly, then he said, "But your wiles are terrible."

"They are not. I'll have you know, I'm extremely wily."

"It didn't get you your marriage."

"That was just bad luck."

"You aren't easily defeated, are you?"

"Well, I'm not often squashed," Robin said. "I like to face every situation with a spring in my step and a song in my heart." He observed the revolted look on Hart's face with satisfaction. "Did you mention dinner?"

"I think I've lost my appetite," Hart muttered, and led him through.

The food was laid out, with chafing-dishes to keep it warm. There was a chicken pie, cabbage, parsnips and potatoes, as well as a good ham. Hart poured glasses of rich red wine, and said, "Tell me something."

"What?"

"Anything. Tell me something of yourself."

"A topic of absorbing interest." It was anything but. There was very little he wanted to tell.

"Where are you from?"

"Cheshire, originally." He really didn't want to talk about his childhood. They'd left it behind them: that was the whole point. "Something about me? I learned to play cards from a nobleman who lost his family home at the gaming tables to his own brother, and was obliged to pretend he was dead and live under a false name."

"I *beg* your pardon?" Hart demanded.

"That's what he said when he got drunk enough. He insisted he was actually an earl and his brother had stolen his title. Now I think about it, I'm not sure it was true."

"You amaze me."

"He was terribly gentlemanly when he was sober."

"And you learned to play cards from a man who lost everything? That explains a lot." Hart had a bite of pie, chewing ruminatively. "Tell me something. How did you find out about Alice's portion? I know you asked the lawyer, but how did you know to?"

"You are aware of how two people can keep a secret, yes?"

"If one of them is dead."

"Quite. There are information brokers who provide hints and tips on possible"—he considered and discarded 'targets'—"heiresses, for a fee."

"Great God!"

"Oh, you can have anything for money."

"As we have established," Hart said, then grimaced. "I beg your pardon."

"Why? It's true."

"It was belittling. I didn't intend insult by it. I too often speak before I think."

"I do almost everything before I think," Robin assured him. "It keeps me on my toes. Tell me where you learned to play piquet like that. I refuse to believe you have a story nearly as interesting as mine."

"I learned thanks to being repeatedly and humiliatingly beaten by a small girl."

"Ah. Maybe not."

Hart told him of his piquet-playing with Alice. Robin, on a wave of benevolence, praised her ability with numbers and led Hart to applaud her skills, and thence to explain his family.

"Edwina married Fenwick, a widower, as a practical proposition while Alice was a baby. Our mother didn't approve." He sounded a little distant. "She—many people felt that Edwina was marrying beneath herself. We are a very old family, and Fenwick was a tradesman, many years her senior, with a child. And yet their marriage was one of the happiest I have known."

"She seems an excellent mother to Alice."

"She is. And to George, her son by her second husband, a delightful little rascal. He's at school."

"And you are breadwinner for the whole family?"

"Not at all. The brewery is Edwina's; I merely manage it."

"If it's hers— Sorry."

"What?"

"It's none of my business," Robin said. "It just seems a little hard on Alice that her father's property should go to her stepmother, who I suppose will leave it to her son, and that she has nothing of her own until her marriage."

"I quite agree with you," Hart said, somewhat to his surprise. "Fenwick's will was trusting to the point of foolishness, and could have been disastrous for Alice with a less kind or principled stepmother, but Edwina was entirely worthy of his faith. She is very concerned to ensure the well-being of both children, and we talk a great deal about what is fair and equitable. As it happens, she need not worry, since the baronetcy can descend through the female line so George will be heir to my title and lands. She doesn't expect that, since she hopes I will marry one day, but it is no bad thing if George doesn't grow up taking too much for granted."

Robin felt a stab of envy of Alice and the absent George, with adults who took it on themselves to love and look after them and think about their well-being. He wondered if the stepsiblings would grow up like Edwina and Hart, in what seemed a highly practical relationship of quiet affection and respect. Probably better that than like himself and Marianne, clinging desperately to one another because there was nobody else.

He didn't want to think about families any more. "Do you enjoy the work of running the brewery?"

"More than anything."

They, or rather Hart, talked of brewing and the iniquitous price of Kentish hops, and his intention to form a partnership with another brewer and expand his business. Robin knew nothing of business or beer, but he knew how to listen, and to read the signs of a speaker fascinated with his subject. He asked intelligent questions, and drank wine, and by the time they had finished the meal with good apples and strong cheese, he'd learned a great deal. That Hart's heavy brows didn't move much, but his deep-set blue eyes wrinkled at the edges when he was amused. That he smiled more he was less conscious of himself. And, mostly, that he could have simply tupped Robin and sent him home, but that wasn't what he wanted to do.

Finally the meal was over, and they were at the table together. Understanding one another better, no doubt, very much aware of the other's presence, and still in this absurd situation.

"Well," Robin said.

"Well." Hart looked just a little uncertain. He was really not confident at all. It was quite endearing.

Robin drained his glass and licked a drop of wine off his lips with a deliberate tongue, noting how Hart's eyes followed the motion. "Tell me something."

"Whatever you like."

"You told me to please you, yesterday. Did I?"

"Christ, yes." Hart's words were flatteringly unguarded.

"I mention it because you could say that again, if you chose. *Pleasure me*, and I will. I wouldn't do it the same way each time of course, so it rather depends if you like variety. If what you want is me kneeling in front of you again, you should simply tell me to come over and suck you." Hart's lips moved, just slightly. Robin would have put money he was trying the words out, and felt a tingle of satisfaction. "But if you don't care to decide, or you prefer to give a general instruction and let me fulfil it as I think best, I can use my imagination. I do have a very good imagination."

"I realised that yesterday." Hart's voice thickened notably when he was aroused, putting gravel in the deep tones. "It's remarkably vivid. Perhaps you could use it again?"

"My pleasure. Would you care to know what I dreamed of last night?"

Hart leaned back in his chair. "Tell me."

"We were in your sitting room, where that big desk is," Robin said, watching his eyes, his lips. "I say 'we', but you know that people are often different in dreams. I told you I couldn't pay my debt, and you told me that I was ruined. I begged you for time, and you refused. I begged you for mercy, and you refused that too. 'You are entirely in my power,' you said, and I told you I would do anything—anything at all.

And you pointed to the desk. You stood over me and told me that I had no choice but to surrender to your demands—"

Hart recoiled in his chair. "What? No!"

That was not the effect Robin had expected. "In the dream only," he hastened to explain.

"That is not a dream. That is a nightmare."

"It's just a game. There is no harm in it. A lot of people like to play games of that sort."

"I don't."

Hart sounded uncomfortable to the point of unhappiness. Hell's teeth, Robin had misjudged this. Especially since he had *said* he wanted willingness, and Robin had nodded along without thinking twice, and now he'd made the man uncomfortable and ruined the atmosphere. Idiot. He'd promised to give Hart exactly what he wanted, and failed at the first hurdle.

"Understood," he said. "I'm sorry. My fault for not listening better."

"No, but—Robin, if that—that sort of thing is what you like—I don't wish to be difficult but I cannot—"

"You don't have to! I like to play, that's all, but if you would rather not play in that way, or at all, we shan't. And of course it isn't being difficult to say if you dislike something. You made me promise to do that, so why should you not?"

Hart didn't look convinced. "Yes, but if you want such things—I am not experienced at this, at 'play'. I don't know how to proceed."

He sounded miserably self-conscious. Under the table, Robin dug a punitive heel onto his other ankle. He would have liked to believe this wasn't his fault—who would have guessed the imposing Sir John Hartlebury was so uncertain? How was he to know the poor sod had never had any fun?—but he should have known, and he had nobody to blame but himself, again.

Well done, Rob, good job. That four thousand must seem like a bargain right now.

Right. Deep breath, go back to where things *had* worked, and start again. "Well, that can be remedied, but it seems to me you play very well," he said, keeping his voice light and encouraging. "After all, you enjoyed our game yesterday, did you not? You certainly took me in hand most effectively."

"Yes," Hart agreed cautiously, shoulders relaxing a little. "That was good."

"Well then. Play is just—oh, developing an idea that entertains us both. Nothing more complicated. For example, yesterday, we were talking about getting me into a state of desperation. Aroused to the point of begging you for satisfaction, so you could hear exactly how much I want it. I think we both liked that idea?"

"Very much."

"So, if that would please you, would you care to put it into action?"

Hart nodded, wordless. Robin shoved his chair back so he could sprawl in full view, and ran his hand over the front of his breeches. "I can think of all sorts of ways to get into such a state. I could use my hand while you watch, perhaps tell me what you want to see. Or you could do it, if you prefer. I'd like your hand on me again. Or—"

"That."

Robin rose, walked over to where Hart sat, and pushed the various plates out of the way. He swung a leg over Hart's thighs, straddling while still standing, rested his arse on the edge of the table, and unbuttoned himself., Hart's eyes were on his face at first, then they dropped as if drawn downwards.

"Touch me," Robin said softly.

Hart's hand was tentative. Robin leaned back. "Mmm. Yes. You had me so hard yesterday, on your lap."

"That was down to your imagination."

125

"My imagination, your hand, match made in heaven. Your prick too at some point, I hope. Uh, do you like that?" he added, realising he should assume nothing. "Fucking, I mean?"

"I do."

"Phew." Robin pushed against his hand, undulating his hips. Hart's movements were firmer now. "If you want to see willing, keep doing that because I'll be pleading for satisfaction soon, and then you can decide just how you want to give it to me. How long you want to make me wait for it."

"Do you like to wait?"

"I enjoy anticipation, but the problem is, I have very little self-control. None, really. That's why I'll be begging and pleading and offering to do anything you like if you'll only fuck me."

"Last time." Hart's voice was a bit raspy. "You said you'd like to be, uh—"

"Put over your desk," Robin offered helpfully. "Yes, I did."

"Was that imagination?"

"Think of it more as a subtle hint."

"That is *very* subtle," Hart said. "I'm surprised you haven't considered a career in diplomacy."

There was a laugh in his voice, and his thumb was doing good work over the tip of Robin's prick. Robin could have collapsed with relief. He leaned back instead, letting himself enjoy the sensation and the anticipation. "I would have, but it would be all too easy for an ambassador to wring concessions out of me."

"Your lack of self-control again?"

"Exactly. Oh God. *Are* you going to fuck me?"

Hart paused, then said, so deliberately that Robin could barely hear the nerves in it, "Not yet."

Good boy. "Not fair." Robin moaned theatrically and thrust into his hand; Hart loosened his grip to the lightest touch, eliciting a real moan. "Oh, *not* fair. I have thought of you having me for weeks."

"Then you can surely wait a few minutes more."

He seemed to be getting the hang of this, and it wasn't long until Robin was whimpering with frustration that wasn't entirely play-acting. "Please. *Please*, Hart. What do I have to say to get put over the table? I need it—Fuck!"

That was quite genuine, because Hart had abruptly let go. Robin made a strangled noise. Hart's eyes were dark. "This might be better continued in other surroundings, with stronger furniture."

"Lead the way."

The desk in the sitting-room was impressively sturdy. Robin perched provocatively on the edge, and felt a wave of something like pride in a pupil as Hart leaned over him and clamped a hand between his legs.

"Sir John!" Robin said, with wide-eyed mock shock.

"I can see you are keen. But—uh. You said, yesterday, I should ask—?"

"Indeed you should, for whatever you want."

"It strikes me that if you wish to—to have me use this desk properly—that perhaps you might—"

"That perhaps I should see about you first?" Robin suggested, since he seemed to be stuck there. "On my knees, with an aching prick begging for satisfaction, just as we imagined?"

Hart's expression was glorious, a combination of bafflement, embarrassment, and something like wonder. "Exactly so."

"Tell me," Robin said softly. "Please. I would like to hear you say it."

Hart licked his lips and tightened his grip. "I want you to suck me. Pleasure me. I want you to do it while you are desperate for relief, just as you said."

Robin slipped downward. Hart was extremely ready for him. Robin mouthed his substantial prick, and made sure he was noisy about it, moaning and grunting his enjoyable frustration against the flesh until Hart gasped, "Up. I want—"

Robin had carefully not worn garments that required too much undignified wriggling to remove. He shoved his breeches and his drawers together down to his knees, and turned.

"Oh." Hart's hand slid over his arse, caressing the curve and muscle of it, then down between his legs, cupping his cods. Robin whimpered. "Do you like that?"

"Touch me and find out."

Hart put his other hand round Robin's waist. Fingers wrapped round his prick. "Oh God. This feels…oh. So good."

Robin rubbed against his hand. Hart pulled away after a moment to take hold of Robin's arse with both hands, and a firmness that sent a quiver of pleasure through him, the more so when Hart gently pulled the buttocks apart and slid his thumbs down the crease. Not an entire novice, then. "You have a delightful backside."

"Thank you, I'm fond of it myself. I sit on it a great deal, but if you have better uses for it, you could put them into practice at any time you like."

Hart snorted. "That is another of your hints?"

"Master of subtlety."

Hart's hands were roaming, pressed against him. "Oh God." He sounded like he couldn't breathe. "You—This is perfect. Now?"

"Definitely now. I have oil," he added.

"Thank Christ for that."

Hart was fairly well sized. Robin didn't cry out as the slick stand breached him—he really did not want to put Hart off again—but it took an effort of will. Not for long though, because Hart was careful, and Robin was practised, and both of them needed this. Hart wrapped an arm round Robin's waist and Robin breathed into the movements till he was comfortable, whispered encouragement, and braced himself against his partner's size and strength.

"You do want it," Hart whispered, sounding almost awestruck. "Tell me you want it." It was not an order, more a request. Possibly a plea.

"I've wanted your prick since I first saw you. I wanted you to pull me into the shrubbery in that garden and have me there against the wall."

"Oh Christ. So did I." Hart was moving a little faster. "I touched you. I wanted to do—I don't know what."

"When you came to me at Wintour's, I'd have left with you for the asking. Oh God, fuck me, show me you want me now."

Hart made a noise in his throat. His hand came round to grip Robin's prick, so Robin thrust into his hand as Hart thrust into him, and then there was no possibility of coherent speech, just urgent movement and the hard drive of flesh against flesh.

Hart came first, letting go all restraint, hammering Robin with a few almost brutal thrusts that flattened him against the desk, crying out as he did it. Robin hung on through that, gritting his teeth, as Hart's movement slowed.

"Great God. Dear God. Robin." He shifted back a little, pulled Robin with him, and closed his hand round Robin's prick again. "Can you spend with me still in you?"

"Might be hard not to."

Hart's hand moved. His hips pressed close, his other arm was wrapped round Robin's waist, holding him tight, and he bent forward to set his lips against Robin's neck, sending sensation shooting over his skin. "I want to feel you do it."

"Make me," Robin whispered, and Hart did, bringing him

off with quick strokes and biting gently at Robin's neck as he cried out and spasmed over the desk.

They stood together then, Robin's shoulders heaving. Hart had got his breath back but it still sounded ragged.

"That's probably going to ruin the surface," Robin observed after a moment.

"What is?"

"Well, I just spent all over your desk. I don't suppose it's good for the wood. Or is it? They use beeswax in polish. And tea-leaves to clean carpets, and piss in tanning leather, so perhaps—"

"Ask a housemaid. No, please don't." He eased himself out of Robin's body and winced. "I'll get a cloth."

He did more than that, bringing tepid water that had presumably not been left for that purpose, and two cloths so they could both clean themselves up. Robin pulled up his pantaloons but didn't fasten them. "Was that good?"

"Magnificent," Hart said. "Did—did I hurt you?"

"Of course not."

Hart put a hand out as if to touch, then pulled it back. "I want you to say if I do. If I am clumsy, or excessively forceful."

"I like forceful, it shows a flattering enthusiasm. Excessive is in the arse of the beholder."

"In the—" Hart put a hand over his face. "You are astonishing."

"I try."

Hart nodded slowly, at what Robin wasn't sure. "Do you need to return home?"

"No, but I will if that's a hint. If not, we might retire somewhere more comfortable between bouts?"

Hart's eyes widened. "Between—?"

"Well, since I'm here." Robin fluttered his eyelashes.

"I assumed your, uh, obligation was met for the night. Is that acceptable? Do you mind?"

Did he *mind*? Robin examined his face. "Good Lord. You really are worrying about what I want, aren't you?"

"Of course I am. I told you that."

"Then let me tell you what that is. I want to tup you spineless over the next month. I want to fulfil every desire you have, and all the ones you didn't know about. I want to be your fantasy, your incubus, the perfect fuck that you'll remember on your deathbed. That's what I want, and I suggest you let me get on with it."

Hart's mouth hung open. The look in his eyes was delicious. "Uh. Why?"

Because they were both lonely, and this could be fun, and he might leave someone better off for having met him, which would make a change. "Because it would please us both," he said in lieu of admitting that.

"It sounds more like you pleasing me."

"Yes, but I *like* to please. If it's good for you, it will be good for me."

"That doesn't always hold true," Hart said carefully. "As a general rule."

"Not if one's partner is only concerned with himself, but you don't strike me as a selfish or a careless man."

"Oh." Hart's cheeks darkened visibly. It was a *blush*. Robin had made him blush. That was utterly delicious. "Uh. Thank you."

"And in any case I'd be quite ashamed of myself if I struck this bargain and didn't put any effort in," he went on. "If one is to do anything, one should do it properly. And I've always thought I'd make an excellent courtesan, so this is my opportunity to find out."

"I," Hart said, then passed a hand over his face. "I have no idea what to say."

"'Good idea, Robin,' would do."

Hart exhaled. "If you care to remain—to sit a while—there is the settle."

So he wasn't going to be invited into the bedroom, or at least not yet. That was a perfectly reasonable boundary. He was here as a whore, even if Hart was treating him like a mistress.

He smiled. "The settle it is."

CHAPTER 13

Robin Loxleigh *was* an incubus. Hart was sure of it.

He was absurdly perfect. Beautiful in the way Hart most liked, with his solid build; outrageously wanton; and now he'd stopped mouthing sugary platitudes, he was thoroughly enjoyable company, an excellent listener, with an irrepressible cheerfulness that didn't falter even when Hart misstepped with some unfortunate bluntness.

He did that as early as the second day, after Robin, chest heaving at the end of a lengthy bout, had complimented him on his stamina with that laughing light in his eyes. Hart had wanted to reply in the same vein, to talk of lovemaking with the uninhibited enjoyment and pleasure Robin displayed, but what had come out of his mouth was, "Got to get my money's worth."

He could have kicked himself even as the words sounded, but it was too late, it always was. He started to apologise, and Robin had shushed him at once, with the unanswerable words, "I don't know what you're apologising about. I have the highest-priced arse in England. I'd take out advertisements if I could." And had gone on to make Hart call him a thousand-a-week whore as they fucked a second time, which was so obscene he'd barely been able to say it, and, in the moment, ridiculously erotic.

Your fantasy, your incubus, the perfect fuck that you'll remember on your deathbed.

He was there to pay off the debt. Hart knew that, and he was careful not to let himself believe otherwise, but it was frighteningly easy to forget, all the same. Robin was very good at enthusiasm that seemed unfeigned, and his physical responses didn't suggest a reluctant man: the very opposite. He was unquestionably taking pleasure from their liaison, which salved Hart's conscience to a probably excessive degree, and by God he was giving everything he had promised.

If Hart had dared, he'd have kept Robin in his rooms the whole time, so as not to waste a single moment of this impossibly easy, magical situation. He didn't dare. It was risky enough that he was visiting nightly, even if Hart arranged the times Robin would come so he could open the door himself and not alert Spenlow. And in any case, he had to show his face to friends and family, and Robin had to appear at parties, supporting his glittering success of a sister.

Parties which Alice attended. That was a little awkward, but she seemed inexplicably happy to meet and speak to Robin, even to dance, which Edwina permitted given Hart's assurance he had taken care of the situation. It was undeniably better that nobody could mock Alice for failing to catch her man, or call Robin a dangerous flirt for dropping her. There was no scandal to be made out of two people on good terms.

It also meant that Hart and Robin could attend the same event, a soiree, which did indeed lead to a ludicrously risky encounter in an upstairs room. Hart had stood, heart and blood pounding together, listening for footsteps as Robin pleasured him with frantic, gleeful haste, and had to bite his wrist as he spent to restrain himself from crying out. It was stupid and dangerous, and it felt like something he'd never known. Freedom, perhaps, from the nameless, joyless sating of desires he'd given up trying to stifle but hadn't known how to pursue. Freedom, if only in his own mind, from what he was supposed to think and feel, and the routine he'd established of work and gaming and his few friends.

He didn't know any men of his class who shared his tastes: they must exist, but he had no idea how to identify most of them and feared to approach those who made themselves obvious in case he was found out by association. He was simply too clumsy to tread the delicate path that would keep him clear of the law. He'd gone to molly houses instead, bought company as politely as possible, felt trapped in a grimy pathway that led nowhere and which he walked alone.

Robin was brightness. He didn't give a damn for the done thing. He lived with an exuberant amorality that wrapped itself round Hart and helped him ignore everything that had led them here in the constant thrum of arousal, and the even more seductive pleasures of casual intimacy, smiles, light-hearted touch.

That lasted for all of ten days.

He woke late on the eleventh morning. Robin had left him near three, and Hart wondered, not for the first time, if he might safely stay; Spenlow never came into his bedroom before ten. That would of course mean inviting Robin into his bedroom in the first place. He'd vowed not to do that—it was so intimate, such a thing lovers did, and he had to remember that they were not lovers. He had less than three weeks of Robin before his rooms would be empty again. He didn't want his bed to be a permanent reminder of a temporary pleasure.

Perhaps that was foolish. Robin's joy sprang from the way he lived in the moment; Hart continually thought of the future, and hadn't made himself happy that way. He'd made himself secure instead, while Robin's course was far more likely to end in disaster, but was it truly enough if the most one could say for a life was that nothing had gone horribly wrong? He lay in bed for a few moments thinking of the previous night, how Robin had made him laugh till he cried, and found he was smiling at the memory. The fucking had been spectacular, but the laughter stuck more in his mind.

He was still smiling when he got up and rang for breakfast. The letter Spenlow placed beside his plate, addressed with urgency in Edwina's hand, put paid to that.

Come round at once. I must speak to you about Alice.

Hart left Edwina's house around three that afternoon. He considered stopping in at his club, but he was too angry for company.

Angry and hurt, and furious at himself that he was hurt. He should have known; he should have bloody known. Why had he trusted a man who lied, who cheated, and sold himself for debts?

He sent a terse note to Robin requesting he pay a call at once. He didn't logically expect the man to be waiting in at his convenience, but it was still two grating, enraging hours before Spenlow announced, "Mr. Loxleigh."

Robin came in with a polite word and a smile that faded as he took in Hart's expression. He waited for the sound of the door that indicated Spenlow's departure, and said, "You look stern."

"I am extremely angry." Hart spoke through his teeth.

Robin raised a tentative eyebrow. Hart said, "I am not playing, damn it! I have just spent the day with my sister and Alice, discussing your plans to elope with my niece!"

"I have no plans to elope with your niece." Robin took a hasty step back, all the same. "I really haven't."

"Are you calling her a liar?"

"Could you possibly tell me what she said?"

Hart took a deep breath. "She told us—Edwina, then me —that she intended to marry in order to get her hands on her portion. She told us that you had agreed to marry her for that reason! You promised me! How the hell could you—after this week—my God, man, have you no shame?"

"Did she tell you why she wanted the money?"

"What the hell does that matter?!"

"Of course it matters. She wanted it for a very reasonable purpose." He ignored Hart's explosive reaction. "I told her to ask her mother for it first, and to hold me in reserve if her request was denied. I take it Mrs. Blaine refused?"

"That's none of your damned business. We had an agreement! You told me you would leave her be, and you lied to me!" His voice was shaking with rage. Definitely rage; nothing else.

"She asked me to marry her a week and a half ago, in order to get her money," Robin said, enunciating with odd, crisp clarity. "Me, a gazetted fortune hunter she had known for a matter of months. Did you want me to turn her down, so that she might request the same of someone else? Can you think of any ill consequences that might result if she took some random swine's word that he'd leave her untouched and hand over her money? Of course I said yes! And I told her to speak to her mother with that in her back pocket, in the hope that she'd be allowed to do what she wants with her life instead of being trotted out to be married for her wealth!"

"That is grossly unfair," Hart said savagely. "Edwina only wants her happiness."

"And Alice told me very clearly what would make her happy. You said yourself she's brilliant. It's what she wants to do, and you wouldn't think twice were she a boy."

"But she isn't a boy. Where does mathematics get a girl, especially one her age?"

"I have no idea where it gets anyone. She wants to do it, so why shouldn't she?"

"She is talking about spending her marriage portion!"

"Because Mrs. Blaine doesn't want to pay for it out of the money from her father's brewery."

Hart clenched his fists. "That is not true, and none of your damned business!"

"I dare say not," Robin said. "But I think Alice had this in mind from the first: she wasn't truly interested in me until I listened to her talk about mathematics, and she trusted me then because she thought I'd sympathise. She wants this, she obviously isn't marriage-minded yet if she ever will be—and if you're talking about where things might get her, by the way, I have to observe that making her sit through a Season is clearly as futile as any academic study."

"You needn't tell me that," Hart said involuntarily. "It was Edwina's idea. And none of this is the point!"

"What is the point?" Robin asked. "Why I told her I'd marry her if she saw no other way through? Because it isn't pleasant to be trapped, that's why. It leads one to do desperate things." The usual lurking humour had gone from his eyes. "It isn't entertaining to be helpless, and not listened to, and have no control of your life. I didn't want her to do something even more stupid than asking me to marry her."

"What 'more stupid' could you possibly you have in mind?"

"I'd have done it for five hundred and not touched her or the rest of the money. Is that so bad?"

"Bad? You've spent the last week fucking me!"

"Well, I hadn't when I offered! We had that conversation before you and I came to our agreement!"

"You proposed our arrangement having *already agreed* to marry my niece? You told me you would withdraw your pretensions!"

"I didn't sodding propose to her!" Robin shouted over him. "What I said was, if she couldn't come to an agreement with her mother then she should come back to me!"

"And what were you planning to do then? Move from my bed to Alice's? Christ almighty!"

"I wasn't going to bed her and I wasn't planning anything," Robin said, more calmly. "I didn't think I'd need to. I assumed Mrs. Blaine would relent."

Hart sat down and put his face in his hands. A rustle of movement suggested Robin was perching on the desk. He didn't want to think of Robin and the desk.

"Do you understand why I cannot stomach you becoming my niece's husband?" he enquired.

"I sincerely hope it isn't in question. Will Mrs. Blaine really not let her go?"

"Of course she bloody will. She is resigning herself to the prospect now, with much tearfulness. She only ever wanted to do what was best for Alice—"

"But they don't have the same definition of best."

That summed it up nicely. "Edwina is deeply conventional. She can't understand why Alice wants to do such an extraordinary thing. She was quite sure she'd forget about mathematics when she grew to womanhood, and I suppose she didn't want to believe she'd misjudged things so. She loves Alice deeply and it is upsetting to discover you have done badly by someone you love."

"Yes. It is."

Hart sighed. "So Alice will have her way, though I can't say Edwina is enthusiastic at having her hand forced."

"But she wasn't enthusiastic anyway, and at least she's made the right decision."

Robin sounded just a little smug. Hart narrowed his eyes. "And you expected her to relent. Did you and Alice cook this up between you?"

"I might have suggested she offer marriage with me as an alternative," Robin said without any obvious signs of repentance. "To remind her mother there are worse things than mathematics. Oh, come, it needed doing. This is what she wants, and why should she not have it?"

Hart flopped back in his chair. "Doubtless she should. God knows she has an apprehension of figures far beyond my capacity. I had wondered about her taking over the brewery, but she told me she prefers numbers in the abstract."

"She gave me remarkable advice on rolling dice. So if she will get her way and has no need to marry me, why are you so angry?"

The rage and betrayal had been overwhelming, the thought of Robin scheming against him all the time, the feeling he'd been played for a fool. He wanted, desperately, to believe him now. "You promised to leave her alone."

"And I have. I haven't approached her except in a friendly and public way as we agreed."

"And if she had asked you to fulfil your promise? What were you going to do then?"

"I honestly don't know. I'd have burned that bridge when I came to it."

Hart had to look up at that. Robin was looking down at him with a little frown. He dropped to a squat and tentatively, too tentatively, put a hand on Hart's knee. "I wasn't going to cheat you, I swear it. I'd probably have set up an elopement, something sufficiently drastic to make her plans seem the lesser of two evils. She asked me to help her, Hart. And I owed her something. I wasn't fair to her."

"You weren't, no."

"I didn't want to let her down. But I wasn't going to cheat you," Robin said again. "Well, you must see I wasn't: there was nothing in it for me."

"Alice's fortune?"

"My price was five hundred pounds. That's a couple of good nights at the tables."

"If you win."

"Winning can be arranged. And if you're about to say I could have consummated the marriage and taken all her money—well, I could, but I promise you Marianne would have hunted me down and cut my balls off long before you got to me. But I wouldn't do that, Hart. I'm not virtuous, but I don't think I'm cruel."

"You have a fascinating approach to morality."

"I wasn't brought up a gentleman."

Hart watched his face, his hazel eyes that were green and gold and brown, like a forest opal. "I assumed you intended to run. To take her and her fortune."

"The current arrangement suits me considerably better."

"Better? Being trapped into desperate things? Having no control?"

Robin blinked. "Eh? I wasn't referring to us by that."

Hart reached out, taking hold of his chin, resisting the urge to caress with his thumb. "If you find our arrangement intolerable, you must tell me, now. I will gladly—"

"Mother of God," Robin said. "How many times must I say it? And if you think I have no control, you haven't been paying attention for the last week."

Hart's breath caught in his chest. He stared. Robin met his gaze and his jaw hardened in Hart's hand before he jerked it away. "Are you going to keep assuming the worst every time I speak? I didn't mean I'm proposing to blackmail you, for Christ's sake."

"What did you mean?"

"Since you ask, I meant that I am doing all the work here. You aren't telling me what to do: you're accepting my propositions, every time. Don't delude yourself that taking your cock makes you my master. I'm leading you by the hand through this, so stop behaving as if you've got me under the thumb, because really, you do not."

Hart could feel himself reddening. "I don't think that."

"You do. You cannot rid yourself of the thought that you're compelling me to this. That's why you can't trust me, because you believe you're wronging me. You simply can't bring yourself to believe I truly want to fuck you. You insist it's about that bloody gambling debt, as though I wouldn't have been here for the asking, or even for you noticing me asking you. And I don't know if that's something I've done wrong, or if you feel that every man you touch must be repulsed—" He stopped abruptly.

Hart felt like he'd taken a right hook to the gut, leaving him winded. "I... You resented me. We were enemies. You owed me money. Naturally, I realise you cannot entirely—"

"Details," Robin said. "I assure you, I *can* entirely. Or I could, if you'd let me, but you won't. I don't know how to persuade you, Hart. I am, or was, perfectly happy with where we are, and I'm certainly not proposing to hurt you when you have been—not unfair to me."

Not unfair. The words stung. Was that the best he could say? Christ, maybe it was. "I did assume the worst," Hart made himself admit. "You're right about that."

"Then stop it. Stop assuming the worst, and telling yourself I must be lying in every word and deed, and persuading yourself I cannot bear your touch in the teeth of the evidence. Because if you can't trust me not to turn on you, you should have thought about that before, and you should say so now. That is no way to fuck."

"Is there another? Given our situation under the law—"

"Not everyone betrays," Robin said.

"Everyone lets you down. That is the state of humanity."

"No." There was something odd and bleak in his eyes.

"Some people don't. Not many, maybe hardly any, but some people will stand by you. Betrayal is not inevitable, it is *not.*"

"Robin?"

Robin stood, jerkily. "And if you believe I am harbouring some great resentment or that I will turn on you—well, perhaps that is rational. Most people would call it ill advised to trust someone like me. But you could, if you wanted, because I dare say I will let you down somehow, with your high standards, but I really don't want to, and I won't do it deliberately. I like you, Hart. You might try believing that, and if you can't, you're a fool to consort with me at all. Think about it and make your decision. But don't shout at me because you're afraid."

He turned on his heel. The outer door slammed a moment later, and Hart was left alone.

CHAPTER 14

The next afternoon, Robin was lying on the settle full length with his hands over his face when Marianne came in.

"What's wrong with you?"

Robin considered telling all, assessed how much sympathy he was likely to receive, and decided not to bother. Marianne had been frying bigger fish for both their benefit, while he was miserable because a man who knew he was untrustworthy treated him as such. He deserved Hart's suspicion, and if he'd made a mull of it all, he had only himself to blame.

He swung himself upright and round. "How did it go? How was the dragon?"

Marianne had finally had her long-awaited luncheon with the Dowager Marchioness of Tachbrook. It was not a friendly gesture, but very much a test. Robin had spent two hours dressing her that morning.

"Dragonish," Marianne said. "Stiff-rumped, condescending, consequential. She gave me two fingers and a nod, and spent half an hour enumerating the Tachbrook lineage before deigning to ask me about my people."

"And?"

"As we agreed. I told her my family was of no note whatsoever, that you were my only living relative, that she need not worry about hangers-on and claimants coming out of the woodwork. I freely confessed that I had neither portion nor birth, and sat with my head modestly lowered while she impressed my worthlessness and Tachbrook's glory on me."

"Sounds wonderful. So…?"

"I don't know. It may be nobody is sufficiently conscious of their unworthiness for her son, but she told me twice I was pretty enough."

"Pretty enough for that inflated lump of dough she calls a marquess?"

"Quite."

"I'm not going to ask again if you're sure, because it is very trying to be continually asked if one is sure," Robin said. "But, just to note, if you would rather accept another invitation there, fill your pockets with everything valuable that isn't nailed down, and disappear, I will very gladly keep you company."

"Things not going well with Hartlebury?" Marianne asked. "Told you so."

"He thinks I'm going to blackmail him for sodomy."

"He shouldn't have sodomised you, then."

"That's what I said."

"Some people won't be told." She flopped down beside him on the settle. Robin put an arm round her waist and she rested her head on his shoulder. "Lord, Robin."

"These bloody people."

"If I were rich—when I am rich—I shall enjoy myself. I shan't spend all my time making other people miserable because they aren't as rich as me."

"You won't have to, because you have other qualities to recommend you than wealth."

"True. Why do the worst people have it? Or why have we all decided that the most important and to-be-respected quality is the one possessed by the worst people? Ugh. Tell me something good, Rob."

She'd used to say that a lot, when they were huddled together against fear or misery. Marianne had strength of character and an ability to think ahead that Robin could only envy, but her disposition was choleric and melancholic. She turned to Robin, sanguine and phlegmatic as he was, when she was lost in the dark and needed to see brightness.

"There is good news for Alice: she may yet get to pursue her dream of mathematics."

He recounted events without touching on his argument with Hart as best he could. Marianne listened and made the right noises, but he wasn't surprised when she said, "That was what you fought about?"

"Did I say we fought?"

"Obviously you did."

Robin sighed. "That started it, yes. He thought I was going to run away with her, despite the agreement."

"I don't think he can have thought that, can he? Because it's quite clear that you were at most a means to an end, in her eyes."

"Lowering, isn't it? I think I should give up fortune hunting."

"You just need a stupider victim," Marianne said consolingly. "And it sounds like you've got one."

"What?"

"Hartlebury was jealous, oaf. And he's given up four thousand for you already—"

"Only nominally."

"All the same, it sounds to me like he's cockstruck. And he's rich enough, and considering your incapacity with women—"

"I'm not going to batten on him, if that's what you mean." Robin pulled his arm away.

"Why not? What's the difference?"

"It wouldn't work."

"Sounds exactly the same, then," she muttered. "Why wouldn't it work?"

"We're fucking because of the arrangement, or at least that's what he's telling himself. I expect that's why he got angry today: he doesn't want to have feelings about this. We haven't gone to his bed, not once. He's never kissed me." That came out sounding embarrassingly plaintive.

"You care too easily, Rob," Marianne said after a moment. "You aren't meant to do that."

He sighed. "This is embarrassing. I'm not even good at being a courtesan."

"You're marvellous at it," she assured him. "You're being the lover, or rather bed-partner, or rather *not* bed-partner that he wants. That's the job at hand. Just remember it is a job."

"What if I don't want it to be?" The words came out before he could stop them.

"Then you're a fool. Have you forgotten Manchester?"

He wished he could forget Manchester. "It doesn't have to be like that."

"But it always is. We use them or they use us, and this time we're using them."

"I didn't want to use Alice. I don't want to use Hart. I just want—"

"—him to forgive a massive debt, and forget your sordid dealings with his niece, and not put a spoke in my wheel," Marianne finished. "You're getting all that along with a good shagging, and you're complaining because he doesn't kiss you? Good God, Rob, at least you like him. If I snare Tachbrook, I may never be well-docked again, and do you hear me whining about it?"

147

"It's only a matter of time."

"When I start, you can remind me that I chose this path," Marianne said. "We may be sold, but at least we can set our own price. Why don't you?"

"Why don't I what?"

"Set a price with Hartlebury. Extend your arrangement. You like him, it's what he wants, why not try? Four thousand a month is a *bit* steep—"

"If we'd wanted to be whores, we could have stayed at home," Robin pointed out.

"That was cheap whores." Marianne rose. "I intend to be very expensive indeed. Have you plans for the evening?"

"No. I was expecting to go to Hart. I might go to my club, I suppose. I paid a fortune for the place, I should probably use it. Do we need money?"

"We always need money. Why don't you come to Lady Rule's with me? She is rather fast, so you can be sure Alice will not be there."

"Would the Dowager approve of you visiting a fast woman?"

Marianne indicated, crisply and vividly, where the Dowager could put her opinions. "Anyway, Lady Rule is visited by the most respectable."

That was true, Robin knew. For example, Giles Verney was a very respectable man, and he was a friend of the Rules. He was likely to be there, and where Verney went in London, so did Hartlebury.

Robin knew both those facts. Marianne knew both those facts. Neither of them, apparently, intended to discuss them further.

"Good idea," he said.

Lady Rule's Evenings were a minor legend. She opened the tall house in Mayfair for dancing downstairs, music, conversation, and gaming on the first floor. It could not be called a hell, or even a club, but the play was always high, and since it was a private home, there was no risk of a raid for illegal gambling. Robin had been a couple of times, but had not wanted to give the impression of a hardened gamester amid general society while he was pursuing Alice, so had kept to the salon. This time he joined the play.

It was the first time he'd picked up the cards since his spectacular loss to Hart at Lady Wintour's and he felt a moment's trepidation. No piquet, he decided. He found a game of whist where the stakes had not yet risen too high, and settled in.

He wasn't going to cheat tonight. If Marianne didn't catch her prize after all this, he intended to spend a couple of hectic evenings clearing out the pockets of every member of the ton fool enough to sit at the tables with him and then disappear; until then, with victory within their grasp, he would be impeccable, even if it meant losing a little. That virtuous resolution was immediately repaid by a run of good hands. Chance, not luck, he reminded himself, and smiled at the thought of Alice's earnest interest.

He played for a couple of hours, until one of his opponents mumbled his excuses and left the table, pockets lighter than they'd been on arrival. Robin was still winning, but he recalled Alice's dictum that it all averaged out in the end. He might as well stop now, before he started losing. So he smilingly announced that he should find his sister, rose, turned, and all but walked into Hart.

"Oh," he said.

"I beg your pardon." Hart's terrifying brows were set in their usual scowl, but the eyes under them were uncertain. "Have you finished playing? Or would you care for a game?"

"I'll give you a partie or two of piquet," Robin said. "For chicken-stakes. I have learned my lesson there."

They took a table in the corner, next to a noisy game of hazard. Hart shuffled the cards and said, low, "I owe you an apology."

"You do, yes. More than one, really."

"I wasn't fair to you, and I should have thought before speaking. The truth is, I am leagues out of my depth in this matter and I don't know how to think of it. Of you."

"Deal the cards," Robin said. "I realise that, and I also realise you have no reason to trust my good intentions. But I don't see how we can carry on our agreement unless you do."

"I do have reason. I asked Alice. She told me your bargain, and that you made her promise she would give Edwina another chance to listen. Thank you for that."

He'd checked the story, rather than taking Robin's word for it. Well, that was fair enough, and at least he *had* checked.

"Edwina is, if not happy, at least resigned to the scheme. Alice is positively luminous with excitement," Hart went on, scanning his cards. "And I...I can only reflect that she didn't come to me."

"Well, it is a very unconventional proceeding, and I don't suppose she sees you as an unconventional man," Robin pointed out. "Whereas she could expect me not to be easily shocked."

"She trusted you. I asked her why, and she said that she believed she could. I might have been tempted to call her rash, but she was right." Hart played a seven, apparently at random. "She is wiser than I. I'm sorry. I hope you can accept my apology."

Robin let out a breath. "Yes."

"Which leaves us where?"

"That's up to you. I'm at your disposal, remember?"

Their eyes met. Hart's were hungry, and hopeful. "Will you come back with me?"

"I'd prefer that to piquet."

Hart left first. Robin went to find Marianne, couldn't, and left after five minutes' fruitless search. Well, she was a grown woman. He bade farewell to his hostess, who gave him the vague wave of a lady with no idea who he was, and slipped outside, joining Hart on the next street where he had secured a hackney.

The journey only took a few minutes at this late hour. It felt longer, with neither of them speaking, or touching.

There was a good fire in Hart's rooms. He stoked it while Robin shed his coat in silence, then straightened, looking into the flames.

"Is the arrangement still in force?"

"Of course."

"Because I want—I would like—" Hart made a frustrated noise. "This feels like an unfair demand, especially under the circumstances, and I wish you will refuse. If you want to, that is, not otherwise. I mean, I want you to feel absolutely free to refuse, without any more justification than that you'd rather not, and I shan't take it amiss. But you said—you told me you wanted this, and I am attempting to take you at your word, so I am going to ask."

"Go ahead," Robin said, wondering what this could possibly be leading to. "You have my word I'll refuse if I don't like whatever it is. Though I'll be impressed if you come up with something I can't stomach. What on earth is it?"

"It is not—it's rather that— Oh, for Christ's sake. May I kiss you?"

Robin had to adjust his mind to that, it was so far from his expectations. "Sorry? You want to *kiss* me?"

Hart was still looking away, but Robin could see his ears redden. "You need not, if it is not to your taste."

"Jesus wept. Of course it is to my taste. I thought it would be spikes and a dildo."

Hart made a spluttering noise. Robin came up, took his shoulder, turned him firmly, took his face in his hands to avoid awkward bumping of noses, and kissed him.

Hart didn't respond for a second, long enough to make Robin wonder, and then his lips parted, and his hand came round the back of Robin's head, and Robin found himself thoroughly, inexpertly, overwhelmingly kissed.

Hart's lips were hot and hungry, but he wasn't using his tongue. Robin licked into his mouth, felt the quiver run through the body against his, and then Hart's tongue met his, and their mouths locked together as completely as bodies could.

Hart was desperate, and he was also strong, his arm tightening round Robin's waist and pulling him close. The only possible response was for Robin to hook a leg over Hart's hip, and that eventually led to them both sprawling on the rug in front of the fire, still kissing, slowly and deeply, then wildly, then almost lazily, for the pure pleasure of closeness and reconciliation. Perhaps they weren't lovers, not really. It still felt like it.

He wasn't sure how long it lasted, and was in no hurry to stop, but eventually Hart pulled away a little. Robin was on his back by then. Hart propped himself on his elbow, looking down, and traced a finger over his lips. "These look bruised."

"Merely well-used."

"I would like to kiss you while I make you spend," Hart said softly. "May I?"

"Do you think I might conceivably want that?" Robin enquired, nudging his hips a fraction to press his stand against Hart's thigh. "Can you spot any evidence to support that theory?"

Hart's eyes met his with a faint, rueful smile. "Subtle hint?"

"So very subtle. What are you going to do, Hart?"

"I'm going to lie over you and pleasure you, and feel you moan in my mouth when you come. I think you will enjoy that."

"Correct," Robin whispered. "Do."

CHAPTER 15

They lay in front of the dying fire some time later, in a tangle of bare limbs. Hart had been as good as his word, and then brought himself off fucking Robin between the thighs, kissing still. Robin felt sticky, sated, and dizzy with foolish optimism.

You care too easily, Rob.

Hart's dark head, spangled with threads of early grey, was heavy on his chest. He stroked his fingers through the thick hair. "May I ask something?"

"Mmm?"

"Why did you not think I would want to kiss you? Did someone not want that before?"

"No. Or rather, yes, they did not. The first simply pushed me away; the second voiced his revulsion more strongly. I assumed there was a convention I had not understood."

"The convention that you have failed to understand is the one whereby we don't fuck horrible people," Robin said with some heat. "It is an excellent convention and I commend it to you for the future."

Hart's shoulders shook. "I think I am learning that."

"Tosspots. Them, not you."

"Thank you for that clarification."

"I am going to speculate," Robin said carefully, "that you have not had a lover before. Not just the act, I mean, but someone who cares for you."

"No."

"And, possibly, that you cared for someone who did not return your sentiments and let you know it."

A long pause. "Yes."

"And that he was a prick with no taste."

"Er—"

"Well, he must have been. Because you are not—that word you once said, which I never want to hear again, and whoever made you believe it was a swine. I'm very glad you wanted to kiss me, Hart. I've been hoping you would." And could have asked for that himself, he realised, with a pang of something—guilt, maybe, or a sense of lost opportunity. "I didn't want to presume."

"Nor did I." Hart reached for his hand.

Robin squeezed his fingers, feeling their strength, their urgent grip. "I don't know who persuaded you to feel undesirable. I do know that you can tell a lot about people by what they attack you with."

"How do you mean?"

"I have noticed that when people want to hurt someone very much, they often reach for the thing that would hurt themselves most deeply. Someone who calls other people cowards is probably terrified of being found out as one, do you see? People who lash out at others for low morals are usually stinking cesspits inside."

"You say that with feeling."

"Experience. And someone who might tell a good man who cared for them that he was unlovable or repulsive—I wouldn't want to be that person," Robin said. "I think that person might have a pretty face, but they'd have very little else to boast of, and I suspect that deep down they'd know it.

Beauty is all very well, but if the best thing you can say about yourself is that you have a pleasing arrangement of features, that's a sorry state of affairs."

"You have a pleasing arrangement of features," Hart observed.

"I do, yes, which is how I know exactly what that's worth. You, on the other hand, have strength, and loyalty, and a heart that cares for people and looks after them and—" *Christ, Robin, stop.* He wanted Hart to believe him; he really didn't need to blurt out his own painful longings. "*And* beautiful eyes and utterly magnificent thighs, may I add, although I've just been arguing those don't matter, but I feel I should point them out anyway. So I don't want to hear any more nonsense from you, because you really are a very desirable man, and I'm sorry for the fool who couldn't see it. His loss."

There was a long silence, long enough to make Robin start to feel rather stupid, before Hart broke it. "Thank you for saying that, Robin. It—it means a great deal."

"I hope you believe me. Well, you have to, because as a professional fortune hunter and amateur courtesan, or possibly the other way around now, I am an expert on masculine attractions."

That got a chuckle, which felt like a victory in the circumstances. "I bow to your experience."

They lay together in silence a while longer. Robin wasn't quite sure what to say now. Everything felt a little raw, or perhaps just naked, feelings stripped bare when it was more comfortable to have them safely clothed. Still, Hart seemed to be comfortable with the silence, or possibly to be thinking, so he let the silence run until Hart broke it.

"Robin? May I ask you something?"

"Go on."

"When we argued, earlier, you said you weren't brought up a gentleman. How is that, when you sound and look and sometimes behave like one? How is it you are obliged to be a fortune hunter at all? Who are you, really?"

Robin had not expected that, or anything like. He stared at the ceiling. Hart pushed himself off and up on an elbow, into a position where they could see one another's faces. "I dare say that is a great deal more than I am entitled to ask, and of course you aren't obliged to tell me, not at all. It was merely that I might understand you better if you did. I don't understand you, that much has become clear to me, and I would like to. I want to know you better."

Robin grimaced. "Maybe you would know me too well."

Hart didn't say anything more, and after a moment, Robin sighed. "I need this to be in absolute confidence. Not for me, but for Marianne."

"You have my word already that I will not stand in her way."

"Absolute confidence, Hart?"

"My word of honour on it."

That was a puff of air, an insubstantial thing to hang Marianne's ambitions on. Robin well knew that gentlemen lied, that the honour on which they prided themselves was porcelain-fragile, and as easily disposed of when broken.

Not everyone betrays, he told himself, needing it to be true.

He took a deep breath. "You remember I told you a ruined not-actually-earl taught me to play cards?"

"Yes."

"Well, that's how. We called him Lordship. He taught the three of us—me, Marianne, and Toby, his son—how to speak and how to behave. How to hold ourselves, how to pass for gentry. Drills. Accent. Vocabulary. We learned to mimic him. If he wasn't an earl, he certainly knew how to ape one."

"What was your relation to this man?"

Robin shrugged. "He was Marianne's father. My stepfather, I suppose, at least in common law. He took up with our mother when I was very young, after Toby's mother had died."

"And he was a gentleman?"

"I think he must have been. He got an allowance from somewhere because we had money four times a year, after quarter day."

"Who was your father?"

"No idea. My mother sometimes said he was the squire's son, but that was to make me feel better, with the other two being Lordship's children. She may not have known."

"And this man, Lordship, he wasn't married to your mother?"

"Certainly not. He was far too far above her in birth, as he pointed out frequently. Above all of us except Toby. Toby was his lawful son, born in wedlock, and should be a real gentleman." He made a face. "That didn't happen."

"And was that his aim in teaching you all to speak well? To achieve a better station in life?"

"Hardly." Robin exhaled. "Lordship never did a day's work in his life, you will be amazed to learn. Our mother earned the money, and then us, when we were old enough." They'd begged, picked pockets, cozened, disguised by borrowed speech and stolen clothes. "He taught us to play at Quality because, as I'm sure you've noticed, rich people are generous to other rich people and miserly to the poor. Well-spoken children are terribly persuasive, especially pretty ones. He taught us to make money one way or another, and to be fair, he taught us well. We had a good living for a while, before it fell apart."

"That sounds…"

"Sordid? It was."

"You spoke yesterday of letting people down." Hart said that tentatively, not quite making it a question. "Of betrayal."

There was a cobweb in the corner of the room, covering

the plaster cornice. Robin glared at it and listened to the clock tick, Hart breathe, his life dwindle away second by second. "Toby left us. Up and vanished one day. He was our big brother, our best friend, the one who stood in front of us when Lordship was free with his fists, but he didn't even say goodbye, and we have never heard from him again. He'd fought with Lordship every day of the five years before that, you'd have thought they hated each other, but Lordship was never the same once he'd gone. Well, he was worse, and by then our mother was drinking too. They slid steadily downwards, and he wanted us to slide with them. Marianne and I had become an affront to Lordship, you see, because he'd lost Toby, and because he'd brought us up to be better than our birth, when he was so much worse than his. He resented that; he wanted us to share in his degradation. That—well, it came to a head eventually, and we left."

The last sentence covered a multitude of sins, all of them better left unspoken. Perhaps Hart guessed as much, because he paused a moment, then asked only, "Have you heard from them since?"

"Both dead. Things ended poorly."

"I am extremely sorry to hear it." Hart touched his hand gingerly. "I truly am, Robin. It is a disgrace that children should brought up like that in a Christian country."

"It could have been a great deal worse. We had our lessons, and we have each other. We are doing very well."

"You certainly will be if your sister marries a marquess. That would be a vindication for your teacher."

Robin sat up at that. "Tachbrook wants her for her beauty, which is real. He knows she has no birth or wealth worth boasting of. Does it matter that the truth is a bit worse than he thinks? Is she less a rose because she grew out of shit?"

Hart started to say something, stopped himself, and spoke carefully. "She has far more beauty and charm than Tachbrook deserves, and he has enough birth and wealth for two. One might say, if he's fool enough to marry an unknown, he deserves what he gets."

"But you wouldn't want her to marry into your family."

Hart hesitated on that, which was answer enough. Robin waved a hand. "Never mind."

It wasn't unreasonable on Hart's part. Of course Marianne wasn't good enough for his family; Robin wasn't even good enough for his bedroom. Hart had still wanted kisses and sought to understand him more, so it wasn't as though he were being brutally spurned. It was just...

"Robin?" Hart said softly. "If I have been clumsy, I'm sorry."

"Not at all."

He evidently didn't make that sincere enough, because Hart searched his face with troubled eyes. "I swear I won't repeat your confidence. I truly don't give a damn for Tachbrook."

"But if you did, you would feel differently? You know, given the choice I'd have preferred not to be the fatherless son of a woman of the town," Robin said. "I'd very much have liked to have a comfortable childhood with a real family, and get my education in a more formal manner than a tutor who was resentful when sober and raging when drunk, and who brought me up for fifteen years then wanted to put us up for sale. I didn't have the choice. I'm not a gentleman; I can only play at one. And if that bothers you, there's very little I can do about it. Except crawl back to my gutter, I suppose, but I'm not going to do that."

"I disagree. Your character and conduct are nothing to do with your birth, and you can control those."

"Conduct depends on your options. Yes, you can be poor but honest, except I don't want to be poor. I've tried it and I didn't like it. And if I had the best character in the world, I still wouldn't be a gentleman."

"I dispute that," Hart said, to his surprise. "My mentor emerged from a situation of greater degradation than yours. He is unquestionably a gentleman, and I am proud to call him a friend."

Robin blinked. "Really? Who is he?"

"His name is James Alphonso, and he was born a slave on a plantation. He was purchased by a wealthy family and well treated, but until his twenty-fifth year, he was a possession, a chattel. He was fatherless and motherless from the moment he was sold away. And you can hide your origins, but he wears his on his skin. So—"

"I should probably stop feeling sorry for myself," Robin said, grateful for the chance to move the conversation on. "How is he your mentor?"

"His master, a Midlands brewer, relied on him as his right-hand man, and left him a generous legacy along with his freedom in his will. James used it to set up his own brewing company, which soon rivalled his former master's, then set out to take its business until it was struggling to survive. The family was forced to sell to him, and now the business is in his ownership and his name."

"Oh, now, that is brilliant. Vengeful *and* profitable."

"He is a remarkable man. I came to know him when Edwina was left the brewery. She was devastated by Fenwick's unexpected death and needed help, but I was only twenty-one and had no idea how to oversee its running or what to do. We had been through so much, and this was a devil of a blow. I was in despair when James visited to offer his condolences. He spoke very kindly to Edwina, and then took me for a walk and asked if I was all right, and I broke down."

"Really?" Robin found that hard to imagine.

Hart looked a bit self-conscious. "I was young, and had

been under a great deal of strain, and he is a very easy man to talk to. I told him everything in the end. Poured my heart out and asked him what I should do—he, a business rival of Fenwick's. He could have taken full advantage of my inexperience, but instead he took me under his wing. He taught me everything I know about brewing and the business, and helped me unstintingly, and we have been friends ever since. He even turns to me for assistance now and again these days, and we are to embark on a joint venture soon, if the details can be agreed. Don't mention that to anyone please."

Robin mimed that his lips were sealed, as if he knew anyone who would care about breweries. "He sounds a good man."

"A good man, a gentleman, and a friend. So I hope you believe that I would not deny you my friendship either."

"Friendship?"

Hart gave him a slightly wary smile. "I hope we are friends? It was not the best of beginnings, granted, but I am enjoying this. Not just the, uh, arrangement, but your company. I only realised how much yesterday, when you left me."

Robin's lips parted involuntarily. Hart stroked the lower one with a finger. "You look startled. I dare say that is my fault. In truth I didn't expect to like you as much as I do." He winced. "I don't mean to offend you by that. You did present yourself as a rather ghastly individual."

"You cut me to the quick," Robin said. *He likes me. He wanted to kiss me because he likes me.* "I like you too, Hart. I would be very glad to think you saw me as a friend. And a devastatingly attractive lover, of course."

"Very much that," Hart said, and leaned in to kiss him again.

CHAPTER 16

Hart had been looking forward to his meeting with James Alphonso, which took place in the third week of the arrangement. It was always a pleasure to see James; they had important business to conduct; and mostly, Hart was in urgent need of a reminder that his life encompassed a great deal more than Robin Loxleigh, even if it didn't currently feel like that. Robin was always on his mind, not to mention his skin: he carried the other's scent with him like a perfume. Or perhaps that was his imagination, which had turned out to be a lot more vivid than he'd ever realised. Maybe he hadn't used it before.

They fucked, a lot. They laughed more than Hart could remember doing, because Robin was amusing and absurd and unsquashable. They ate together when they could, always at Hart's rooms. That was doubtless sensible, even if it felt a little peculiar to know nothing more of Robin's home than his direction: the arrangement entitled him to Robin's body, not his personal life. Hart wasn't sure if Marianne knew of her brother's proclivities. He could not possibly have told Edwina his, but she was a respectable woman.

He was having a lot of thoughts like that these days. About

when and how he could see Robin, and what they could do, and how their lives intersected. He tried not to think about the fact that they intersected because of the arrangement, and in a diminishing number of days that would no longer be the case.

He had booked a private room in his club for lunch with James. It was a courtesy he always offered his friend, since in a public place one never knew when some numbskull might try his patience with an offensive comment.

James was waiting when he arrived. He was still hale and hearty in his late sixties, with white hair in striking contrast to his dark skin.

"John, my boy!"

"James. Good to see you." They embraced, rather than shaking hands. Hart had never known precisely what generous impulse had caused the ruthlessly practical James to offer assistance in his moment of despair; his respect and gratitude for his rescuer had only grown over time. He'd attempted to repay the debt a little with assistance and support of James's various concerns once he was in a position to do so, and over the years a warm affection had developed between them, along with a very satisfactory working relationship.

"Let's get business out of the way first," James suggested as Hart poured wine. "Now, what about the Tring site?"

Hart had long held ambitions to start his own brewery, at a sufficient distance from Fenwick's Aylesbury site to avoid direct competition with his sister. That required a substantial outlay, and James had proposed to put in part of the money. They thrashed out terms and ideas over two courses, and reached a very satisfactory conclusion.

James sat back with a sigh once they were done, and topped up both glasses. "Very well. I look forward to working with you, John."

"I too. I have a great deal still to learn from you. How is Theodora?"

James always smiled at the mention of his wife. Hart wondered if he even knew he did it. "A touch of rheumatism, but still pretty as a picture. And Edwina?"

"Well enough." Hart updated his friend on the goings-on in the family, drawing his rich laugh.

"Alice is a wonder. Send her my love."

"I will."

James raised a brow. "And who are you sending your love to?"

"What do you mean?"

"I still have the use of my eyes, boy, and you have a spring in your step. It's rare enough that I see you with a smile. Of course I want to know who you have found to smile about."

Oh Christ. Hart felt a pulse of panic, and hard on its heels, one of choking resentment. "There's nobody." The words came out harshly.

James looked puzzled, as well he might. "Really?"

"Nobody," Hart said again, getting a grip on himself. It wasn't James's fault that he couldn't answer a perfectly normal question. "I, uh—"

"Don't want to tell me," James finished for him. "You need not. I beg your pardon for prying."

He sounded a touch offended and Hart couldn't blame him. "You did nothing of the sort. I'm sorry. It's just—"

He didn't want to talk about Robin to James, except that he did. He wanted to talk about his intimate affairs, perhaps not as freely as others talked about theirs because that was not his way, but at least with the man who'd been father, partner, and friend to him. He resented the world that denied him that, suddenly and savagely.

"It's a little complicated," he said, feeling himself flush. "I have—well, yes, there is a young person—"

"That much is obvious. Does she return your sentiments?"

Oh God. "I don't know what my sentiments are. And if I did, there is no way I could pursue the matter, so—"

"An offer of marriage is traditional," James pointed out.

"That's not possible."

The humour vanished from James' eyes, replaced by concern. "What? Why not?"

"It is a difficult situation. Marriage isn't on the cards, now or ever."

James frowned. "That doesn't sound good, John. Not good or right."

"It's not my fault!" The words came out rather more loudly than Hart intended. "It's not a matter of fault on anyone's side. It's circumstances."

"Is she married?"

"No. It's— Don't ask me, James. It's a great tangle and I don't want to discuss it."

"Well, I'm sorry to hear this. It doesn't sound like an association that will bring you joy."

"It does," Hart said, because to deny that would be to deny everything. "It brings me great joy, more than I have known in my life, and does no harm to anyone. Nobody is betrayed, nobody suffers—"

James was looking sardonic. "The woman usually does, in the end. Especially if Nature takes its course."

"That's not—" Hart bit that off, reminding himself that he and James were having two slightly different conversations, which was not his mentor's fault. "The situation won't arise."

James snorted. "No? What if she loses her name at your hands? Can you protect her then?"

"The situation isn't of my choosing, curse it! And I'm not a damned rake. I don't abandon people I care for."

"No," James said more gently. "You don't, do you?"

"If I had a choice, if I could conduct things otherwise, I

would. But I don't. So I will grasp the happiness I can have, and do the best I can within that because it's all I *can* do!" The words rang off the walls.

James regarded him for a few seconds. "I will take your word for it. But I must say, you don't sound like a man who doesn't know what his sentiments are."

That left Hart lost for words. James sighed. "Well, you are a grown man, and I dare say you have considered your position. I am sure you will do your best by her in whatever way you can. But I'm sorry."

So was Hart. He was sorry he'd mentioned it at all; he was sorry he couldn't tell James the truth; he was sorry he couldn't have done that *anyway* because to admit that Robin was tupping him in lieu of a debt and that Hart had given his situation damn-all consideration would be to lose James's respect for good, and deservedly so.

He put his face in his hands. James slapped him lightly on the arm. "Ah, don't despair. After all, if people make vows and keep faith and conduct themselves as they should, does it truly make a difference if a parson didn't pocket his fee?" He was a Nonconformist, with strong views on Church rates. "I dare say the Lord will understand what's in your heart, even if men don't. Just be careful of your lady, John. You have responsibility there, and I am sure you know it."

"I will. Thank you, James." Hart felt the tension in his shoulders slacken a little. "Thank you for listening to me."

"For what good it does."

"It does," Hart assured him. "I have needed a dose of good sense from someone. Actually, can I ask you something else? In confidence?"

"Of course."

"This isn't my situation, though it is related. Suppose you knew of a woman who was not what she pretended to be. Who came from unfortunate beginnings and had a dishonourable past. And suppose she was masquerading as a woman of birth and might soon marry a very wealthy and well-born man who would turn from her in horror if he knew the truth. Would you feel you had an obligation to warn him?"

James frowned. "Is she an honest woman now?"

Hart considered Marianne Loxleigh. "I don't know about her chastity, and she is certainly deceiving him. She has many excellent qualities, I am told."

"And does she love this man or is she marrying him for his money?"

"The latter, unquestionably."

"Can you be sure she hasn't told him the truth?"

"Quite sure. He does not have the character to prize anyone's virtues over their origins. He is a damned fool, in truth, and I dislike him intensely, which has no doubt affected my judgement. I am watching a wrong being done, and I wish I did not know of it so matters could go ahead without my complicity. But since I do know, have I a moral obligation to speak?"

"Eh. If this man is the fool you say, he will make any wife unhappy, and if she is offering a Smithfield bargain, she will make any husband unhappy. Why not let them make each other unhappy and save two less deserving people from that fate?"

Hart had to laugh. "That was roughly the conclusion I had reached, but I have other reasons not to speak out and I was concerned I had let that sway me from what was right." James raised a brow. Hart shrugged awkwardly. "The lady in question is very close to, er, my cher ami." Blessed French, with its indistinguishable genders saving him from a lie.

"Then keep your mouth shut like glue," James said firmly. "Believe me, John, and I have been married thirty years: any woman worth a man's having will fight him to the death over her friends. Theodora might forgive me if I struck her, but if I informed against her cronies?" He sucked air through his teeth to indicate the scale of the potential disaster. "Is your lady the same? Of unfortunate background?"

"I— Yes."

"If that's all that stands between you, then wed her, you trifling idiot. Is that it? Preserving the Hartlebury lineage? Because let me tell you, after a few years in the grave, the baronet and the pauper look very much the same. What a damn fool way to go on."

"That isn't it at all," Hart protested. "My situation is different. But if I were to marry, I hope I should put character before any other consideration, including birth. My sister's example alone should teach me that."

James acknowledged that sorry truth with a nod. "I'd stay well out of this business, John. It sounds like you have trouble enough of your own."

"By God I do. More than I had realised." He made a face. "I said I would look after my, uh, cher ami, and I will, but how one ought to go about proposing that—"

"There, my friend, you are on your own. I've never kept a mistress. You can tell because Theodora has left my manhood intact."

Mrs. Alphonso was a redoubtable lady, and not to be crossed. "No, I wouldn't dare in your shoes," Hart agreed. "I suppose one just offers?"

James shrugged. "With the right sort of woman, I suppose one does."

◈

The luncheon left Hart with a great deal to think about, much of it unflattering to himself. He felt raw all over, from revealing—well, hardly anything, but still more than he ever had of his love life. And from James's scorn, too. That was foolish, since he'd been working off the misleading information Hart had given him, but it still hurt from a man Hart loved and respected.

And it contained enough accuracy to sting. Hart could not be blamed for the hidden, trammelled, precarious way he was forced to conduct his affaire, but that didn't absolve him from seeing and shouldering his responsibilities. He wouldn't have taken a mistress without considering her means of support. Robin's life was chaotic and insecure, frighteningly so. It was only right Hart should help, and if that meant he could extend the arrangement, put them on a firmer footing, a longer term...

Robin would want that. Surely he would. He liked Hart, he'd said so, and he needed help, and Hart could give it. The conclusion was obvious.

He was all but pacing the floor when nine o'clock finally arrived, and brought Robin with it.

"Good evening. How was your day?"

Robin smiled brilliantly. "Tolerable. Did you have a good meeting with your friend?"

"I did, thank you. We are agreed we will set up a joint venture together, a new brewery. I shall have a great deal of work to do." Before Robin, he would have been thoroughly satisfied with his new prospect and nothing but excited at the work. Now he couldn't help a tiny sense of a task that would need to be fitted into his life. "And you? Has Tachbrook declared himself yet?"

"Not so far. His mother has graciously indicated her conditional approval, so now it is a matter of him making a decision."

"But you feel confident?"

Robin gave him a quizzical look. "I didn't realise you were so interested in Marianne's machinations."

"I wish her all success in her ambitions," Hart said with entire truth. "Here is to the future Lady Tachbrook." He handed Robin a glass of wine.

"To her happiness." Robin tapped the glass to his. "Are you all right? You look preoccupied."

"I have had a great deal to think about. And there is something I should like to talk about, but perhaps later."

Robin looked up through his lashes. "Later than what?"

"Than this, for a start."

Hart extended an arm. Robin came willingly, curving his body to Hart's, kissing him with a waft of wine on his breath, the two of them perching against the desk. They kissed, tongues tangling, and Hart got rid of his glass and stroked Robin's back and the curve of his arse until his lover was breathing fast and magnificently pliant.

"I have a demand," Hart said in his ear.

"At your disposal."

"I want to make you spend. Just that, several times. I want you naked in my bed, lying back while I take charge of you."

Robin's eyes widened and his perfect lips curved. "Well, now. If you insist."

"I do." Hart took his free hand. "The bedroom is this way." He wasn't in any way as certain as his performance suggested, but he felt a need to prove something, to Robin or himself. He didn't need his hand holding any longer. He could take control.

Robin was soon sprawled naked across his bed, looking like some Greek deity in a painting lacking only cherubs, fruit, and a tactfully placed urn. Hart knelt over him, caressing his member to full strength, then he crouched down, and took it in his mouth.

"Oh," Robin said. "*Well.*"

Hart had not yet done this, though he'd wanted to for some time. He indulged himself now, caressed Robin's cods, let his hands roam freely over his firm thighs, took his time experimenting with teeth and tongue. It helped that he'd handled Robin enough to know his rhythms and sounds, so he could feel confident in his work. He stroked him and sucked him, and felt a ludicrous sense of achievement when Robin cried out and spent in his mouth.

"Hart," he said hoarsely. "Oh Christ, that was good. God."

Hart sat back, and took a hasty gulp of wine to wash the taste down. Robin was watching him with something in his eyes that gave him a stab of sudden, inexplicable pain. "That was a pleasure. Thank you. May I reciprocate?" He nodded at Hart's own very solid stand.

"You may not. I told you what was going to happen. What did I say?"

Robin lowered his eyes mock-submissively. "That you will take charge of me."

"Then you will lie there and be fucked."

Robin stretched luxuriously. "Yes, Sir John."

Hart felt he had something to live up to now. He used a well-oiled finger to probe Robin's arse for the sweet spot, and tormented him while they kissed, until Robin was hard again and whimpering for release, and Hart's own arousal was near-intolerable. Out of both malice aforethought and also necessity, he stopped and withdrew his hand. Robin gave a strangled moan.

"Quiet," Hart said, kneeling over him and moving his hand to his own prick. "And stay there. Don't touch yourself. Learn some self-control." It was more than he could do; he was painfully desperate. He worked himself as Robin watched, eyes bright, lips wet and parted, and brought himself off in a few frantic jerks, spending in ropes over Robin's chest.

He shut his eyes, gripping his prick as the tide subsided and, as ever, climax was followed by a sudden doubt as to whether proceedings had been a good idea, or ridiculous and undignified.

A hand touched his thigh, a sliding caress. "That was the most arousing thing I have ever seen," Robin said softly. "If your aim is to torture me, be assured I will tell you anything."

He was smiling into Hart's eyes, a reassurance without words, and Hart felt his chest contract. He wanted to blurt out incautious things, to hold Robin and weep for the glory of being known and understood.

He didn't. He resettled himself so they could kiss, and went back to work, more comfortable now he could take his time. He did so, using only his fingers inside Robin until his lover was thrashing wildly and all but speaking in tongues, and it took no more than two strokes to bring him off. And he didn't stop there, despite the now-late hour, but set about business again, telling Robin to beg for a fucking now because of how much that aroused them both, and took him splayed across the bed, slow and steady, holding back until he could wring a third climax out of him. His fantasy lover, his incubus, his Robin.

They fell asleep together, entangled in sheets and sweat and spunk, and one another.

CHAPTER 17

Hart woke first. Robin was still there, warm and golden in bed. In *his* bed.

He hadn't really intended that. He'd just wanted to do things in the way he might if Robin was truly his lover, and if he wasn't afraid.

"Morning," Robin murmured. "Do you want me to go?"

"No."

"Ought I go anyway?"

"No." Creeping out early would look more suspicious. "Say you drank too much and slept on the settle." He would throw a blanket on it, perhaps empty a second bottle of wine. He wondered about the state of his sheets.

Robin nodded, shifted on his side, and flung an arm over Hart's chest. "Mph."

"You're still half asleep." His hair was dark gold in the shafts of light through the shutters, his eyes shadowed. Hart wanted to kiss his eyelashes, his nose.

"You wore me out."

"Sorry."

"Not at all." He shifted forward so he was lying closer against Hart. It was possible the word was 'snuggled'. Robin, snuggled against him. Hart put his own arm over the warm shoulders and tried to ignore the feeling that gave him.

"Hart?"

"Mmm?"

"Thank you."

"For what?"

"Last night. Sleeping with me. That thing with your finger, that was marvellous."

"My pleasure."

"Really mine."

"Both," Hart said. He'd felt a joyous power working Robin's body, making him respond, thinking *I brought you to this.* "I liked it when you told me how much you needed my prick."

"I tell you that a lot."

"You do. Is it good? Being buggered, I mean?"

"Well, I enjoy it," Robin said. "Each to his own. Ever tried?"

"No."

"Would you like to?"

Hart gazed up at the ceiling. "Yes."

"That sounded heartfelt." Robin gave the words a touch of a question.

"I am a big, intimidating man with a scowl. Nobody has ever suggested—and I have never known how to ask for it, still less how to do it."

"And you didn't feel you could ask a paid boy to deflower your virgin arse?"

"Good heavens, you have a turn of phrase."

"It's a gift. I will fuck you all you please, my Hart. I suppose now would be indiscreet."

It was the morning. People were about in the house. "Probably."

"Then next time, or whenever you care to. And I can't

promise you'll like it, but if you don't, it won't be for lack of trying."

"You make it so easy," Hart whispered, because his throat was closing. "How is all this so easy for you?"

"I think I have a different idea of what makes life hard."

Hart couldn't find a response to that. After a moment Robin said, "Sorry. That didn't come out quite as I intended."

"Happens to me all the time."

"But it was stupid. Something difficult for you isn't less difficult because other people have different problems."

"More serious ones."

"It's your life. You decide what constitutes a problem in it."

"And you don't feel I have any, because I am a baronet and a wealthy man."

Robin gave a small shrug. "I don't know what your problems are. Money and birth would have solved most of mine, but for all I know I'd have a different set to worry about in their place."

"Well, that is probably true. For example—" He stopped.

"What?"

"Nothing. It doesn't matter."

"This isn't a contest," Robin said gently. "If it hurts, it hurts."

"For example," Hart said again. "I think I told you my father died when I was a boy?"

"Yes."

"And you had no father at all, which is surely worse."

"It doubtless depends on the father."

"Mine was decent enough," Hart said. "He always seemed busy. He married my mother when she was seventeen. She was twenty-five when I was born, thirty-six when Father died and she decided that she was free from his penny-pinching ways."

"Was he miserly?"

"Perhaps. I don't remember it. It's possible he was merely

doing his best to restrain her. Because when he died, she spent everything. She had the house refurbished with satins and silks. She bought clothes by the trunkful. Vases, trinkets, pictures, perfumes. My trustee was her brother and he did nothing at all to stop her draining the lands and amassing debts. Edwina tried, but she had never liked Edwina. She never liked either of us. We were such Hartleburys, such repulsive things with our great ugly features, and she couldn't bear it."

Robin sat up. "Wait. Your *mother* said that? I thought—"

"She was a very beautiful woman," Hart said, voice sounding remote even to himself. "I was brought home from school because she couldn't, or didn't, pay the fees. She sold land that had been in the family since the fourteenth century. When the bailiffs came, I went to a solicitor, and hired him with a five-pound note I had found in her bureau. I was only fifteen, but I had heard they were men who did things for one, so I walked into his office and asked him to act for me, and he didn't laugh and send me home. Good God, I have been fortunate in my friends. With his help I told my uncle I would sue him for failure to do his duty as trustee, and my mother that I would repudiate her bills."

"That cannot have been pleasant."

"No. She called me a variety of names. Told me what a disappointment Edwina and I were to her, that she was simply trying to have *some* beauty in her life."

"Jesus, Hart."

"The solicitor was a tower of strength. I still use his firm, though he's retired from practice. I slowly got control of the finances, wrested back the management of the land, and learned what to do, but God, it was hard. Humiliating. I had to take out advertisements, first telling local traders not to give her credit, and then in the London papers to stop her sending orders. Every day she was in the house it felt like disaster waiting to strike. She wouldn't stop, and I couldn't let it go on." He sounded in his own ears as though he was pleading for understanding. "That was why Edwina accepted Fenwick: her portion was not protected and it had all been spent. Of course the marriage was for the best, very much, but at the time it didn't seem so. Our mother said she was debasing herself, as if she had left Edwina any choice. That was when Tachbrook stuck his nose in."

"Tachbrook? What did he have to do with it?"

"My mother is his cousin. There was naturally a scandal about the advertisements I placed, and then a fuss about Edwina's marriage, and he came to see us while on a visit to Lord Aylesbury. He told me I was shaming his family and disgracing mine, that I was disrespectful to my mother and uncle, and a great deal more. He spoke as if the money were trivial, called me a young muckworm—he was perhaps thirty then and spoke to me as though I were a child—and complained that Edwina's marriage stained his family. But I was no child any more. I was sixteen, and I had had quite enough, and I lost my temper as badly as I ever have in my life. It almost came to blows, but he would not lower himself so far, or possibly didn't dare. He left in high dudgeon, and cuts me to this day."

"That would be why you are not concerned for his family line?"

"I hope Marianne spends every penny he has."

"She will," Robin said confidently. "So what happened to your mother?"

"She married again, thank God. Another baronet, Sir Roger Asperton, a very wealthy man from up Birmingham way. Or he was. Perhaps she has spent all his money by now."

"Do you see her often?"

"I have not seen or heard from her since she left the house to marry him. We were not invited to attend the wedding."

"Oof," Robin said. "She just forgot about you?"

"I wish she had forgotten. She complained bitterly about my unfilial cruelty, and took her grievance all over London while Tachbrook called me a violent savage. I came to London when I was eighteen or so—of course I could not attend university—to discover that I already had a reputation as a misanthropic, miserly, mannerless brute. I had not the grace or wit to win people to my side, and in any case, she was, is, my mother and to tell everyone what she had done to us—no. It was miserable. I was an awkward youth anyway, but the whispers and humiliation, the stares... I couldn't abide it. People talking about us, looking at me and laughing or sneering—I don't know how you are so unsquashable by insult. It broke me."

"It did not. You are not broken."

"I am a damned awkward clumsy man because I never learned to fit as a boy. I dare say I would have been unsociable anyway, but it didn't help to be mocked and ostracised." He hadn't quite meant to say all this. It had come spilling out, the pain and fear and crushing responsibility, and the deep scar carved by repeated rejection. He let out a long breath. "But I was fortunate, too. My solicitor was a hero. The Verneys didn't turn their backs on us. Edwina had Fenwick, and when he died James Alphonso saw I was desperate for help, and extended his hand, for which I will be forever grateful. I made friends among Cits who had either never heard of my mother or had strong views on people living above their means. I righted the ship and restored the finances. It took years, but we, Edwina and Alice and I, were on an even keel once more." He stared at the ceiling. "And then Edwina married Blaine, her second husband, and it all started again."

"What did?"

"I suppose he'd picked Edwina as an easy target—a wealthy widow, not used to flattery. He was charming until they married and then it fast became apparent he was another spendthrift. A selfish greedy swine with no thought of anything but his own fleeting satisfaction, running up endless bills. This time he was draining the lifeblood of Edwina's business rather than my lands, but it was still my family, my sister helplessly watching as her future was destroyed. It felt like being trapped in a nightmare. I couldn't stop him spending her income; I had a great deal to do to prevent him ruining the brewery with his endless demands for funds. He seemed to believe it was his right to bankrupt them all. He even tried to make Edwina send Alice away, a slip of a girl who barely ate, because he said she was a drain on the household while he ordered the best wines and new coats. I could have killed him. I could have throttled Edwina for bringing that on us. We had got back on our feet, and she opened the door and let him in."

"Is that entirely fair?" Robin asked carefully.

"Of course not, but it's how I felt. It seemed I would be working all my life to pay for other people's self-indulgence."

"Was it your responsibility? In law, I mean."

"Oh, I had no rights at all except that she had given me a minority holding in the brewery."

"You could have retreated to your estate, and left your sister to deal with her own mistake. But naturally you could not. How did you make him listen to you?"

"I shouted," Hart said, with something of a snap. "He could rule a wife, or bully a child; he didn't dare bully me. But when it came down to brass tacks, I could not stop him spending, because he had the right. It still makes me feel sick. Edwina was frantic. The desperation of being tied to someone who doesn't care if they ruin you—"

"Yes." It was all Robin said, but the single word brought Hart up short.

"Of course. You know."

"Lordship positively wanted us ruined by the end. He hated us because we were young, and not rotting away from pox, and not Toby. He wanted to put us on the town as a pair. We'd sell better that way. Brother and sister, pretty as a picture. That's what he said."

"Dear God."

"It was only talk. He was a gin-soaked husk, nothing but fumes, but to hear him make those plans was the outside of enough. Anyway, you hadn't finished. What happened to Blaine? He's dead, yes?"

"He bought himself a very expensive and nervy colt, which promptly threw him. He broke his hip, and died of it. The marriage only lasted two years, thank God."

"Good." Robin's shoulders heaved with a deep breath. "And then I came along to batten on Alice and her money, and you must have thought it was all starting again."

"You see why I wasn't welcoming."

"I really wouldn't have ruined her, I swear. I only ever wanted to be secure. I'm so sorry, Hart."

"I know you wouldn't have." Hart spoke with certainty. "You have a heart. Not to insult your capacity for wiles, but I really don't think you're in the right line of work."

Robin's fingers groped for his, gripped them. Hart squeezed back. They lay in silence for a few minutes.

"Thank you for telling me that," Robin said eventually. "It sounds appalling."

"Maybe someone else could have handled it better. I have sometimes wondered, if I had been less hostile, more understanding, if I had had my mother's affection—"

"If you had been more lovable."

The words were stark and painful. "Well," Hart said. "Yes."

"If you were more lovable, she would not have treated you so. If you were charming and graceful and handsome, other people would have been kinder to you. The former maybe, the latter undeniably, but do you know what, Hart? *I* am charming and graceful and handsome, and there is only one of us in this room who is worth a damn."

"That is not true."

"Yes, it is. And if people care for nothing but a pretty face, they deserve what they get when the charming, graceful, handsome one empties their pockets."

"Blaine was handsome," Hart said. "Charming too, at least until they were married. Edwina didn't deserve that."

"All right, no, but I maintain the principle. If you can only treat a pretty child well, you have no business with children. And any charlatan can learn social graces. I learned them at a drunkard's knee, and have used them to cozen, cheat, and fortune-hunt, while you have worked damned hard at the expense of your own comfort and social standing to help your family. I don't know about lovable, but I bloody know who deserves to be loved."

He sounded ferocious. Hart looked at him, startled, to see that Robin looked somewhat shocked himself.

"Thank you," he said inadequately. "I, uh, appreciate that."

Robin squeezed his hand. "Well, someone had to tell you."

Hart wanted to hug the words to him, to start a diary just in order to write them down. He took a steadying breath instead. If this wasn't the perfect opportunity to raise the subject that had been consuming him, he didn't know what was. "Speaking of fortune-hunting, Robin. What will you do at the end of the month?"

"In what sense?"

"Financial. The Season is well underway. Do you plan to pursue another..." Not *victim*, for heaven's sake. He went with "Lady?"

Robin made a face. "I have to agree with you: I don't think I'm cut out for this line of work. I don't know what I'll do. It will probably depend on what Marianne, or rather

Tachbrook, does. I can't make a decision until I know about that."

"Could I offer a suggestion?"

"What's that?"

"A proposition for you. I like you very much, and our arrangement has been extraordinary. You said you wanted to be my fantasy, and you have fulfilled that beyond imagining. I have never had anything like this—like you—in my life."

"I like you too," Robin said softly.

"And I listened to what you told me about your situation. Of course you want security. That is quite reasonable."

"It stays with you, doesn't it?"

"But I don't want you to be forced to, uh, drastic action to find that security. So I wondered if we might put the arrangement on another footing."

Robin looked a little wary. "You want to change the terms?"

"Our agreement isn't fair to you. It never was."

"Of course it is. We agreed a month where we could fuck without any other considerations, and that is what we have."

"That wasn't what we agreed."

"It was really," Robin said. "I wanted you, and you wanted me, and the arrangement let us have that. Me paying off a debt and you getting your money's worth was a, a framework. We both knew where we stood when we started. Or I did anyway, and you grasped it in due course."

"Perhaps. All right, yes. But we aren't where we started, are we?"

"No, we aren't, but we still know where we stand. We both have the right to walk away at the end if we want, either of us. Nobody is *obliged*."

"But I don't want to walk away," Hart said. "Do you?"

"We have ten days still. I don't want to think about it yet."

"Yes, but you don't think ahead. I do, and ten days isn't

much. It isn't enough for you to make plans for your future and it isn't enough for me at all, and— Robin, I could look after you. I have the funds—"

"No," Robin said. "No, no, no. Stop. Please."

"Why?"

"Because I don't want to think about it! We have our arrangement, the rules are simple and clearly laid out, and we don't have to worry about anything more. Can we not leave it there?"

"You haven't heard me out."

"You are proposing to offer me carte blanche or some such, yes? That's all I need to hear. You must not. It's absurd."

That was stark. "Absurd, why? I want to give you choices, Robin. Pursuing wealthy women or cheating at cards isn't a choice. Or if it is, it's the choice between a louse and a flea."

"Being a kept man is better?"

"You were looking for a rich wife. Is a protector so different?"

Robin's lips moved slightly, as though he was trying out an argument. Finally, and in a steady tone, he said, "It is a kindly meant offer. But I would be a knave to take it, both for your sake and for mine."

"Why?"

"For your sake, *because* you have never had anything like this. For God's sake, you have only just learned what it is to kiss a man. Perhaps you should try some others before you decide where to spend your money. For mine—" Robin looked up at him, his eyes entirely without light or humour. "Because you have just told me what you think of parasites, and I saw your face as you spoke. I don't want you to look at me like that."

"What? That is an entirely different—"

"It isn't," Robin said. "Please stop. I don't want to talk about it any more."

Hart felt his chest tighten with alarm. "I had no intention of offending you."

"I know that, and I'm not offended. It was a generous thought, but it isn't necessary." Robin smiled, his unusually grim expression relaxing. He always smiled, always made the difficult moment easy. "We have a very satisfactory arrangement for now. Let's stick to it."

CHAPTER 18

Hart was still fretting about that conversation a couple of days later. It didn't help that he'd had very little time to reflect. He'd been busy with a lawyer drafting terms for his agreement with James, which had required another meeting with his mentor; he'd had a great deal of correspondence accumulate over the last weeks, since it seemed he had inexplicably failed to give work his full attention; he'd spent hours in Bill Richmond's boxing saloon, pouring his confusion and frustration into punishing exercise. And then there was Edwina and Alice.

Edwina had capitulated to Alice's scheme, but was clinging to her new position, which was that Alice must travel with a companion—a competent woman, not merely a maid—and a responsible British connexion must be found in Heidelberg so that she had assistance at hand.

"It's not unreasonable," Hart said, seeing Alice's mulish expression. "For your well-being."

"It is perfectly reasonable as a condition but how will we do it?" Alice demanded. "How long will it take to find these people?"

"We'll ask Trelawney's help, and I'll talk to Giles Verney. Foreign Office, remember? He will know someone."

"That is an excellent idea, Uncle Hart," Alice said, beaming. Edwina agreed, less enthusiastically.

"And we will advertise for a companion. There is bound to be someone who wants a passage. I'll have that done at once. Don't worry, Alice. We'll find your way."

Edwina gave him a rather jaundiced look once Alice had left them to go out with her friends. Hart said, "What now?"

"Anyone would think you are keen to be rid of her."

"Nonsense. She wants to do this, and it is not fair to drag our feet."

"I am not dragging my feet, I am insisting on reasonable precautions. Going overseas, fending for herself—"

"So we will find a capable companion."

Edwina sagged. "I don't want her to go. I don't understand why she wants to."

"But you understand *that* she wants to. Your choice is to thwart her efforts and earn her resentment, or to help her do it as well and safely as possible."

"Those are extremely trying choices," Edwina said crossly. "Suppose she dislikes it after all? What if it goes badly and she is thousands of miles away and I can't help her?"

"Then she will have failed. But if she doesn't try, she will have failed too. You cannot protect her from failure, so you might as well give her the best chance to succeed. Edwina, you have done all the protecting and teaching you can, and have brought up a remarkable young woman. Trust her and yourself."

Edwina glared. "Don't you dare be wise at me John Hartlebury. It is intolerable from one's little brother."

"I could pull your hair if you prefer."

She leaned back and rubbed her face. "I absolutely insist on a responsible and respectable companion and I shall not budge on that."

"Duly noted. I'll put it in motion."

"Thank you, Hart. I am grateful, really." She took a deep breath and sat up. "I feel I have not seen you in an age. Have you been busy?"

"Somewhat. I have been working on my plans with James Alphonso."

"Not every evening, surely." She gave him a shrewd look. "I will not interfere, but if it is That Woman again, I trust that you will keep your affairs to yourself this time."

"Eh?"

"Lady Wintour. We had quite enough of that."

"I have not been involved with Evangeline Wintour in years," Hart protested. "She is a friend only."

Edwina sniffed. "Then who is it?"

"Who is what?"

She sighed heavily. "I do know what it means when a gentleman is privately engaged all the time. Sara Verney says that Thomas Verney told her that Giles Verney thinks you are in love."

Hart was resigned to this sort of thing in a general way. The extensive Verney family came from Drayton Beauchamp, the next village, and had been on good terms with the Hartleburys for generations, and hostile ones with the Tachbrook marquessate for decades, thanks to an endless dispute over a five-acre strip of land. That had doubtless underlaid Tachbrook's interference in his affairs. Interference was a tradition as old as family itself, and one taken up enthusiastically by the Verney clan.

"Giles, Thomas, and Sara should all mind their own business," he said. "I shall tell you at such time as I have anything to tell you, which I currently do not."

"I'm sure you will," Edwina said. "As long as I am not quite the last to know."

"The way they gossip, I imagine *I* shall be the last to know."

He mused on that as he strode home. He had no fear of Edwina prying—she took no great interest in his personal life as long as he didn't embarrass her—but he was unnerved to hear that Giles was speculating. He'd had a drink with his friend the other night, but they'd only talked about prizefighting and politics. Christ, was his affaire written on his face?

Perhaps it was. James had been able to tell the state of his mind at a glance, after all. Hart was not used to having his expressions read, since most people only ever saw the scowl, and he wondered what those who knew him well saw when he thought of Robin. Was it something like the light in James's eyes when he mentioned Theodora? He should take care.

And he should consider. Consider what his sentiments might be, since his best friends clearly had ideas on the subject, and consider what he was going to do about it. Robin had refused his offer, but that was because Hart had gone about it badly. He had not meant the offer as a payment for services to be rendered, or to imply that he might regard Robin's affections as purely financially motivated, but clearly that was what Robin had understood it to mean, and that was Hart's fault.

He could, and should, do better, to make Robin understand. Maybe he should ask him to come over now, rather than waiting till night once more. If they spoke outside the bedchamber, he might be able to explain himself properly.

He arrived home, and was greeted by Mrs. Spenlow telling him, "A gentleman is waiting in your sitting-room, Sir John."

Hart's pulse jumped. Could it be?

Robin was a mind-reader at times. "Thank you," he said, and hurried up, absurdly pleased. To come home and find him there felt like a gift.

He threw open the sitting room door. "Are you here? I was just— Oh. Giles?"

"Hello, Hart." Giles looked startled. "Were you expecting someone else?"

"No. Yes, I was, but on a matter of business. I must have misunderstood Mrs. Spenlow." He pulled himself together. "I'm glad to see you. Did I know you were coming?"

"I knocked in the hope you'd be in and Mrs. Spenlow suggested I wait. Hart, I need to talk to you." Giles sounded urgent, even desperate.

"Of course. What is it?"

"I don't know what to do. I just don't know. I dare say there is nothing at all but I cannot bear to think that and—" He put his face in his hands. "It's Marianne."

"Miss Loxleigh?" Hart said, with a sense of impending doom. "What's wrong?"

"*Wrong?* Have you ever been in love?"

"I don't know."

Giles looked up, jolted out of his misery. "How can you not know?"

"I don't know what 'in love' is supposed to convey. I have never found it hard to distinguish my beloved from the moon and stars, no matter what poets say."

"Of course you haven't. Love is—I don't know. That one thinks of her all the time in her absence—what she might say were she here, what she must be doing elsewhere—and there is very little that can distract one for long. That one's pulse quickens at the sound of her voice and one's heart heaves in her presence. That to be without her for an hour is an irritation, and to be without her for the rest of your life would render it a desert. It is a constant pain and a constant pleasure, and you would give anything to have her place her hand in yours and say she chooses you above all else."

"You would call that love? Not, uh, fondness, or

infatuation, or the sort of thing one might feel during a mere affaire?"

Giles gave him a look. "If you feel that way, it is not a mere affaire."

Hart sat down. "I see."

"I have never felt like this before," Giles said. "I will never feel like this again. She is everything I have ever dreamed. And she is going to marry Tachbrook."

"He's offered?"

"Not yet, but he will."

"Have you spoken to her?"

"She knows my feelings."

"Does she return them?"

"She asked me not to declare myself." Giles's face was twisted. "She said, *Don't make me refuse.* And how can I persist? What have I to offer her except my love, compared to him?"

"Yourself. God's sake, man! What has *he* to offer her except wealth and a title?"

"Oh, yes, trivial. You are asking her to turn down the position of a marchioness!"

"No, you are," Hart said. "And if she loved you, wouldn't she do it? Granted, Tachbrook could elevate her to the first rank, and make her wealthy beyond counting. She would never have to worry about material things again, or about the opinions of others. He could give her a place. Security."

He stopped there. Giles waited a moment. "Is there a 'but'?"

"I thought there was." Hart grimaced. "Maybe not."

"Thank you so much."

"No, there is a 'but': he won't make her happy. I'm sure of that."

"Do you imagine that's a consolation? Dear God, if I

thought he would I'd wish her well if it broke my heart to say it. I'm not entirely selfish."

"I didn't mean it as consolation. She is a clever woman. She must know what Tachbrook is, and she is choosing the path of wealth and ambition. Does that not tell you something of her character?"

Giles sat up, eyes angry. "I cannot think that. I *don't* think it. I know her better."

"Can't we be judged on the choices we make?"

"What sort of choice do I offer? A younger son with no fortune but what I earn, against a marquess?"

Hart's mind was full of Robin's face, lit with anger as he spoke of being left without choice and desperate situations, and how desperate Marianne's situation had once been, and if it might become so again. "An impossible one, maybe. And perhaps she doesn't truly believe happiness is in her grasp either way, in which case she is making the only sensible decision. Perhaps the world has taught her that she is a commodity to be traded, so she should hold out for the best price."

"I beg your pardon?"

"It is called the Marriage Mart, isn't it?" He'd very nearly slipped there, and knew he had to be careful, but the thoughts were pressing as he teased out the Loxleighs' situation. "It is a frightening thing for anyone to trust a will o'the wisp of feelings that come without guarantees. And if you are seeking security, if you *need* it, would you trust a declaration of love over a solid income? I drove my own mother away because I had a choice between her and security."

"You did nothing of the kind," Giles said heatedly. "Her behaviour was disgraceful and you were right to act as you did."

"She was still my mother, Giles. I stopped loving her because I had to, and if she ever loved me, she does not now.

Love is not guaranteed to last. And if you picked it over a lifetime of certainty and then it died and you had nothing left —that is a great leap of faith to ask of anyone."

Giles was staring at him, open-mouthed. Hart shrugged, suddenly self-conscious. "Or so I suppose. I can't pretend to know what Miss Loxleigh thinks."

"No, you are right. I'm sure you're right. I cannot believe she is selling herself for a coronet merely out of cold ambition. That is not her nature. I need to make her understand that she can believe in me. That I have something to offer far above a coronet, that she can trust me to be faithful unto death. I will swear it is what she truly wants. Thank you, Hart, you're a genius. I honestly didn't expect you to be helpful." Giles jumped to his feet.

Hart had a distinct sinking feeling, in large part because he was sure Miss Loxleigh was extremely keen to sell her person for a coronet. He'd tried to work up a sympathy he didn't truly feel, for Robin's sake and in order not to insult Giles's sentiments, and now look what he'd done. "Wait. What are you going to do?"

"Plead my case, and do it properly. I have to go to her. Tachbrook is expected to declare himself at any time."

"But—"

He'd promised Robin not to impede Marianne in any way. It would be a gross breach of his word if he told Giles his secret. But for Hart to let him pursue a woman from whom he would recoil if he knew the truth—and suppose his friend prevailed? Suppose Miss Loxleigh did abandon her ambitions and Giles married her in ignorance of her character? The Verneys were not the most notable of families, but their name was old and respected and had never been tainted by scandal. He couldn't imagine the devastation if Giles invited such a cuckoo as Miss Loxleigh into the nest.

He'd told Edwina so smugly that she needed to let Alice make her own mistakes. What a fool to think that was easy.

Marianne would say no, he told himself. Of course she would say no, because she was an ambitious schemer marrying for money. She had to say no, and then she would have her riches, Giles would forget his sentiments, and Hart would not have broken his promise to Robin.

"Good luck," he said weakly, and hoped that his words would have no effect.

CHAPTER 19

Two days later, Robin was waiting at home for Marianne. She had been invited to luncheon at Tachbrook's mansion once more. This was, surely, it. Tachbrook had paid such marked attentions that he'd be vilified if he didn't propose, and it was three o'clock now: she'd been there for hours. When she came back, she'd be all but a marchioness.

Robin wished he were happier about it.

Marianne had been...wrong, these last days. She was as lively and charming as ever in society, but silent and bleak-faced when she was not observed by anyone but Robin, who didn't count. He'd tried to discover what was wrong, and been roundly told to mind his own business.

He'd have *liked* to mind his own business. He'd have liked to do nothing but enjoy every remaining moment he had of the dwindling month with Hart, without care for anything else. He didn't even want to come back to his own bare rooms, still less to worry about why Marianne looked like she'd lost everything when she was about to win it all, and he very much didn't want to think about what he'd do when the month was over.

He'd need to live off something and he wasn't convinced it

would be Tachbrook's money. Marianne would find it easier to act the marchioness if she wasn't saddled with a parasite brother reminding her of her old life. No, he would not hang off her sleeve. Which meant he'd need to do something else.

He could keep gaming but he didn't know many rich old gamesters. You could do well for a time, but time always ran out. So did youth. Robin's face might not be the fortune Marianne's was, but he could still trade on it for now. That wouldn't last forever.

A small, frightened part of him wished he'd asked for terms rather than flatly declining Hart's offer. There could be nothing better for him than to be kept by a kind, wealthy, generous man who was a good fuck and a good friend and a joy to please, and with whom he'd been reasonably honest, for once. He'd been prepared to marry for money: this was infinitely better. It was so obviously the perfect answer that he hadn't dared tell Marianne he'd had the offer and declined, in case she threw things at him.

He simply couldn't do it. His chest had constricted as Hart spoke; he'd had to restrain himself from putting his hands over his ears. An absurd overreaction to a perfectly reasonable suggestion. Hart had money, he didn't, and a carte blanche was hardly an insult under the circumstances. The offer had been thoughtful, kind, and considerate, and Robin hated everything about it.

Why? he imagined Marianne demanding. *It's perfect! You like him, he likes you, what's wrong with it?*

Because he likes me. Because I like him. Because I want something else, something that I already know I can't have, but if I take his money I will make it certain.

It was about money from the start, the imaginary Marianne reminded him.

Robin didn't have a glib answer to that. *Everything's about money. I want one thing in my life that's better.*

Do you deserve something better? Marianne asked in his head, except Marianne would never say that. She'd tell him he deserved Hart to lavish him with riches and treat him like a prince, and she would refuse to listen to him argue otherwise.

Robin wished he could make himself agree. Hart was going to return to the subject, he was sure. The question was whether it would be an offer to keep him so that Robin wouldn't pursue wealthy women or cheat at cards, or if he would simply suggest they continue their relations while ignoring how Robin lived off other people. They could see how long *that* lasted.

It was, he now realised, a bloody awful idea to pose as someone's fantasy lover when you were quite so unsatisfactory in reality. Hart didn't believe Robin was a worthless parasite. Hart looked at him with wonder and happiness. Hart was hopelessly cockstruck and bedazzled by Robin's performance, living in a dream, and one day he'd wake up and realise he could find a respectable gentleman to shag instead, one who wasn't a sham from the gutter. Robin didn't want to be there when he woke up. He didn't want to see Hart's face then, because he knew how the waking felt.

Robin had lived in his own dream once, he and Marianne together. They'd both thought they'd found care and affection, and they'd been wrong. Marianne had vowed she would not be fooled again, and set out, a virgin reborn, bent on taking some gentleman fool for everything he had. Robin, lacking both her drive and her ever-smouldering rage, would have preferred to forget about the whole sorry business. But he couldn't, because he kept remembering that plunging, sick, *stupid* feeling as he realised that he'd been held in contempt all along, and imagining Hart feeling that same baffled hurt towards him.

He didn't want that to happen, but it would. Hart was fooling himself, and when he stopped, he'd believe that Robin had fooled him and either blame him for it or, even worse, blame himself for being fooled. Neither would be fair to a man who had tried so hard to do right by him, and who didn't deserve another leech in his life, and Robin was not going to take advantage of him just because he'd never had a solid tupping before. Which was inconceivable, by the way, and made Robin quite angry. Could not a single backdoor gentleman in the whole city tell a good thing when they saw one? Was he truly the only man who noticed Hart's kindness, and passion, and thighs? The vast majority of Society's shallow, self-centred fools deserved whatever came their way and Robin would happily have taken any of them for all he could get, but instead he'd found himself with the one man who didn't deserve it. Typical.

Robin wished he were more like Marianne. Marianne thought about things in advance, and made clear-sighted decisions. She was going to make a bargain with Tachbrook, who had all the choices he could possibly want in life and had used exactly none of them to make anyone happier. She would take the money and the title and wear them like a cold queen, as a damn-your-eyes to the aristocratic world that had used and rejected them, and Robin wished quite desperately that she wouldn't.

He was relieved when he finally heard her feet on the stairs. He was no sort of company for himself today.

She came in, walking steadily, her face unreadable, closed the door behind her, stood. Robin jumped to his feet. "Well?"

"I said yes. He told me he would marry me, and I said yes."

Robin had imagined this moment many times. A month ago she would have shrieked it, and he would bound over and lift her off the floor and swing her around in their triumph. They ought to be celebrating, but instead they stood together, caught in stillness.

"His exact words were that he would stoop to elevate me,"

she added after a moment. "That he proposed to overlook the manifold ways in which I do not meet his station. And the Dowager Marchioness told me I must always be sensible of my husband's great condescension. Did I say she was in the room for the proposal? Not that it was a proposal, as such, because that implies asking, and he did not ask."

"Marnie—"

"Marianne."

"*Marnie*," Robin said. "Is this worth it?"

"It's what we wanted. It's what we did everything for. It's the *point*."

"You're going to be as miserable as sin."

"I'm not going to be happy anyway." Her stormy eyes met his. "Giles Verney asked me to marry him. Two days ago. He told me—he said— He doesn't know me!"

Robin put a careful arm around her. She was as stiff as a lamp-post. "He said he loved me. That he could not offer me anything except love, but he would never falter in that, and try every day to make me happy. And it was a lie, Rob. Such a lie."

"How do you know?"

She made an impatient movement. "He loves the woman he thinks I am. Not me, because he doesn't know me, so he is lying to me. And if I married him without revealing the truth, I would be lying to him. Suppose I told him, my mother was a doxy, my father a drunken wreck, my education all in the service of shamming and stealing. Do you think he'd propose to me then, Rob?"

"I don't know. If he loves you—"

"Men have died, and worms have eaten them, but not for love."

She quoted that line a lot. Robin sighed. "And you couldn't just not tell him? Would he ever find out?"

Her face hardened. "If I must lie to my husband every day, I will make sure he deserves it."

"Then tell him. There's nothing to lose, is there? See what he says."

"There is everything to lose. I don't want to see him turn from me in disgust or anger, still less for him to tell Tachbrook what he is marrying. Give him the truth and be left with nothing? No, thank you."

"Do you think Verney would do that?"

"He'd want to revenge himself for the mistake I didn't let him make, because he'd feel a fool for wanting to make it. There is very little cruelty a man won't stoop to if you dent his self-esteem. You should have learned that by now."

"*I* don't, and people dent my self-esteem all the time," Robin pointed out. "It's a wonder it still works so well."

Marianne's arms came round him then. He hugged her properly, and she put her head on his shoulder and held on to him, and after a moment, she started to cry.

Tears provided a temporary relief, but not a solution.

"We wait until he gives you the ring, I clean out the tables at the Laodicean, and then we run away," Robin said as they sat on the settle together, supplied with gin and cake. The situation definitely called for cake. Marianne was on her third slice.

"No."

"You marry him, get a settlement, and run away with Verney."

"Don't be stupid."

"I borrow a dress and a wig and go through the ceremony in your place?"

"Shut up."

"You never listen to me," Robin complained, and saw the reluctant twitch of her lips.

"You're too optimistic," she said. "It's unbearable. And what about Hartlebury?"

"What about him?"

"Other than that you are heels over head for him—"

"Am not."

"Yes, you are. Whenever you see him, or are going to see him, you look like a dog that expects to be taken for a walk. All bright eyes and frantic wagging tail."

"I do *not*."

"Of course you do. I don't know why you can't have a tragic love affair and stare into the abyss of your hopes like everyone else."

"I'm being well tupped. It helps."

"I find that astoundingly hard to believe. The man's a gargoyle."

"He is not," Robin said, with a startling wave of anger. "What rubbish. He's got the most magnificent legs, and beautiful eyes, and I *adore* his nose, and actually he's had plenty to scowl about but if you ever looked at him properly, you'd see—"

Marianne was giving him an exceedingly smug smile. Robin thought back. "Cow."

"Heels over head. And if you were a marquess's brother-in-law—"

"No."

"Listen. You'd be respectable, you'd have status. You'd be safer. You could go and stay with your friend the baronet at his country house and nobody would think twice."

"That would be very nice. If you were happy marrying Tachbrook, I'd be delighted about it."

"I'm marrying Tachbrook, happy or not, so we might as well get the benefits. I'd be happy if you were secure, Rob. That would make it worth while to me."

"Indulge me a moment," Robin said. "Suppose you believed Verney."

"Rob…"

"Suppose he didn't care about where you came from, only who you are, and he still wanted to marry you, and you did. What would that look like?"

She knocked back most of her glass. "Tachbrook angry and humiliated at being jilted for a penniless younger son, perhaps bringing suit for alienation of affections. A notorious wife for Giles to support. The scandal doing him out of his position."

"Would that happen?"

"I don't know. Probably. Ruined prospects and disillusionment, and scrutinising his children for signs of bad blood—"

"All right, all right. But maybe it wouldn't look that way to him. Maybe he sees what I see," Robin said. "Someone clever and wonderful and loyal unto death who is worth defying the world for."

"Maybe he saw a nice pair of tits and got overexcited."

Robin sighed heavily. "If you didn't think you'd hurt him, would you marry him?"

"But I would hurt him, so it doesn't arise."

Robin slid onto the floor so he could wrap his arms round his knees. "You're determined not to be positive about this, aren't you?"

"When I marry, that is the end of my choices unless my husband dies. I will not throw my one chance away for sentiment."

Robin sighed. "Marry Tachbrook and be Verney's mistress, then."

"He'd be shocked at the very idea. Why did I have to meet a virtuous man, Rob? Couldn't he have been a wealthy rake who wouldn't care?"

"I still think you should tell him. If he's worth it, if he's the man you think, he'll forgive you."

"I'm not going to beg forgiveness for what I can't help," Marianne said harshly. "He doesn't know me, and he fell in love with a liar, or with a lie. More fool him. I am going to be rich, titled, and safe, and stop trying to argue me out of it."

"Have you a date for the wedding?"

"September will be convenient, I am informed. An announcement is being sent to the newspapers. We are to attend the Aylesburys' ball as an engaged couple—the ring will be ready then, it is a family heirloom, but the Dowager has fingers like twigs and it must be resized. You will have to meet Tachbrook."

"Oh God."

"Be charming. Don't get caught at anything."

"I won't."

"And I will marry him and we will be secure and in a year's time, I will be a fashionable, beautiful, adored marchioness, and all will be well and we'll wonder why we made such a fuss," Marianne said. "So you needn't look at me like that. What are you doing tonight? I'm going to the masquerade in Vauxhall."

"Marnie—"

"I'll be back late, I expect. If it's very late I may stay with Florence. Don't wait for me. And don't look at me like that. I will do very well and I don't want to hear any more."

CHAPTER 20

Robin had no particular plans for the evening. He went along to his club, where he played a few desultory rounds of hazard because he didn't have the energy for cards.

"Something wrong, Loxleigh?" Mowbray asked. "You look worried."

"Do I? I'm just a little worn down. Burning the candle at both ends, I suppose."

"Go on a repairing lease," Tallant advised. "Best thing for it. Bit of country air."

"He lives in the country, you fool," Mowbray said. "*This* is his repairing lease."

"That's right," Robin said. "I just don't have the stamina of you town-bred men."

"Always suspected it. I say, you will mention it if I can help, though? If you're short of the readies or what-not? Happy to do you a service if I can."

"That's…very kind of you. Thanks." Robin searched his mind to discover what Mowbray might be after and came up with nothing. He was after nothing. He wasn't clever, or scheming. He was just expressing concern for a man he thought was his friend.

"Thanks," Robin said again. "Very much. I have to go."

He left the club quickly, almost running. He wasn't even sure what he was running from, only that he couldn't stand still while his and Marianne's decisions caught up with them. He wasn't supposed to go to Hart's until later, but he couldn't wait. He wanted, painfully, to talk to him. Or even not talk, just to be together and pretend that none of it was happening.

Robin was Hart's fantasy, a likeable, enthusiastic, accommodating fuck who didn't offer complications or difficulties or the word 'no'. He wasn't meant to bring troubles to his door. That was what you did with a real lover. He had a terrible feeling Hart would react as a real lover might, that he would be kind and caring and supportive, and that would put paid to one more line of defence between Robin and a broken heart. But he kept walking anyway because he needed Hart and he had nowhere else to go.

He duly knocked at the door, and Spenlow answered.

"Good evening. I don't suppose Sir John is in, is he? I was passing by—"

"He is engaged, sir. I will see if he is available."

"Oh, there's no need at all. If he's busy I'll call another time. It isn't important."

Spenlow ignored him. "Kindly wait one moment, Mr. Loxleigh." He disappeared up the stairs. Robin cursed himself but waited, since it would look odder to leave.

There was quite a long pause before Spenlow returned, inviting him to go up. Robin went, adjusting his bearing to 'distant acquaintance,' knocked politely, and went in.

Hart was in his sitting room, his habitual scowl looking like he meant it this time, and so was Giles Verney.

He looked shocking, as if he hadn't slept, eyes hollow, face grey. He clutched a glass of brandy, and he looked up at Robin with a dull horror of recognition which was entirely mutual.

"I'm obviously intruding," Robin said, desperately trying

to think of a good reason he might have called on Hart, since Verney surely knew they had been at odds. "I beg your pardon. I'll go."

"No, don't," Verney said. "Tell me, has she accepted him?"

Hart grimaced. "Giles…"

"I just want to know. Will she be his marchioness? Is that what she wants?"

"My sister has accepted Lord Tachbrook's proposal, yes."

Verney shut his eyes. "I hope she'll be happy. I hope she will be very, very happy. She deserves to be a marchioness. I wish he were a better man for her sake, and I hope he becomes one."

At least he seemed too consumed by his sentiments to ask awkward questions. Hart sent Robin a somewhat wild-eyed look over Verney's head; Robin returned an equally panicked one. He had no idea what to do now. He'd have liked Verney to come up with a wealthy great-uncle on his deathbed and sweep Marianne away, but he clearly didn't have one, and anyway Marianne was not easily swept.

"I'm sorry," he said inadequately.

"So am I. I'll go, I think. Sorry to pile my troubles on you, Hart."

"Don't be a fool. No, Giles, stay."

"I'd rather be alone. She's made her choice and there is no more to say. I'll see myself out."

They stood in silence for a moment after he had gone. "He's left his hat," Hart said at last. "And a glove. Look at it, lemon-coloured. Fop." He sounded like he was hurting.

"I could run after him? It's cold."

"I doubt he cares. My God. I haven't seen a man so hollowed out before. My poor Giles."

Robin walked up to him and buried his face in Hart's shoulder, needing the comfort. "I'm so sorry. You should see Marianne."

"Are you serious?"

Robin pulled away, startled by his harsh tone. "Of course I am. She's devastated."

"Why? She has exactly what she wants."

"And you think she's happy about it?"

"Satisfied, at least. She has made her choice, and she must be aware that money doesn't buy happiness."

"She also knows that happiness doesn't buy food."

"Giles has a good position. She had the chance to be the wife of an excellent man who would love her, and she preferred to sell herself for a coronet. It is a glittering match in the world's eyes: it merits no sympathy from me."

Robin took a deep breath, feeling the anger rise and for once not pushing it down with a smile. "She did *not* have the chance to be Verney's wife because she believes that if he knew the truth about our past, he would spurn her. Is she wrong about that?"

"I don't know what he would do. I do know that her birth may be repellent but I find her behaviour worse."

"No, you do not," Robin said. "If she was a lady born you'd be shocked if she threw her cap over the windmill and married for love. You're condemning her ambitions because you don't think she deserves to have them."

"I have never objected to her marrying Tachbrook."

"Yes, as punishment for him!" The flush on Hart's cheek proved the truth of that. "You don't *want* her to marry Verney, you're just angry because she presumed to reject him. You don't think she is good enough for him."

"You are putting words in my mouth."

"Am I wrong?"

Hart glowered. "If she truly cared for him, she would have told him the truth already, before things reached this point."

"Balls," Robin said explosively. "It is not her responsibility to coddle the men who fall in love with her.

Should she tell them all how unworthy she is? When, exactly, should she reveal she's a whore's bastard to prevent them forming attachments? How could she trust him not to ruin her?"

"He loves her! She could trust that!"

"So he says, and she should just take his word for it, should she? Believe he will never regret his passions? Why do his feelings matter more than her future?"

"Evidently they don't. And if she doesn't care for his feelings, then it is undoubtedly for the best that she doesn't marry him."

"She does care. She cares a great deal too much. She won't be his ruin, and she has denied him for his sake and cried her eyes out over it, and you *dare* to condemn her because she doesn't also destroy herself in the process? What, if she can't marry Verney, she should marry nobody? Does she have to become a nun to satisfy you?"

They glared at each other for a moment, then Hart put a hand over his face. "I see. I do see. Damnation."

"She's breaking her heart," Robin said, voice lower. "I can't bear it."

Hart pulled him into his arms again. Robin resisted for a second, then let himself collapse. "I'm sorry. Giles is in so much pain and I thought— I didn't realise she felt for him too. I thought she didn't care. Oh Christ, what a tangle."

"It's not fair," Robin said, muffled. "This ought to have been a triumph. A *marquess*. I wish she'd never bloody met your bloody friend."

"So do we all. Giles is not prone to falling in love. He's devastated."

"I suppose she couldn't tell him the truth, could she?" Robin suggested. "He would feel as revolted and deceived as she fears?"

"I don't know, and—I don't wish to offend you, but if he

did accept her past, would she really accept his proposal? He is only a younger son, with no prospects but what he can earn."

"If she refused, it wouldn't be about the money. I assure you that. If Marianne marries Tachbrook, he can't hurt her, you see."

"I think probably he can," Hart said carefully.

"Yes, of course, but I meant—Ugh. It happened before, is the thing. A gentleman who loved her but not her birth, and it hurt. She'd rather not be loved at all than have that hurt again."

Hart was frowning. "I don't quite follow."

Robin sighed. "It was after we left Lordship and our mother. She acquired a protector in Manchester. A gentleman, rich and well-born. He promised he would marry her, and she believed him. She was very young then, and very much in love. And I had *also* found a lover, a man for whom I cared and who was very generous to me in return, although I didn't realise it was in return at the time. My mistake. We were happy, Marnie and I. We thought it was perfect. And then I overheard my lover talking with friends, and one of them was offering to pass his mistress around to the rest of them. He had a fair bit to say about her. I recognised his voice."

"Oh Christ."

"Yes. And as if that wasn't bad enough, my lover capped that with a few remarks of his own. He said I was 'reasonably priced'. That's what stuck in my craw the most—on my account, I mean. I don't know whether I'd have preferred expensive, or even cheap, but 'reasonably priced', like a roll of cloth—he might as well have said I wore well, or didn't show the dirt. It was rather lowering."

That was an understatement. He and Marianne had wept, then raged, then pulled themselves together, and left Manchester six days later with quite a lot of money and jewellery that was not, technically, theirs. That had paid for their travel to Salisbury, a new wardrobe, another start. There they had stayed two steps ahead all the way, and when they'd fled again, this time for London, it had been with full pockets and a burgeoning confidence in their powers that now felt wildly misplaced.

Hart was looking quite sick enough without Robin telling him all that. "Oh, dear heaven. I'm sorry."

"That was the last time Marianne believed in men's promises. It's why she won't believe Verney, and even if she did, she has her pride. She doesn't want to be stooped to."

"Surely Tachbrook is stooping?"

"Yes, but she doesn't care what he thinks."

"Fair," Hart said. "Is she not afraid he will discover the truth?"

"If he does so after the marriage, it's his hard luck and he'll have to pay her off. If he finds out before—well, there's no reason he should. There's no reason Verney should either; that's not what she's worried about. Tachbrook is the sensible choice, and Marianne thinks sensibly about the future. My future, even. She thinks if she becomes rich and titled, if I can say *My brother-in-law the marquess*, I will be safer."

"Aristocratic connections won't save you from the law."

"You should try not having them," Robin said. "I told her not to consider me but she's done it all her life."

Hart took a breath so deep it lifted Robin as he leaned against his broad chest. "Would it help to take that off her shoulders?"

"How do you mean?"

"I realise this is far from an ideal time to raise the subject, but it sounds like it might be relevant. I want to talk about us. In a few days the month will be up and our agreement will end. I don't want it to. I offered you, or attempted to, a new arrangement before. I did it poorly, though in fairness you didn't let me speak. I didn't tell you that I care for you, Robin, very much. You occupy my thoughts to a remarkable degree and I want more of you. Granted, I lack experience, but I cannot imagine anyone suiting me better than you and I don't feel any need to test that. You truly are everything you promised." He ran a finger down Robin's neck, making him shudder. "My incubus. I know what it is to fear for the future, and I don't want you to feel that way. I don't have a great fortune, but my land and the brewery do well enough—"

"Don't offer me money," Robin said wretchedly. "Please."

"I'm offering security. It's what you need, and it would make me happy to give it to you. You often say you like to please me. Well, I would like to look after you."

"In return for me pleasing you?"

Hart flinched. "That is unfair. I am not trying to purchase you but to help you. What choices have you: card sharping? Hanging out for a rich wife? Hoping Tachbrook will be a generous brother-in-law?"

"I am well aware that's all very contemptible," Robin said, trying not to speak through his teeth. "So you want to be my protector?"

"I want to be with you, and the best way for that to happen is surely that I support you. Because you need it, and I can do it."

"And I can't." There was a painful knot in his throat. "After all, I have only two professional skills, and the other one is cheating at cards, so I dare say it's very reasonable to pay me to fuck instead—"

Hart let him go, recoiling as if struck. "Robin, that is not what I said! I'm not trying to insult you, for God's sake. I want to help. You have always said you want security, and I can do that for you, so why should I not? What's the alternative, that I demand your time for nothing?"

"That is what people do when they like one another, yes! Do you bill Verney for his visits, for Christ's sake?"

"Giles isn't in need of a protector, and it's not the same thing at all. I'm proposing a practical solution to a practical problem. I want you with me, and I don't live in London. You couldn't make a living in the hells of Aston Clinton because there aren't any. I don't know why we are arguing about this."

"We are arguing because—" Because Hart hadn't so much as mentioned wherever the hell Aston Clinton was, far less asked Robin to go there; because whatever Robin might want of him didn't include a bloody 'practical solution'; because he and Marianne had once more sought safety through rich lovers, this time achieved exactly what they'd wanted, and got it all horrifically wrong *again*.

He sagged. "I dare say this is my fault. I told you I'd be your fantasy lover, and I was, and I don't want to do it any more." The look on Hart's face hurt. He pressed on desperately. "I want to be real to you, and I'm not. This proves it. I'm simply not."

"Of course you are. How could you not be?"

"Because you don't want *me*. You want the obliging man who always smiles, and makes it a joke when you hurt him, and cares only to please. You can buy that man; you already have. You don't want the jumped-up fortune hunter who tried to run away with your niece, or the courtesan who might suck other men's pricks if you don't pay him to do yours, or the card cheat, or the man with the shameful sister."

"For Christ's sake, is not the point for you to escape all that?"

"But I can't escape it by doing the same damn thing! You want to rescue me, and I would...I would very much like to be rescued, actually, but that's the problem, isn't it?"

"I don't understand."

Robin rubbed his face. "It has always been about money because that is what I made it. I realise that. But there's another me who doesn't care for that, who cares far more for other things. For you. And I don't think you see him and—I don't think you ever will."

"What? Robin—"

"No. You might have if my past wasn't in the way, but it is, and you can't see beyond it, any more than you can see beyond Marianne's. She will never be good enough for Verney, which means that I am not good enough for you. You know I am not, because if you thought I was, you would never have offered this. And I realise that's mostly my fault, but it's yours too." He was, quite suddenly, exhausted: of himself, of the effort it took to wring the words out, of the look on Hart's face and the knowledge he'd put it there. "I think I understand why she would rather marry a man she despises than be despised by the man she loves. I should have listened to her. I'm going home."

"Wait. Robin, for Christ's sake! Will you please talk about this?"

"I've talked and talked." He picked up his hat and coat. "And you can't argue with me because I'm right. You want to buy me, however nicely you put it, because, in truth, you can't envisage us, you and me, as lovers on equal terms, choosing one another freely. You can't believe I'd want you just for yourself. Can you?"

Hart's stunned look said everything. Robin couldn't do this any more. He pulled open the door to walk away from everything he wanted and wasn't going to get, and saw, on the landing just outside, a single lemon-coloured kid glove. The twin of the one on Hart's table. Right by the door.

And, as he stared, the slam of the outer door, downstairs, as someone left the house.

"Oh, *fuck*," he said.

CHAPTER 21

"Breathe," Robin said. "Breathe."

He'd been saying it for some time, and Hart was trying, but his lungs didn't want to cooperate. Or perhaps the air no longer worked, because no matter how much he sucked in, it did no good.

Giles—his best, his oldest friend—had heard everything. He'd heard what Marianne was, and what Hart had known about her, and he'd heard that proposal to Robin and that meant he'd know Hart not only fucked men but, far worse, tried to buy them, and he'd think Robin was some creature to be bought. He could go to the magistrates, lodge a complaint, *talk*—

"Hart! *Breathe*. Do I have to slap you? I will slap you. Honestly, one might think you never had your life fall about your ears before. You baronets are soft as kittens."

Hart had to look up at that, although not far because Robin was squatting in front of him, holding his thighs for balance, or perhaps even comfort.

He was still here. He'd been in the middle of walking out, but he hadn't gone. Hart made a powerful effort to fill his lungs and steady himself.

"Better," Robin said. "I need you to stop panicking. I'm not saying panic isn't appropriate, but it won't help. We need to talk about what we're going to do."

"What is that?"

Robin moved so that his elbows were resting on Hart's thighs instead, which let him put his head in his hands. "I don't know, but not panic. For all we know he dropped his glove as he left and that was somebody else going out, or Spenlow at the door." He shrugged at Hart's look. "It could have been. We have to assume he listened to everything, of course, which means I need to warn Marianne, and when my body is fished out of the Thames tomorrow you'll know how *that* went. And you need to find out exactly what he heard."

"I can't."

"Of course you can. He's your friend."

"Was."

"Maybe. Maybe he'll surprise you. Maybe he's known for ever. Maybe he isn't on his way to let Tachbrook know he's engaged to a strumpet, sweet Jesus. Do you think he would do that, and if not, where do you think he might be?"

"I don't know. I should have gone after him." The shock and, yes, panic on top of his realisation that he'd got it so horribly wrong with Robin had hit him too hard. He hadn't been able to make his legs work.

"Can't be helped. First, we go to Marianne, all right? That's the most important thing. Then we will look for Verney."

We. Hart stared into Robin's face. "Why are you staying? Why haven't you gone?"

"That was an argument. This is a crisis. When we've dealt with the crisis, we'll go back to the argument." Hart felt fingers close on his. "Come on, up. I've had lots of unpleasant surprises, and the best way to feel better is to do something."

"This unpleasant?" Hart demanded, and could have kicked himself as Robin said, simply, "Yes."

"Sorry. That was stupid. I'm sorry."

"Don't be." Robin stood. "You know, it would help if you weren't ashamed of yourself. You've done nothing wrong. Illegal, perhaps, and we need to avoid the consequences of that, but not wrong."

"Yes, I have," Hart said harshly. "I kept the truth about your sister from Giles—"

"Because you kept your word to me."

"I doubt he'll see it that way, considering I've lied to him about so much else."

"You don't have to endanger yourself for his benefit any more than Marianne does. Why do you think he deserves that? Come to that, why can't you trust him, if he's such a good friend?"

Hart couldn't answer that easily. He'd grown up wanting to be like the Verneys, with their loving, stable family, their rectitude and respectability. Giles had never had an embarrassing affair, or had his name bruited around town, or been the object of anyone's scorn. Hart had always felt as though he had something to live up to, by comparison. Something to hide.

"I haven't done well by him," he repeated, because that at least was clear. "And I have not treated you well at all."

"Oh, you have," Robin said. "Perhaps not exactly as I'd have liked, but that's not the same, is it? And none of that is anyone's business but ours. Frankly, Verney's more in the wrong for eavesdropping. I thought gentlemen were above that sort of thing."

"You'd have listened in his position."

"I'm not a gentleman. Look, best case, he didn't hear anything at all. Worst case, he tells the magistrates and we deny everything. We can say he was drunk, he's malicious—"

"He's my best friend!"

"In that case he won't tell the magistrates, will he, so

problem solved. Look, Marianne is the one at immediate risk. I don't know if Verney has our direction, but I don't want him turning up there angry if she decided to stay at home. You don't have to come if you can't manage it, but I have to check."

Hart took a second to realise what he meant. The thought was grotesque, but he made himself stand anyway. "I'm coming, but I would swear on my life he wouldn't hurt her. He isn't that sort of man."

"I don't share your confidence in men, and there are many kinds of hurt." Robin's voice was flat, but then he glanced at Hart's face and produced his ready smile. "And to be honest, I wouldn't swear she won't hurt him. However, the *actual* person who is going to get murdered here is me. Got your coat? Let's go."

They looked for a hackney for some minutes, but there was a drizzle starting and the evening was closing in. Eventually they gave up and walked. It was better than doing nothing.

Hart wished they could have ridden in private so he could hold Robin's hand for strength or comfort. If he'd had to imagine a crisis where one of them collapsed and the other was a tower of strength, he wouldn't have pictured it this way round.

"Have you been exposed before?" he asked, low-voiced, as they walked. "Caught?"

"Never arrested," Robin said. "Shouted at a few times, got away by the skin of my teeth a couple more. And had plenty of people not care because it's none of their business. Not everyone is an arsehole."

"I hope that's true."

"So do I, and this might yet be bad. But it will be survivable."

"Unless Marianne kills you?" Hart suggested, trying for humour because Robin deserved the effort.

"Always a possibility."

They reached Robin's unfashionable street eventually, and walked up the stairs together. Robin let them in, calling, "Marianne? Marnie!"

No reply. He went into what seemed to be the only bedroom. Hart stayed in the small sitting-room, noting its bareness of pictures or furniture. There were blackbeetles on the wall—not many, just enough to suggest a slovenly housekeeper and a lack of servants. The Loxleighs spent everything they had on clothes, it seemed. They were nothing but appearances.

Robin emerged a moment later. "Well, it looks like she went out. I think I need to stay and wait for her. Unless I should go to Vauxhall in case Verney went after her there? No, that's stupid. Oh God."

Hart came up, slowly enough that Robin could back away. He didn't, so Hart wrapped him in his arms. Robin didn't resist, just leaned against him. "What a day, Hart. What a bloody day."

"I'm sorry for my part in it."

"So am I. Drink?"

Hart wasn't sure where to sit. The settle seemed rather presumptuous, as though he expected Robin to cuddle up to him. He took the sole armchair, which was not comfortable. Robin handed over a tumbler of oily, pungent gin, and perched on the settle.

"I want to apologise for earlier," Hart said after a while. "Not to return to the argument while we still have the crisis, but simply to say I'm sorry. I don't know how to do this, to conduct an affair, and I raised the subject at entirely the wrong moment anyway. I'm sorry that I offended you."

Robin sighed. "It isn't the easiest situation. I shouldn't have shouted."

"You should."

"No, I shouldn't, because if I hadn't, Verney wouldn't have heard me."

"Good point. You shouldn't have shouted. But you were entitled to, all the same."

He wanted to say *Please tell me what I did wrong*, but the fact was, he ought to know. He'd known Robin in the Biblical sense for a month, talked to him, listened to him. If he hadn't understood, that was due to his own ineptitude, which it was his responsibility to amend.

"Could we talk later?" he asked. "When I have thought a little harder. Only if you want to give me a hearing, of course."

Robin contemplated him. After a moment he stood, still holding his gin, walked over, sat down on the rug by Hart's feet, and leaned against his legs. Hart reached down, feeling his heart thump, and ran two fingers through his honey-brown hair. Robin made a mildly pleased noise and shifted a little closer. Hart stroked his hair, slipping into the absent rhythm he might with a cat, and they sat in silence together.

He'd had various ideas over the weeks on how he'd spend their remaining nights together—acts, games, gifts. At first he'd assumed he'd spend them wringing every ounce of pleasure he could from the affair. More recently he'd thought of giving pleasure instead, had even dreamed he could be Robin's fantasy in return, as if that might make him stay.

Four thousand two hundred and twenty pounds over thirty-one days was a hundred and thirty-six pounds a night. If the money mattered—if it had ever mattered—he was paying a hundred and thirty-six pounds for the privilege of sitting in an armchair that badly required reupholstering and stroking Robin's hair, and it was worth every penny because he was here when he was needed.

Except that he hadn't purchased the privilege of being Robin's comfort in trouble, still less that of Robin's instant, unquestioning support. Those things had grown out of knowing each other, and caring, and surely to God they showed that there was something between them that was real.

No: Robin's anger was what showed that. Robin had been angry because he had expected Hart to know better.

And he should have done. He hadn't *thought*. He'd had plenty of opinions on Marianne as a scheming fortune hunter and seductress, and it hadn't crossed his mind that she was Robin's little sister. She might be queenly, beautiful, poised enough for a marchioness, and seemingly older than her years, but she was his little sister and Robin had always, always spoken of 'us'. And he'd talked so casually, so rudely of her as a fortune hunter and offered Robin money to fuck almost in the same breath and…

You can't believe I'd want you just for yourself.

Robin had sounded so hurt then. And he was wrong. Hart knew Robin wanted him, he'd had proof, and been told, and he had come to believe it, incredible though it still seemed. Why would Robin doubt it? Hart had not accused him of wanting his money, or implied that would be his only reason to stay: he'd just tried to help. Was it really so wrong to offer help? He wanted to provide for Robin because that was a natural urge when one cared. He worked for Alice and Edwina because he loved them, not in order to buy their love, and they would never have thought otherwise.

But Robin thought otherwise. Because he didn't take love as his due, and he was used to having a price put on him, or putting one on himself.

He'd worked so hard to make Hart believe he was lovable. He'd said, *There is only one of us in this room who is worth a damn*, and *I bloody know who deserves to be loved.* And Hart had lapped it up, basking in the words, and hadn't even noticed that, when Robin praised him, it was at his own expense.

Robin didn't need another protector. He very specifically

needed *not* to have a price on his head, reasonable or otherwise. He wanted to be valued, but not like that.

And what had Hart offered him?

"Hell's teeth," he said aloud.

"Are you all right?"

"Just thinking."

He'd failed, catastrophically. That much was clear. But he had the tools to improve, if he picked them up and used them. What he needed now was time and peace to work out how, and he had those, sitting here stroking Robin's hair by the dying fire, both hurt, both afraid, still together.

He'd touched Robin in so many ways in the past month. He'd never felt as intimate as this.

"I suppose there's a reason you're in my chair."

Hart jerked into wakefulness. His neck hurt, he had the nauseated feeling of bad, broken sleep and he was trapped by some constricting—no, it was a blanket. He was sitting in a chair with a blanket over him.

He blinked, looking around the room, where the light suggested it was early morning. There was no sign of Robin. There was, however, Marianne Loxleigh, standing watching him.

"Good morning, Sir John," she added. "Where is Robin?"

Hart just blinked. Marianne swept past him into the bedroom, shutting the door behind her. Muffled voices rose.

He should probably make himself scarce. It seemed the most tactful thing, but he didn't want to look as though he was running away. He hovered awkwardly, folding the blanket for something to do, and was relieved when Robin at last stuck his head out of the door.

"She's back," he said unnecessarily. "Thank you for staying with me. Uh, would you mind—"

"I'll go."

"Probably best. There's quite a lot of shouting to be done."

Will you come around later? Hart didn't want to ask. And had no right to, because though the month of their agreement had a few days left to run, he knew it was over. They could no longer hide behind that paper wall; whatever was between them needed to be established anew, and properly, if it was to exist at all. Assuming that nobody needed to flee the country, of course.

"She's safe with you," he said. "Everything else can be dealt with. I'll go and see Giles now, and tell you what he says at once."

"Thank you," Robin said, and Hart took some pleasure from his smile.

He went home first, to wash and change because there was nothing like sleeping in an armchair to make a man feel filthy. He put on new clothes, shaved clean, adjusted his cravat with a care he never normally took, told the man in the looking-glass that he was a coward, and went to see Giles Verney in his rooms.

He was admitted by Giles's man, Stanford, and sat to wait in the drawing-room for an uncomfortably long time before Giles came in. He wore a banyan and looked as grey as Hart felt. It seemed nobody had had a good night's sleep.

"Good morning," Giles said. "Have you been offered coffee?"

"Stanford is bringing a pot, I think. I came to return your hat and gloves. You left them at my rooms."

"So I did. Thanks." Giles looked painfully awkward. He started to say something but at that point Stanford came in bearing a coffee-pot and the next moments were taken up with thanks and pouring. Hart had wanted to stay on his feet—to be ready to leave without ceremony, frankly—but he couldn't refuse the cup that was handed to him, in part because his head hurt from the lack of sleep, and he found himself sitting down to sip the dark, bitter brew.

"I need this," he muttered.

"Don't we all." Giles was staring into his own cup. "Look, Hart, I'm glad you came, or I should have sought you out. I wanted to say—"

"Yes?" He braced himself.

"Well, first, thank you for listening to me yesterday. I was rather distressed. I was desperately in need of a friend, and you were there, as you always are. I hope you know how much your friendship matters to me." His eyes met Hart's, though it seemed to require an effort. "We've been friends for a long time. I hope that won't change due to any act of mine."

Hart swallowed a hard lump in his throat. "I feel very much the same."

"Good. Because I have to admit that I overheard things I was not meant to. It was not intentional, I assure you, but I came back for my hat and your voices were raised. And I listened for too long, rather than walking away at once. I'm sorry. I have no excuse."

"I must ask what, exactly, you heard."

"What you said of Mar—Miss Loxleigh. That her birth, her past, are unworthy of a decent family. That she has lied and deceived me, Tachbrook, all of society."

"Is—is that all you heard?"

"Is it not enough? Or is there something else? I heard that much and then made myself go downstairs, where I sat to recover my composure. Is there something more, some excuse —was it not true?"

His expression was one of desperate hope. It hurt to look at. It hurt doubly because Hart had thought, just for a minute, that his friend had seen his truth and accepted it.

Clearly not. Giles didn't know, and had other things on his mind, and it was absurd to feel such crashing disappointment. He ought to be relieved that the matter didn't arise after all. He told himself that as firmly as he could.

"There is nothing else," he said. "And it is true as far as I know, though in fairness I don't think she ever claimed to be well-born. Only to be beautiful, and that is surely indisputable."

Giles sagged. "But she did claim it, at least by implication and omission. They lied to establish themselves in society, both of them. I don't know why you've taken up with the brother, knowing this, and with all you've said of him in the past."

"He is my friend, and I don't give a damn for his birth."

"Really?"

"Yes, really. His character is better than I realised. Considerably better than he initially showed, because—you're quite right that one cannot excuse their behaviour entirely—"

"Entirely?!"

"—but Miss Loxleigh's beauty, wit, intelligence, and steadfastness are real."

"Her honesty is not," Giles said. "And I do give a damn for birth, and so should you. I have a responsibility to my family, to society as a whole. Honestly, Hart, I am appalled you should have kept this secret."

"I gave my word."

"All the same— No, I hear you." Giles rubbed his face. "I cannot speak of this easily. My feelings are somewhat overwhelmed."

"She feels for you too, I'm told."

"If I had known that two days ago, I should have been in seventh heaven. Now... I suppose I will count it a lucky escape soon. At this moment, it seems like the end of the world."

"You're a fool," Hart said. "What the devil does it matter if she has no parents to speak of? They're dead anyway. Haven't you enough ancestry for two? Don't we all spring from Adam and Eve?"

"Tripe. Would you marry her, knowing all this?"

"I have no fancy to play the misshapen Vulcan to an acknowledged Venus. But someone like her who I loved, and who loved me? Yes. I would beg their hand and think myself lucky if it was granted, and be damned to what society thinks. Society is a consequential fool, and I am tired of rules and strictures that do no good and bring nobody happiness."

"There is more to life than the pursuit of happiness!"

"Tell that to the United States."

Giles snorted. "Yes, and I doubt *that* will work out well. Happiness pursued for its own sake is nothing more than pleasure-seeking and selfish impulse. You know that as well as any man. You find your fulfilment in hard work and service, not worldly indulgence and pleasure-seeking, and I have always admired that."

"I have been lonely all my life," Hart said through his teeth. "It is not self-indulgence to seek a companion. And I cannot see the virtue in an existence trammelled by meaningless laws and shibboleths. It is exhausting. *I* am exhausted. And you are throwing away this great love you claimed to feel—for God's sake, Giles, do you truly believe that to be born into misfortune is a permanent stain on the soul? That a sinner can never be forgiven? I'm sure your father would have opinions on that."

"Perhaps, but I doubt he would want me to marry a lowly sinner, all the same. And I don't believe that you, a Hartlebury, would marry a woman of whom such things could be said."

"My father, a Hartlebury, married a woman of impeccable pedigree and unquestioned virtue. I'd rather have had Marianne Loxleigh any day."

Giles looked shocked. "You can't say that!"

"I damned well can. You do remember my mother?"

"Yes, but— Curse it, Hart, why are you arguing this? What good is it? She has chosen Tachbrook, which, as you said yourself, tells us her character and ambition. I should have known, and I wish her well of him."

"If you feel that way, there is no more to be said. But I must require you to keep this secret, Giles. You had no right to know it."

"I realise that," Giles said. "And I am an eavesdropper, not a villain. Though if it was another man— No. I had no right to listen, so I will keep my silence. But you should have told me, Hart. When I came to you for help and you encouraged me to propose—"

"I encouraged you to put yourself in her shoes, that's all. You are constantly saying I should do that, but when I do, you don't like it."

"There's a difference between showing empathy and supporting a liar!" Giles said hotly.

"So I should only have empathy for people who make decisions I approve of?"

"Of course you must exercise judgement. To understand all is not to forgive all. There are still standards to be upheld."

It was exactly what Hart himself would have said a few weeks ago. Intellectually speaking, Giles was probably right. He simply couldn't reconcile that with Robin.

"I suspect it is all a great deal more complicated than a simple aphorism," he said. "I am sorry for your disappointment, Giles, but I hope you understand that I could not break my word."

"I don't understand why you would give your word to such people in the first place."

"You fell in love with one of 'such people'."

Giles winced. "Don't. Please. I can't be fair about this. I am

226

finding it cursed hard not to be very angry indeed. If she had accepted me—"

"But she didn't. She refused you precisely because she thought you would be revolted at her background. She tried to spare you the very pain you are complaining of now. I quite understand that you are hurt, but you haven't been betrayed."

"You think not?" Giles said. "I feel like I have. Would you go, Hart? I'm not fit for company at the moment."

CHAPTER 22

Robin and Marianne weren't speaking.

They had spoken, or rather shouted, an overwrought and overtired exchange of "What do you mean, overheard?" and "Well, if you hadn't—!" on both sides followed by the slamming of doors and a period of cathartic sulking, crying, or both. Marianne had emerged, looking perfect once more, to inform Robin that if he couldn't keep his voice down during arguments, she would appreciate him not discussing her affairs with his fancy man in future, made some highly specific threats as to what she would do if Tachbrook found out, called him a prick again, and swept out to visit Alice Fenwick.

That was disheartening, and also annoying because she had a fair point. He'd been appallingly foolish in telling Hart anything that could reflect on Marianne, and culpably careless during the argument. And he bloody well knew why he had.

He sat by the window, staring out at the aggressively sunny February day, which was really quite unforgivably bright for a man who'd lain awake most of the night, and made himself face the truth.

He wanted Hart to know him and still want him. He wanted Hart to tell him *I love you, I don't care about anything else*. He wanted to choose Hart without consideration, and for Hart to choose him without reservation, and to believe it could last. He wanted to live their entire relationship over again without the taint of money—not just the arrangement, but his and Marianne's fortune-hunting, their need, their greed. He didn't want to do it without the fucking, because that had been glorious, but he wished to hell he hadn't based everything on physical instead of true intimacy. That was all he wanted to change, because he'd lied through his teeth about no longer wanting to be Hart's fantasy. He just needed that to be part of their reality, instead of a substitute for it.

None of that was compatible with becoming yet another worthless drain on the Hartlebury estate. And it wasn't Hart's fault he thought that was what Robin wanted, because God knew he'd spent a month claiming that he only did bad things because he needed money. Hart knew him to be mercenary and grasping and a fortune hunter, so he would never be able to give him his full trust, and it was no more than Robin deserved.

Hart had tried, even then. He'd offered Robin the security he'd always craved. It wasn't his fault Robin wanted something quite different from him.

A note arrived from Hart around noon, assuring him that Giles Verney was no threat to any of them. That should have been a balm to his worn nerves but there was no summons, no request for a meeting, no indication of what next. Had Hart decided this was too dangerous, or Robin too demanding? Suppose he'd decided to take Verney's side against Marianne?

"Oh, stop it," he told himself aloud, and went out to buy some food.

He went to visit Alice that afternoon. He hadn't seen her in a few days and rather wanted to know what Marianne had said to her; he also felt slightly worried about her plans, and his promise.

When he gave his name to Mrs. Blaine's butler, he was kept kicking his heels for a few minutes, then Alice emerged with her maid, and suggested a walk in tones that implied command. Evidently they needed to talk.

"I saw Marianne earlier," she said as they came into the park. "She looked rather... Is she happy?"

"About Tachbrook?"

"Yes."

He sighed. "She will make a wonderful marchioness. I have no idea what it entails but I am sure she will be very good at it."

"So am I. I did wonder if she might make another decision."

"Did you ask her about it?"

"I did, and I thought she looked sad, but it is her choice."

"In the end it has to be."

Alice didn't pursue the subject, to his relief. There wasn't a great deal else to say.

"Have you any news?" he asked.

"On my studies? Nothing new. Mama has thought about coming with me but that would involve being separated from Georgey for far too long, and to be honest, I think the idea terrifies her. She likes her home and her friends and her comforts. She's had so much unhappiness in her life and she wanted more than anything to be settled, and now here I am, upheaving it all, if that is a word. She asked me again if I could not find a tutor in this country."

"Could you?"

"I don't want to. I want Heidelberg." She made a face. "I don't suppose we might get married after all?"

Robin wondered what to say, and decided on honesty. "I know I promised you. But the thing is, I gave Hart my word I wouldn't do it."

She turned to him, looking startled and hurt. "What? You promised me first!"

Robin couldn't even remember which way round it had been. He had promised too much to too many people. "I know, but he's right. He's a capable man with good sense, your mother listens to him, and he wants you to have this. Give him a chance to make it work, please. It would be much better."

She sighed. "I suppose so. I'm just so desperate to get on. Dr. Trelawney wants to leave by the end of May, for the weather, so we must be settled very quickly if I am to go with him. Never mind." She shot him a smile. "I'm glad you're friends with Uncle Hart now. I didn't expect that."

"Nor did I," Robin admitted. "We didn't get off on the right foot, but that was my fault. He's a good man."

"Yes, he is. Most people don't see it because he says the wrong things or growls at them, but they don't understand. He had a dreadful time growing up, you know."

"He mentioned that."

"Did he? I'm surprised. Mama doesn't talk about it often. It's one reason why she is so kind to me, of course. She remembers what it was like to have a mother who was not kind and didn't care. It makes me feel terribly ungrateful that I'd like her—not to care less—"

"To do it from a greater distance?"

"Well. Yes."

"It sounds like all of you went through rather a lot," Robin suggested.

"Their mother was horrible," she said heatedly. "Uncle Hart had to say no to her, and be told he was cruel and uncaring while Mama was ugly and useless— How could a parent say those things? I am a sad disappointment to Mama in many ways—"

"You are *not*."

"None that count. That's my point. We may not always be in harmony, but I have never, ever thought she didn't love me, not for a moment. Whereas it sounds as though theirs hated them. I cannot imagine how it feels to have one's own mother hate one."

"My mother loved me," Robin said. "But she loved my stepfather more, or at least she chose him over us, and he didn't like us at all."

"Oh, I am sorry. Very sorry. I had a stepfather too, and it was not pleasant."

"Hart told me. Not a nice man?"

"No. Mama married him after my father died and he was dreadful. Hateful." She gave a little twitch, like a horse shuddering flies off its coat. "He didn't want Mama to keep me. He said I was not permitted to call her Mama because she was not my mother and I was not part of the family. I have never seen Mama so angry and there was the most appalling argument, which only ended when Uncle Hart came round and held him against the wall by the neck."

"Did that help?"

"Well, he stopped pretending to be fond of Mama after that, so she could stop pretending to believe him. He kept away from us and just spent her money. She and Uncle Hart were working on the terms of a separation when he was thrown from his horse. Which was a blessed relief and I shan't say otherwise, but poor Mama felt—still feels—so guilty for how he behaved to me. I'm sure that is why she is so protective of me now, and I really ought not be ungrateful about it. Goodness, people are complicated. But you can see why poor Mama wants a little peace, and why Uncle Hart is so prone to growling. He had a great deal to growl about, and he has worked so hard to help the family and worried so much about us."

"It doesn't sound as if anyone has worried much about him."

Alice gave him a swift, startled look. "Should we? Is something wrong?"

"Not wrong," Robin said, cursing his too-ready tongue. "Just—well, he carries everyone's burdens."

"Oh, but he wants to," Alice said, with absolute assurance. "He's one of those people who does things, which is lucky because he's dreadful at saying things. If you listen to him and Mama speak they sound like the merest acquaintances, but she was the only person who ever cared about him when he was a boy, and he has spent his whole life working on her behalf, even though he was horribly ridiculed for going into trade. He doesn't remember her birthday or bring her silks, or ever do thoughtful things like that. He just works to make her safe and happy, because that's how he loves people. I suppose it's one reason he's never married," she added thoughtfully. "I can't imagine him bringing a lady flowers or paying pretty compliments. Although, if I had a husband, I think I'd prefer one who did things rather than one who just said them, but I don't suppose I'm very good at that sort of thing either. Are you certain nothing's wrong? Because he has been preoccupied, and you know Mama and I would do anything to help him."

"I'm sure you would," Robin said faintly. "I'm glad you have each other. And if you know he does things for people he loves, then you know very well he will help you. Perhaps he's a little busy right now."

Robin felt rather better for that conversation, if also quite a lot stupider. Maybe Hart was right about his lack of wiles: he certainly couldn't pride himself on his cunning understanding of human nature, given how badly he'd failed to see what was in front of him. He probably ought to marry Alice after all, or at least hire her to manage his correspondence: she had more sense than he suspected he ever would.

Less inspiring was the absence of any further communication from Hart. He kicked his heels waiting, for a note or for Marianne to come home. The second happened before the first.

"Have you stopped sulking yet?" she greeted him.

Robin decided to ignore that. "Hart spoke to Verney. He says—well, see for yourself."

"I don't need to. I have spoken to him. To Giles."

"When?"

"This afternoon. It's over. I told him the whole truth."

"What?"

"I felt I owed it to him. As I expected, he was grateful for his escape."

"Did he say that?" *I will kill him. I will stab the fucker. I will end him.*

"No, of course not. He said all that was reasonable, didn't upbraid me, and wished me well in my marriage. So there we are."

There they were indeed. Of course love didn't conquer all. It never did, not for long. It had no strength against the massed armies of reputation and birth and privilege and *what people would think*. One would be a fool to risk all for love, rather than protecting oneself.

Verney was a cowardly, sentiment-spewing tosspot, all the same.

He exhaled his fury. Marianne didn't need to hear that her lover had never valued more than her face and his fantasy of what lay behind it. "Well, we will take an absence of retaliation and be thankful. What now?"

"Now? I am going to Lady Colefax's soiree as Lord Tachbrook's affianced bride."

She looked beautiful and remote, all feelings hidden behind stony eyes. She'd looked like that when they had left home without saying goodbye.

"Have a good time," he said.

"I suppose you're seeing Hartlebury?"

"Maybe," Robin said, in lieu of explanation.

"Then the same to you."

CHAPTER 23

Nothing had come from Hart by seven. Robin ate at a coffee-house for a fraction of the price of dining at his club. He felt no temptation to go out and play afterwards. He didn't want to gamble, or to talk. He wanted not to feel this horrible sensation of *alone*.

That was childish. Marianne had her ambitions to pursue; Hart had a family, and obligations, and a number of delightful things like name, reputation, and friends that he must yesterday have feared losing because of Robin. They both had better things to do.

Fine. He'd marry Alice, move to Heidelberg with her, and watch her become the foremost woman mathematician of Europe. Or he'd stay here and win at the tables. He would do *something* and he would be very well indeed, even if it felt like all his happiness was tied up in a thick-thighed man who hid his fears and his hopes and his heart behind a scowl.

Because even if Marianne and Hart could not, in the end, be his, neither of them had let him down, and that was important. Marianne had always been staunch. Hart was caring and kind and he'd stayed when Robin had needed him to. That was enough. Or if it wasn't, he wouldn't improve his situation by whining about it.

He went back to his dismal empty rooms in that spirit of dignified resignation, saw a heavy-set man hovering outside the door, and sprinted the rest of the way.

Hart turned swiftly at the sound of his footsteps and a smile broke across his face, real and joyous and open, before it was replaced by nerves. Robin skidded to a halt, looking up, heart thundering with, yes, the exercise. Definitely that.

"Robin," Hart said. "I just called for you. You were out."

"I'm back."

They were staring at each other in the street like gapeseeds. Robin cleared his throat. "Will you come in or shall we state the obvious out here a little longer?"

"Uh. If I may. If you're ready—willing—to talk?"

Robin nodded. It seemed a better bargaining position than suggesting Hart shut up and kiss him until he couldn't feel his lips.

They went up to the rooms. Robin lit a couple of candles and threw some coal on the fire. "I'm sorry. It's not very comfortable in here. Well, you know that."

"My back still hurts." Hart sat in the armchair with the look of disgusted familiarity Robin felt for that misbegotten piece of furniture. "First things first: your sister?"

Robin shrugged. "I don't know. She seems resigned. She isn't really speaking to me, possibly because I'm a prating idiot who could have ruined everything, but I expect mostly because there's nothing to say. Verney has spoken to her and—well. It's over."

"I'm sorry for it, truly. That's the first thing I wanted to say. You're right: I didn't understand, and I didn't make the effort to do so. I have been a great deal more forgiving of my own sins and failings than those of others, and I didn't realise it until I came face to face with consequences."

"That is a terrible thing, to be more sympathetic to oneself than other people," Robin said. "I expect you're the only person in England who does that. How is Verney?" He hoped the bastard caught plague, but it seemed only fair to make a concession.

"I spoke to him this morning. It seems he only heard the earlier part of our conversation, thank God. So our friendship is intact, at least."

A friendship based on Verney not knowing or seeing Hart properly. He deserved a great deal better, but Robin made himself say, "I'm glad."

"He promised not to repeat what he heard about Marianne. Would it help to know I think he's made a mistake?"

"Do you?"

"Yes. I would not have before, but you have changed my mind about many things, or made me see them differently. He should have taken a risk, and he plumped for the world he knew. I believe he'll regret that caution. I told him so."

Robin blinked. "Really?"

"For all the good it did. In fairness, it would be the stuff of nightmares for Giles's family if they ran away together. I don't suppose you have followed the ecclesiastical controversies of the past few years?"

"I've been meaning to catch up on that."

"Suffice to say, it would be a gift to the Archbishop's enemies, among whom Tachbrook is already numbered, if his son seduced an innocent young lady, or broke up a peer's engagement, or however it would be seen. The Verneys trade on their rectitude. Well, I am notorious in the family as Giles's disreputable friend, if that gives you an idea of his virtue."

"What did you ever do that was disreputable? That people know about, I mean."

"I had an affair with Evangeline Wintour."

"You're brave. I'm amazed she left you your prick."

"She is one of my dearest friends," Hart said severely. "Although it was a near thing, to be honest. I know you did not make a marvellous impression on her—"

"She saw right through me, didn't she?"

"At least she didn't have your hands broken. I would like to mend matters between you, though. She is my only friend with whom I speak about my personal affairs—"

Robin blinked. "Lady Wintour knows your tastes?"

"Knows? She *explained* them to me, when she ended things."

"Oof."

"It was salutary. She is a good friend, and I think you might like each other, given a fresh start."

Hart wanted him to meet his friend? As his lover? Robin attempted to keep his posture relaxed while digging his fingers into the upholstery.

"Anyway, I digress. I merely meant to say that Giles is a high stickler, but I hadn't previously seen him so judgemental. He is deeply hurt, of course, but even so. I'm sorry for his choice, and that things have ended thus, for both their sakes."

"Thank you." Robin could feel something hard and angry dissolving in his chest. "Thank you, Hart. That means a great deal."

Hart offered him an uncertain smile. "Talking of people left distraught by their lovers, I wondered if I could speak to you about my offer."

"Yes, you can, but could you just...not do the same thing again?"

He winced. "I think I have finally grasped that. Let me try to explain myself? When I made you that offer, I wanted to give you the security you have asked for, but I also wanted something like the arrangement, because, to be quite honest, it was something I understood. You asked me if I believed you wanted me for myself. And honestly, I do find it hard to believe because you are wonderful, Robin, bright and airy and irrepressible. You find joy wherever you can, and make your own. You are gloriously loyal and kind, and desirable in every possible sense. I want you and I want to be with you, and what do I possibly have to set against that but money? I am not used to—to being cared for, and I certainly should not presume it."

"Hart—"

"No, wait. I need to explain. While I'd have liked to sweep you off your feet, I know I'm not capable of that, but I did think I could serve you. I wanted to make you feel safe. And you thought I was trying to buy you, but I hope you'll believe that I meant the opposite. I thought, if you didn't have to worry about money or your future, you would be able to choose freely, and then…well, I hoped you might choose me."

"But I would have had to choose you to get the money."

"Yes, well, that was where my plan fell apart. It is staggeringly obvious to me now that I had everything wrong, but I've never offered carte blanche before, and frankly I never want to again. It was foolish, but it was not nearly as foolish as my belief that it was for me to offer and you to accept. What I should have done was ask. Ask you if you wanted to have more time with me, and if you do, discuss how we might achieve that between us."

"But you wanted to do something for me, didn't you?"

"I did, but that isn't how I should have gone about it. I have spent a great deal of my life doing things for people—which isn't a complaint, I am a damned lucky man to have my sister and Alice, but clearly I have got into bad habits."

"Habits of seeing what needs doing and pressing ahead in the teeth of other people's objections. I expect a lot of the things you do need doing," Robin said. "But this isn't one. I don't want your money because it would be bad for both of us.

It would be bad for you to give it to me, because you have a lifetime of being responsible for leeches, and it would be bad for me to take it, because I have a lifetime of being an irresponsible leech."

"That's not fair. You had—have—a little sister to look after."

Robin would have answered, but for the quite unexpected sob that rose in his throat, silencing him. Hart's eyes widened. "Oh God. What did I say?"

"Nothing. It's all right. I just— She's very nearly taller than me, and stronger in almost every way and it's been such a long time since she was my little sister, but she is. I didn't know you saw that."

"I should have seen it a long time ago. I'd do anything for Alice or Edwina too." Hart paused. "Well, not become a fortune hunter, but I don't have the qualifications. Robin, listen. I have needed something more in my life for a long time. I thought having my own business would answer that, and then I met you. Well, not 'and then', obviously, it was some time after our first meeting that I came to appreciate you, but the point is, I have been happier in the last month than any time I can remember. And that is not down to a fantasy lover, though heavens knows you were that, but to *you*. Making me see differently, showing me what care and kindness look like. Refusing to be squashed or shamed. Making me laugh, because you bubble with joy. You make me feel loved, and I love you. So the first thing I need to ask is whether you want to be with me too. And if you can't answer me now, that is quite understandable, but maybe you will be willing to have that conversation one day—"

"Hart! I'm free now." Robin was all but hopping on the edge of the settle. "I truly, desperately don't want to batten on you, and it is important that you believe that."

"I never meant to insult you."

"It's not me you insulted," Robin said. "The idea—the very *idea*—that I might not want you for yourself is an outrage. You're wonderful, Hart. You carry the world on your shoulders, and you're so scowling and so sensitive, and your thighs are glorious, and I adore you. I don't deserve you, but I love you, and I want you to love me. And I want all the time I can have, preferably starting here and now while you kiss me a great deal."

Hart lunged. They met in the centre of the room, and Hart put a hand to his face, cupping Robin's jaw. He looked into his eyes with a kind of hungry wonder, and then he leaned forward and kissed Robin, absurdly gently, and everything was all right. Everything was so all right, he could have cried.

Hart's mouth was hot and desperate, his hands sliding up and down Robin's body before settling on his arse. Robin locked both hands on Hart's shoulders and wrapped a thigh around his leg. Hart's tongue delved into his mouth and Robin opened to him, his whole body nothing but a long stretch of wanting and needing, and they kissed wildly, until Robin lost his balance and fell into Hart, who held him as close and safe as if nothing could go badly at all.

They spent the night at Hart's rooms, since Robin had a single bed in the room he shared with Marianne. Neither of them was in the mood for elaborate loveplay. Robin whispered, "Hold me," and Hart did, bare and close in bed, fitting Robin's sturdy body to his own bulky one and bringing him off with a careful hand and his own prick between Robin's thighs. It was…peaceful.

"Where is Marianne tonight?" Hart asked idly.

"Lady Colefax's soiree."

"I don't know how she tolerates all that socialising. I'd run mad."

"I'm not sure she won't," Robin said. "Tachbrook is a domineering prick, and Marianne has a temper."

"She hides it well."

"She can't hide it forever. She could start a fight in an empty room, and she regards a belt as a handy indication of what to hit below. She will only put up with his condescension for so long. And—ugh. Normally I would back her against all opposition, but he's a marquess. All the power, all the family, twice her age, she'll be alone. I don't like it, Hart. I don't think she should do it."

"Have you told her?"

"Of course, but she doesn't back down easily, or ever, and it's a lot of money, and mostly, if she doesn't get Tachbrook now, we're in trouble. She's made too much of a splash in London to hook another rich man without a scandal. If she jilts him now, we'll be going home by Weeping Cross. Except we're not going home. Or anywhere near Manchester, or Salisbury either." He shrugged at Hart's look. "We lit our way to London with burning bridges."

"If it is any use, you would both be welcome to stay with me in Aston Clinton for as long as you needed."

"You plan to invite an unmarried woman who has just broken her glittering engagement to your enemy into your home? I'm sure that wouldn't cause any comment at all."

"Damn."

Robin squeezed his hand again. "You are a darling for offering. As if you and Marianne wouldn't murder one another within the month."

"I would like you to visit Aston Clinton though," Hart said. "My home is plain enough—I had Mother's extravagances sold—but it's a fine old place, and I am proud of my roses."

"You have roses?"

"A garden of them. I adore roses, no matter what they spring from." He planted a kiss on Robin's neck. "You would like it. I wish you would come."

Robin wished that too. He let himself slip into the dream. "What would I do in Aston Clinton? Which, I may say, I have never heard of. Town? Village? Thriving metropolis?"

"Village. There is not a great deal of entertainment there compared to London, needless to say. But—" He stopped there.

"But?"

"It's just a thought I had last night. Not even a thought, a castle in the air. You have your sister, and your life to consider."

"*But*, Hart?"

Hart tightened his arm round Robin's chest. "I told you I am setting up a new brewery in Tring, in partnership with James. It will be a great deal of work and there is Fenwick's to run, plus my manager is to retire next year. I need another pair of hands. I intended to take someone on. That could be someone who needed training up from scratch."

Robin wasn't following. "And?"

Hart hesitated. "I don't suppose you'd consider it?"

"*Me?*"

"I need a bright, personable, capable man. It seems to me I have one here."

"But I don't know anything about brewing. I have never done an honest day's work in my life. I wouldn't know how to start."

"I didn't know anything when I took over. James taught me the business, and I learned. So could you."

"Could I?" Robin said, almost breathlessly.

"I can't see why not. You're quick and clever, and exceptionally likeable, which I am not."

"Does that matter?"

"Well, the point of brewing beer is to sell it, and selling is better done by likeable people."

"I can sell things," Robin admitted. "Myself, for example, or the advisability of increasing the stakes mid-way through the game."

"Beer should be easy. There are always arguments to be settled, bargains to be struck, men to be managed. Personal things, and you are very good at people. And it would be a trade, Robin. You'd have a salary that you earned, and skills you could take elsewhere. And this isn't charity, or payment by other means, before you ask. I have far too much to do and I should work you like a dog."

"It's charity if you need to teach me everything."

"Good Lord, Robin, how do you think people acquire skills? We all have to be taught."

Robin sat up. "Tell me the truth, Hart. Is this something I could truly do, or are we playing?"

Hart propped himself up on an elbow, face serious. "I think you could do it if you chose to apply yourself. You're perfectly capable. I wouldn't invite you into my business if I didn't think you would do well by it; I have too many responsibilities for that. If you don't serve, I will tell you so plainly. But if you do...well, there is no reason the new man I am training should not take a room in my home on arrival, and stay a while, if he cared to. It's a big house for me alone."

"With roses in the garden, who wouldn't stay?"

"It's up to you. You would have to see if the life suits you. No obligation, needless to say. But if you'd care to try..."

Robin curved his neck to bring his lips to Hart's fingers. "If you truly think I could do it, I would do my best. I swear. If you absolutely promise to tell me if I'm no good."

"And if you promise to say if it does not suit. I could ask James to take you for a fortnight to begin with. He's forgotten more than I'll ever know, and I'm sure you will like him. And then we could say you come from Alphonso's."

"Oh God. Hart. Really?"

"Really."

Robin opened his mouth to say yes, and then reality returned. "Marianne."

"Marianne?"

"I need to be sure she's safe," Robin said. "If she marries Tachbrook, I suppose—but if it goes wrong—"

"You need to look after her. I understand."

"Not at your expense. But it's just been the two of us for so long and I have to know she's all right. I can't abandon her."

"You have a responsibility," Hart said. "I *know*, Robin. I wouldn't expect you to do otherwise."

"But if I can't go with you—"

"Shh." Hart pulled him down. "If that's the case, we'll find another way. We've already thought of one, so we can think of others."

Robin buried himself in Hart's chest. "I want this one," he mumbled.

"So do I."

"God, I love you," Robin said. "Who'd have thought it? My castle in the air is a brewery."

CHAPTER 24

There were many things Robin had imagined himself and Hart doing on the last night of the arrangement, all of them more desirable than going to the Duchess of Aylesbury's ball. Yet here he was.

The Aylesbury ball was one of the great events of the Season, and perhaps the most important for Marianne, since Tachbrook was first cousin to His Grace of Aylesbury by marriage. She was to be introduced to the great man as the Marquess's affianced bride, a public acceptance and recognition of her status. The Dowager had sent her instructions as to what to wear.

"This is irrevocable, Marnie," Robin said as he curled her hair in preparation.

"I know."

Everyone would be there, it felt like. The Verneys were going, as were Hart, Mrs. Blaine, and Alice, on the basis of the geographical connection with the Aylesburys. He would have far preferred not to go, but Marianne was suffering under the tension of her lost love and her miserable engagement: he could see lines around her lovely eyes.

She looked defeated already, and that was frightening.

They'd airily assumed she could make a husband do her bidding no matter how rich, but the fact was, she'd be outnumbered by his family, legally his possession, effectively powerless but for her own will, and wills could be broken. Marianne was strong, and savagely determined, but Robin wasn't sure anyone could resist all that weight.

"I wish you wouldn't," he said.

"I know. Don't say any more."

"He'll grind you down, Marnie."

"That's men for you."

"No, it is not. For Christ's sake. I don't do that. Hart doesn't. Tachbrook wants you to be a trophy in public and a victim at home—"

"Enough," she said, and her tone made Robin clamp his lips shut.

After a few moments, she glanced up at him in the glass. "What about you, Rob?"

"What about me?"

"Hartlebury. Are you happy?"

"Very."

She put up a hand to hold his. "You want to be with him, don't you?"

"Yes. Very much."

"Then for God's sake do it. Don't wait around to see me settled. I'm going to be a marchioness. Toddle off and sort out your unwedded bliss."

"You know damned well that you and I stand together until we both choose to part," Robin said. "I haven't changed my mind on that, and Hart knows it too. If I have to wait for you—"

"Will he wait for you?"

"If he doesn't, he's not the man I think. But I believe he is. He knows what it means to love."

She pressed his fingers. "I hope he knows what it means to love you. The poor bastard."

"He may still be coming to terms with the consequences, I grant you."

"I'm glad you have him. I'll be out of your way soon, Rob."

"You have never in your life been in my way. If you want to throw the ring back at Tachbrook and run for it, I'm in. We don't need riches, Marnie."

"And then what? Where will I go? What is my security against age if not marriage?" She glowered at the woman in the mirror. "I *can* do this. I will take the best and live with the worst. Don't worry about me."

❧

The ball was a magnificent affair. The ballroom was strung with apricot silk, wax candles blazed in the chandeliers and candelabra, musicians played, drink flowed. Marianne made a grand entrance on Tachbrook's arm, superb in dark green with emeralds, his engagement gift, dripping from her neck and ears and wrist. She'd said they were hateful. Robin thought they were beautiful, but he was fairly sure that she hadn't meant their appearance.

He wasn't part of Tachbrook's party. The Marquess had indicated that Marianne would have no future need for her own relatives or friends, since he would provide or approve those for her. So Robin arrived alone, and wandered the halls. He spoke to various acquaintances, responded to many congratulations, some of them sincere, on Marianne's engagement, and fended off a few nakedly unpleasant remarks about how well she had done for herself or Tachbrook's remarkable condescension. There had to be more than two hundred people here, a sad crush. God knew what it must cost.

He worked through the crowd into the salon, where there was a hubbub of conversation. Robin caught a flicker of dun-coloured coat and a fraction of bulky shoulder, and his heart skipped before his mind had caught up. Hart.

He squeezed his way forward between people, and as he did, an odd silence fell, rippling out from the centre of the room. Something was about to go wrong.

He didn't know what, but he'd been in plenty of rooms just before things went wrong, and he knew how it felt. People sensed a storm about to break, inched away, kept watching. They did it in gambling dens and low taverns and prayer-meetings, and they were doing it now, at the Duke of Aylesbury's ball.

Robin scanned the room. Marianne stood opposite on Tachbrook's arm. Her face was still, but Tachbrook wore an unpleasant, almost gloating smile. A little way away Giles Verney stood, face tense. Robin felt a single second of pure anticipatory terror before he realised he had it wrong. They weren't at the eye. The storm wasn't coming for them.

Because there was Hart, stiff-backed, face set in a rigid expression that exaggerated his features and made his scowl look almost grotesque. Mrs. Blaine stood slightly behind him, eyes wide, clutching Alice's shoulder with white knuckles. Alice looked confused, and a little alarmed.

Opposite them were two people: a distinguished, portly gentleman with a red face, and a woman who had clearly been a belle in her day. She seemed perhaps fifty or a little more by her face; her elegant dress flattered a very well-preserved figure, and feather sprays and jewels demonstrated that she was both able and keen to maintain her appearance. Her whole presentation stated that she was to be regarded as beautiful, and indeed she was, except for the look of disdain she was casting at the man Robin loved.

"Do you not intend to greet me?" she enquired in a musical alto voice. "Graceless still, I see."

"Lady Asperton," Hart said flatly. "Sir Roger."

The name rang a bell, and so did the raw hurt in Hart's eyes, not at all the expression of a strong, grown man. That was what let Robin place her.

This was his mother. Hart's mother, who had married a rich baronet and never looked back, and who now stood and regarded her grown children with something extraordinarily like contempt.

"Hartlebury." The portly man—the second husband, Robin supposed—gave a dismissive nod.

"I see you have not improved," Lady Asperton remarked. "Neither of you. I did hope for Edwina's complexion—but it was not to be. And this must be, what, that person's daughter?"

"This is Alice, and his name was Fenwick," Mrs. Blaine said.

Lady Asperton gave Alice a look up and down. "Oh dear. Blood will out. I dare say you will struggle to marry her off, but at least she doesn't have the Hartlebury nose. I do feel *one* of my children might have spared me that."

Alice flushed bright red. Mrs. Blaine said, voice shaking a little, "Alice is the very best of daughters. I am sorry for you that you do not know her."

"Good heavens." Lady Asperton gave a little startled laugh, as though she were turning down some encroaching request. "I really am rather busy for that."

"It's your loss," Hart said, voice flat. "I hope you have been well, Lady Asperton. We have not seen you in some time."

Lady Asperton's upper lip curled. "Nor written either. Perhaps you might ask yourself why I have cleaved to my dear

Asperton. But I suppose I am not to be permitted happiness, even now." She pitched that more at the circle of people pretending they weren't listening than at her son. "You take after your father in more than looks. I am sorry for it."

Eyes gleamed around them. Alice looked as though she was about to cry. Hart was dark red with humiliation, and Robin thought desperately at him, *Stop this. Walk away. She doesn't care, you do, so you can't win.*

"Quite right." Tachbrook apparently addressed that to Marianne, but his voice was loud enough to be generally heard. "It is a pretty pass when a man does not honour his mother. Shocking."

"Perhaps the fault lies in my upbringing," Hart tried, but he sounded leaden, almost choked.

"Once again I am made at fault," Lady Asperton jabbed back. "A grown man who must blame his mother. What a sorry state of affairs."

Robin strode forward to insert himself between the Aspertons and Hart, turning his back to Lady Asperton in a manner that would have earned him a blow from Lordship for the rudeness. "Hello there, I was looking for you all." He managed to hit a tone of bright cheer despite the rage that fuzzed his brain, at Hart's mother, and Tachbrook, and Verney, and every damned one of these damned people. "I was hoping both your ladies would dance with me. Would you like an ice first, Miss Fenwick? Shall we go?"

"*Excuse* me," Lady Asperton said, in arctic tones. "You have interrupted a conversation."

Robin swung round. "No, I don't think I have. That wasn't a conversation. It was a malicious, ill-mannered, nasty-tempered scold, and you should be thoroughly ashamed of yourself."

There were audible gasps at that. Robin could almost hear the crackle as his carefully cultivated facade of Humble and

Pleasant went up in flames. Oh well. What good was a bridge you couldn't burn?

"Sir!" Tachbrook was bright puce. "You will apologise at once. How dare you speak to my cousin that way?"

Robin's stomach plunged. Cousin—fuck, *fuck*, he had known that. Hart had told him, and now he'd just insulted Tachbrook's cousin in full view of everyone. Fuck. He'd have to grovel, and Hart would see him take the words back, and he could *not*. He'd swallowed a lot in his life; he couldn't swallow this. Except, Marianne's marriage—

"Who is this ill-mannered individual?" Lady Asperton demanded.

Robin took a deep breath. Marianne cut across him. "He is my brother."

Lady Asperton looked from her to Robin with a curling sneer. "Yours? I *see*. Well, I am astonished at your brother's conduct."

"Marianne is not responsible for me," Robin said wretchedly.

"Perhaps she should be." Lady Asperton gave her little laugh. "But then, so many of us have unfortunate relatives."

Marianne's head went up, setting the emeralds at her neck and ears to a glittering dance. "Very true," she said, voice hard and bright as any jewel. "On which subject, Lady Asperton, you must know that Alice Fenwick will be chief bridesmaid at my wedding. So I must oblige you to mind your manners and treat her with the courtesy she deserves."

Lady Asperton flushed red. Alice, to whom this appeared news, made a strangled noise. And Lord Tachbrook said, "What? She will be no such thing."

Marianne stiffened. She stood tall and absolutely still for a second, an outraged Greek goddess just before someone got turned into a small prey animal, and when she spoke, her voice was very soft. "I cannot have heard you correctly, my lord."

"The arrangements are not made." Tachbrook appeared confused as to why he was not receiving instant obedience. "My mother will make a list—"

"Your mother will choose my bridesmaids? I think there must be some confusion. Alice is very dear to me, as is her family, so she will stand with me. I see no reason for your mother, or anyone else not involved"—she gave Lady Asperton a frozen look—"to interfere."

"A vulgar tradesman's daughter, at Tachbrook's wedding?" Lady Asperton demanded. "I hardly think so."

"You—think," Marianne repeated, enunciating the words with lethal precision. "You *think*. Do remind me. Who, precisely, are *you* to think?"

Lady Asperton's mouth dropped open. Tachbrook looked both baffled and—Robin almost had to admire him—annoyed. Apparently his sense of his own consequence was such that it even obscured the jaws of the mantrap that yawned in front of him.

"I beg your pardon," Tachbrook said. "As my cousin, Lady Asperton may make what observations she pleases."

Marianne turned on him like a tiger, and, for all his pomposity, the marquess recoiled an involuntary step. "She may insult a girl from the schoolroom who has done her no wrong, and dictate your wedding arrangements? What a very remarkable thing it is to be Lord Tachbrook's cousin. Or his mother, indeed. But, clearly, not his wife, since my opinions are to be ignored and my friends insulted with impunity. I quite see what courtesy I must expect." She strode over to Robin in a ferocious swish of skirts. "I should like fresh air. Robin, perhaps you will take Alice and Mrs. Blaine for an ice, and Hartlebury will escort me."

"Excuse me, madam," Tachbrook said. "If you wish for an ice—"

"Oh, will you fetch one, sir?" Marianne demanded, voice thrumming magnificently. "Will you stoop to do me the most trivial courtesy, or must we wait for your cousin to grant you leave? Is there any other family member you should care to consult first? A great-uncle, perhaps?"

That got a general laugh. Tachbrook was a very unhealthy colour by now. "Miss Loxleigh! I must insist on respect to my family."

Robin met Marianne's eyes, questioning. She put an appealing hand on his arm and breathed, very softly, "Kill."

He stepped forward, head up, back straight. "And so, sir, must I. I should like a private word with you, Lord Tachbrook, at once."

"You?" Tachbrook looked as startled if he'd been attacked by a kitten.

"I am of no great account, I am aware," Robin said, pitching his voice to be heard. "But enough is enough, and I will not stand for this flagrant discourtesy to a woman to whom you owe the greatest consideration. You may be a marquess, but you will treat my sister with the respect she or any lady is due, or you will answer for it to me. How dare you behave with such ill manners to your future wife, sir? How *dare* you?"

The murmurs of approbation were loud now. "Quite right," someone remarked from the crowd. "Well said."

Tachbrook's eyes flicked around. It seemed he'd finally realised the situation had slid out of control. "I cannot see any discussion is necessary. This is a great quarrel about nothing."

Marianne inhaled like an opera singer. Robin sidestepped out of the firing line, repressing a well-honed instinct to duck. "Nothing? About nothing? It is about *me*. About the respect I may expect to receive, and the protection too, as your wife, and you call that nothing, sir? Do you say, in front of this crowd, that I am *nothing*?"

Her voice had risen to impressive force and volume. Tachbrook swayed back a little. Lady Asperton said, "Really, what nonsense."

"You keep talking," Marianne said lethally. "I cannot imagine why."

"Am I to be spoken to in this way by this woman?" Lady Asperton demanded.

"Yes, Tachbrook," Marianne flashed back. "*Is* she?"

All eyes turned to Lord Tachbrook. He hesitated, torn between pride and alarm, and failed to speak for just long enough that Robin got in first with, "It seems you have your answer, Marianne."

"So it appears." Marianne dropped the marquess a very low curtsey. "Thank you for your protection, Robin, but I should prefer to have this conversation myself. Perhaps we might speak, my lord, in private, at once. *Without* unwarranted intrusion from ill-mannered, pushing individuals."

Lady Asperton gasped shrilly. Marianne swung past her as though she didn't exist.

"We may certainly speak." Tachbrook sounded congested. Hopefully he was going to have an apoplexy.

"Then let us go," Marianne said, and steered him off to an anteroom.

Robin turned to the Hartleburys. Hart looked stunned; Mrs. Blaine's eyes brimmed with tears. Alice had her arm round her mother's waist, but when she caught Robin's eye, she gave him a sudden, utterly gleeful flash of a smile.

Get them out, Robin mouthed at her, with a quick jerk of his head, then took the opportunity to position himself between Lady Asperton and Hart, adopting a tight-lipped expression as she turned back.

"Well," she said. "What a shocking display of ill temper."

"I couldn't agree more," Robin told her. "You seem to have broken an engagement with it. I hope Lord Tachbrook will not resent your interference too much."

"I beg your pardon?"

"It is my sister's pardon you should be begging, not to mention your children's. Your conduct is extraordinary."

"Sir!" Sir Roger Asperton began.

"Yes?" Robin enquired, close to a snarl. "Do you have anything to say to me? Please do. Really. I'd be *fascinated*."

Sir Roger appeared to read Robin's absolute lack of damns to give on his face, because he said, "Come, Lady A," and urged his wife away with soothing noises. Robin watched them go, breathing deeply, and turned to see that Hart and the others had gone.

"That was magnificent," said a quiet voice by his side. Giles Verney.

"I'm in the mood for telling people what I think of them," Robin said. "So you should probably go away."

"Let me thank you first, as Hart's friend. You might not quite realise how much you did for him just now, but I do."

"I couldn't stand by and watch that display."

"So I saw, and may I say—"

"No, you may not, because *you* stood by and watched," Robin said. "You call yourself Hart's friend but you did damn all when he needed you, so your thanks aren't meaningful, wanted, or welcome. And while I'm on the subject, it's odd that I've never heard him mention any ways you or your family helped when he was in trouble. Lots about what you think, never anything about what you did. What is it you're so proud of yourself *for*, exactly?"

Verney's mouth opened and shut. "I—"

"I'm still talking. You're the one who cares what other people think, so you can hear what I think of you, and that's

257

that you don't have the heart or spine to match Marianne by half, and you have never deserved Hart. So sod off, you smug prick," he finished, with perhaps a slight failure of eloquence.

Verney sodded off, which was wise of him. Robin stood, trying to calm his thundering pulse, and wondering at what point he'd become someone who openly said what he thought. Maybe Hart had rubbed off on him. As it were.

Various people sidled up as he waited for Marianne, making enquiries about the future of the engagement. He told them all, "My sister won't accept insult as the price of a coronet," and added that in his view a marquess had more rather than less obligation to behave as a gentleman. It was a popular line to take, since Tachbrook had offended almost everyone over the years, and there was no shortage of volunteers to regale the audience with stories of his boorish manners while they waited for the next act. By the time Marianne emerged from the anteroom with her left hand bare of rings and a near-purple Tachbrook trailing behind her, Robin had the waiting crowd very much on her side.

Marianne's features were composed but her eyes blazed and a high colour burned on her cheekbones. Naturally, she looked magnificent. She glanced around, apparently oblivious to her audience, and said, "Robin, I should like to depart. Oh. Just one moment, Lord Tachbrook."

He was already ten feet away but he turned at her words, drawing himself up. She put her hands to her nape, removed the heavy emerald necklace, and held out the glittering gold and green at arm's length, and in her fingertips. "This is yours, sir."

He looked blank. Marianne's face was perfect in its haughty chill as the jewels dangled from her hand. "The parure was a gift for your future wife, my lord. It is no longer mine to wear."

The crowd watched, fascinated. Tachbrook hesitated, but

she had him in a vice. He would have to walk back to her and take the discarded thing—*be permitted* to take it, in fact, stow it in a pocket like some vulgar merchant, and stand waiting while she removed the bracelet and earrings too. Robin could only imagine the joy with which caricaturists would fall upon a marquess cravenly snatching jewels from a dignified woman.

He could have got away with a lofty instruction to return the jewels to his lawyer if he'd thought of it in time, but before he could speak, someone in the crowd let out a sibilant hiss of disapproval. A few more arose, and then it was too late. Admittedly, the first someone was Robin, but it was still public opinion.

"It was a gift to you, Miss Loxleigh," Tachbrook said stiffly. "I regret that we could not suit."

"So do I, my lord." Marianne swept a very deep curtsey, inclining her head to display her lovely bare neck, and stayed down. Tachbrook managed a bow, glared around, and stalked off.

"Come, Marianne," Robin said, offering her his arm, and sliding several thousand pounds worth of emeralds into his pocket as casually as possible. "Let us go."

⚜

They maintained a strict silence as they returned to their rooms. It was only with the door firmly shut that Robin said, "You fucking beauty."

"Jesus Christ. What have I done?"

"Got rid of a flaccid pego you didn't need."

"Eighteen thousand pounds a year!"

"I wouldn't have him at twice that. And nor would you. Come on, Marnie, don't pretend you don't feel better."

She met his eyes. "Maybe a bit. A *little* bit."

"Honeymoon," Robin said meaningfully. "Kisses."

"Good point. Oh God. I'm rid of him. I am rid of him, Rob!" She flung her arms round him. "Oh my God, I could fly. Why did you let me think I could marry him?"

"It's all my fault." He hugged her. "What a prick."

"Him and his cousin too. That was really Hartlebury's mother?"

"I'm afraid so."

"The poor swine. He won't mind that, will he?"

"I hope not. And you were superb. A masterpiece of womanly dignity."

"No tosspot talks like that about my brother." Marianne picked up the gin bottle, dragged out the cork with her teeth, and spat it on the table. "To womanly dignity." She swigged a mouthful and passed the bottle.

"To emeralds." Robin tipped a fiery slug of gin down his throat, and coughed. "That was beautifully done. What do we think we can get for them?"

"With the bracelet and earrings? A fortune."

"Plus the three hundred savings and we can sell a lot of the clothes. We're rich. Not marchioness rich, but rich enough to manage without any bloody awful men."

She took the bottle back. "Talking of which, you were adorable, Rob. One day I'm going to find a man who stands up for me the way you did for yours."

"You've got one right here," Robin said. "You always have had, and you always will."

"You're going to Little Wimple and a cottage with roses round the door."

"Aston Clinton, and the roses are a garden. And I'm not."

"Yes, you are."

"I'm not leaving you, Marnie. It's not up for debate."

"It bloody well is. How selfish do you think I am?"

He retrieved the gin. He needed it now. "I know you

aren't, and that you want me to be happy, but I can't be if you're not. If I'm afraid for you, if you're alone— No."

"Robin, I'm a grown woman with a double handful of emeralds. And you've got a chance for a home and safety and someone who loves you. I could never be happy if I took that away from you, so if you care about me at all, you'll go with Hart."

"I'm not letting you down. It's the one thing I said I'd never do. I won't."

"You never could, idiot. Go to your brewer." Marianne plucked the bottle from his hand. "Get your hops and roses."

"He'll be with his family. I'll stay here tonight." He snatched it back. "We've got a lot of gin to finish."

CHAPTER 25

The next morning was exactly the sort of morning you might expect if you'd burned all the bridges and drunk all the gin. Robin dragged himself out of bed at a knock on the door, had a handful of letters thrust at him by the landlady, and was informed in no uncertain terms that she'd been up and down with messages all morning and would thank him to collect them from the hall.

He woke Marianne, dressed while she remembered the eighteen thousand a year and screamed into her mattress, and crawled out to buy something for breakfast. When he returned, she was curled on the settle in a litter of papers.

"Anything good?"

"Three anonymous notes calling me a bitch and whore, two proposals of marriage, five invitations to come over and tell them all about it, and this." She waved a note. "Mrs. Blaine would like us to call."

"We should do that." He looked at Marianne, all tangled hair, red eyes, and dark circles. "When you've primped a bit."

"Speak for yourself. You look like the Fall of Man."

They rendered themselves acceptable for polite society, which involved a lot of coffee and Robin putting his head under the pump, and set off walking, since the day was bright with the promise of spring. Excessively so, for Robin's sore eyeballs. They saw a couple of acquaintances and nodded, but didn't stop.

"If anyone speaks to me with my head in this state, I won't be responsible for my actions," Marianne muttered. "What are you going to do?"

"Stand back and watch. Sod 'em."

"Not that, fool. Hart."

"I told you yesterday."

"And I told you. Rob, I love you, and you love him, and if you spoil this, I will never forgive myself. Which I'll make you regret for the rest of your life, so consider yourself warned. Oh God, it's Florence Jocelyn. Look the other way. Oh no."

Miss Jocelyn and Mowbray approached, faces full of concern. They hadn't been at the ball, but word of the scandal was doubtless spreading like the clap. Robin forced his mouth into a smile and agreed that it was true, it was most distressing for Marianne, they didn't greatly want to discuss it, and they had yet to decide whether to return home to Nottinghamshire. Marianne adopted the bearing of a plaintive nun for the duration of the conversation, but as they walked on, she said, "I am leaving."

"What, London?"

"I'll have to. For one thing, I've used my chance. For another, I don't like the sympathy, but I'll like the malice even less."

"Will there be malice?"

"People do love to see an ambitious woman fall. And Tachbrook will be malicious, I'm sure of that. I have no doubt he'll put his side forward."

"He did that to Hart," Robin said. "When he was estranged from his mother because of her behaviour, Tachbrook made sure her story was the one people heard."

"I'm not in the least surprised."

They made it to Mrs. Blaine's without further incident, and were admitted to the sitting room, to find not just her but Alice and Hart. They all stood as the Loxleighs entered.

Robin hadn't set foot in the house since being exposed as a fortune hunter, and certainly not during the period where Alice was threatening to elope with him. He felt a sudden, belated, and very well deserved spasm of embarrassment. "Uh—"

"Robin!" Alice shrieked, and hurled herself at him, hugging him more like a child than a grown-up mathematician. "You were *wonderful*. Thank you, thank you."

Robin looked over her head in mild alarm, but Hart was smiling at him, and he now saw Mrs. Blaine was embracing Marianne, rocking her back and forth. "You are the dearest girl," she said, voice muffled. "Heroic. I am so dreadfully sorry."

Alice disengaged herself from Robin and flung her arms around Marianne. Mrs. Blaine held out her hand to him from between them, and Robin took it, feeling somewhat startled. "Thank you so much, Mr. Loxleigh. For you both to step in like that—"

"It truly was nothing," Robin said. "Honestly. It was the least we could do, considering."

"It wasn't." Hart's voice was very deep. "I can't tell you what it meant to have a defender just then."

"And you were so wonderfully rude." Alice looked remarkably pretty in her enthusiasm. "It was *glorious*. Someone should have told that horrible woman off years ago, and Tachbrook with her. I've no idea how you had the nerve to do it, but I intend to learn."

"Perhaps I should too." Mrs. Blaine stepped back, wiping her eyes. "Let me ring for tea, and you must tell me, Miss Loxleigh. Is the engagement truly off?"

"Yes," Marianne said. "And an exceedingly good thing too. I had made a very stupid mistake."

"It is a great deal better to discover your mistake before the wedding rather than after. But what will you do now?"

Marianne glanced at Robin. Mrs. Blaine coughed gently. "I should say that I had a long talk with Hart last night. I would imagine you find yourself in an awkward position. And Tachbrook is a vindictive man who does not forgive insult."

"We were thinking of leaving London," Robin said. He didn't, couldn't, look at Hart as he spoke. He didn't want to say it and if he looked, he didn't think he'd be able to get the words out. "I don't want Marianne exposed to his malice."

"*I* was thinking of leaving," Marianne said. "Whereas Robin—"

"We are not having this conversation now," Robin said through his teeth.

"Try me." Marianne gave him a bright smile.

"If I may." Hart was still standing, though the rest of them had sat. "Edwina has a suggestion to make."

"It was Hart's thought," Mrs. Blaine said. "I have been looking for a companion for Alice to go to Heidelberg with her. Someone who I can trust to look after her. A lady with the heart of a lion who I know—I have seen for myself—will take good care of my daughter. I don't suppose…"

Robin did look at Hart then, swinging round with his jaw slack. Hart gave him an exceedingly tentative smile. "It was just a thought. But if it appeals to Miss Loxleigh—"

"But I don't speak German," Marianne said blankly. "I've never been abroad."

"Dr. Trelawney is to go too. And you could learn," Alice said. "He has been teaching me the language. We thought you could stay with us for a little while and have some lessons, if you liked. It isn't difficult, truly."

"And go to *another country?*"

Alice nodded frantically. Marianne's hand flew to her mouth.

"We would pay all the passage fees and accommodation, of course, and make the arrangements," Edwina said. "There's a great deal you will want to discuss. But I want Alice to have someone with her that I can trust. And I believe I can trust you."

Marianne put both hands over her face at that. Robin touched her shoulder, feeling it heave, and shook his head at Mrs. Blaine's worried expression with a smile. "Oh, love. Of course you should, if you want to. It sounds wonderful. Try not to upset the Elector Palatine."

"Who's he?" Marianne asked through her palms.

"Some fellow who lives round there."

"The Electoral Palatinate has been disestablished for some years now, so you need not worry unduly on that front," Hart said. "If you would like time to think—"

"No," Marianne said, lifting her head. "I don't need to think at all. I should love to, Mrs. Blaine. I really will take care of Alice, I promise you. I'm quite sure I can. I've always wanted—so much— Do you really want me to?"

She looked about eighteen herself, the world-weariness and disappointment and defences washed away. She should not have had to be so much older for so long, Robin thought, feeling his chest constrict with love and pain.

"Oh goodness. Will you really? Marianne!" Alice grabbed her hand; Marianne squeezed it; Mrs. Blaine positively glowed.

"And on that, we will leave you ladies to make your plans," Hart said. "Unless you've anything to say, Robin?"

Robin looked between them. He told Mrs. Blaine, "Thank you," hugged Marianne hard, and felt Alice put an arm round his shoulder. It took something of an effort not to cry.

He had to breathe deeply so as not to disgrace himself as they emerged into the street. "Was that your idea?"

"All of ours together."

"Then you're all marvels," Robin said. "I don't think I've ever seen her look so happy. We have talked about travelling, but it was always a fantasy. This—"

"We'll do it properly. They'll have everything they need. And Marianne will be away from Tachbrook and London and everything else, and she will probably declare herself Holy Roman Empress but that's not our problem. It's a choice for her, Robin. Is it what you wanted?"

Robin wiped his face, because he couldn't help it if his eyes were leaking. "It's all I wanted. She—I couldn't leave her, not to go off and be happy myself when she had lost everything. You understand, don't you?"

"Of course I do. I didn't expect you to."

"So you found a way for her to be happy, and it's perfect." Robin gave a little hiccuppy laugh. "She's going to teach Alice to say what she thinks. They're going to be terrifying."

"Unquestionably, but a long way away. Which, by coincidence, is how my rooms feel at this moment. Shall we take a hackney?"

"Let's go to my rooms. They're closer."

They took a hack anyway. Robin led the way upstairs, ignoring the now-towering pile of cards and notes on the hall table. He locked the door, and walked into Hart's arms.

"You are wonderful."

"I am nothing of the kind. You are," Hart said. "I couldn't speak last night. The same hatred on her face after all this time —I had thought she might have relented, somehow—the same jabs, the people watching and sneering and blaming us, the knowledge that people would *talk*. And you drove it away. You did what nobody has done for me in my whole life. You saw I needed defending, and you fought."

"I wasn't sure if you'd want me to," Robin admitted. "Actually, to be honest, I didn't think at all. I lost my temper. Marianne's not the only one with a temper, you know, I just hide mine better."

"An alarming thought, given that display. And she took so much on herself, because nobody will be talking about my mother now, only about her and Tachbrook. I owe her a very great deal, and I am deeply sorry she will have to bear the gossip she spared us."

"Don't overstate it," Robin said. "She was standing for me and you, yes, but she also needed a way out of that blasted marriage that salved her pride, and she took it when she saw it. Let's say, it worked for everyone."

"She is certainly better off not marrying that fool. Dear God, when he said it was about nothing—"

"He should have asked for a kick in the balls instead. Quicker and easier."

"I have said the wrong thing many times, but I've never said anything that stupid in my life." Hart's arms tightened on his shoulders. "And you—you were glorious, Robin, striding to my defence. To think I had the gall to offer myself as your protector when you're mine."

"I wish I could be," Robin said. "I'd like to do something for you because you've done everything for me."

"I've done nothing."

"Oh, you have. It's all different now. You saw me, and believed me, and didn't stop trying for me." He sniffed, rather than wiping his nose on Hart's coat. Not that it was a very nice coat, but there was a principle at stake. "And I really do desperately want to come to Aston Clinton and learn about hops, and I thought I couldn't, and you've made it work—"

"Robin, Robin." Hart urged his face up, brushing the tears away. "If I hadn't found a way, you would have. Or Marianne. Actually I feel certain she would have. She loves you."

"I love *you*," Robin said. "I've been in love with you for I don't know how long. Since—"

"—the fishpond—"

"—yes, the fishpond, and don't finish my sentences just because you know what I'm going to say."

"We have talked about your pernicious habit of making speeches."

"This isn't a speech, it's a statement. A simple declarative statement. I love you. You thought you were renting me for a month and you have me for life. Buyer beware."

"That will teach me." Hart kissed him. "Robin, my Robin. My incubus, my friend, my defender, and I hope my partner. I love you absurdly. I had no idea my life had enough room for anything so bright and warm and free as you."

"You need to stop making me cry," Robin told him. "I'll have a red nose, and then you'll be sorry."

"You will still be beautiful with a red nose. I cannot imagine how I have someone so beautiful in my arms. You might need to keep the red nose, in the interests of fairness."

"Rubbish. Did Alice tell you about all the sixes?"

"What?"

"She said, when you roll dice, any string of numbers is as rare as a string of sixes. People don't notice the ones that aren't obvious, but they're just as precious and special and unique. That's you. You're spectacular, and it's other people's loss if they're too stupid to see that. My Archimedes' constant."

"You are going to have to explain that a great deal more clearly, but not now," Hart said. "Dearest—"

That led to a great deal of kissing, in the course of which Robin found himself very comfortably settled on Hart's lap, tongues and limbs tangled. He slid his hands under Hart's coat and tugged meaningfully at his shirt. Hart pulled away. "Robin?"

"Mph?"

"I had a thought. I wondered if we might make another wager."

Robin felt a tingle run down his spine. He wasn't sure where this was leading, but he'd follow the desire straining in Hart's deep voice anywhere. "Wager?"

"Our arrangement ended yesterday and, while it was doubtless a very disgraceful business all round, it had some benefits, I think?"

"I certainly enjoyed it." It had eased Hart's way, given him something to hold on to. He was a man who liked things spelled out, after all. "Do you suggest we play again?"

"If you'd care to. I have liked learning to play with you."

"What are the stakes?"

"Same as last time. The winner to have whatever he wants of the other. Perhaps for a night, rather than a month, this time, but still—what he wants."

"You might lose," Robin said softly.

Hart met his eyes. "I know."

Oooh. Robin liked this. He liked it a lot. He liked it so much that, if Hart chose cards, he intended to cheat to the top of his bent. "I accept the stakes. What game?"

"Uh…" Hart looked around, and stood swiftly. He went to the wall and scooped a hand along it. "Races."

"What?"

"Racing." Hart opened his fingers to reveal a couple of beetles. "Pick your horse."

"We're going to race *beetles*?"

"Would you rather play a dozen parties of piquet, or wait for beetles to walk six inches?"

"An excellent point," Robin said. "What's the course?"

Hart cast a glance at the table. "This crack to that water-stain."

"Show me the fillies."

Hart put the beetles on the table, trapping each with a

finger. Robin considered. "The left-hand one has a noble bearing and, I infer, excellent pedigree. He's mine."

"Left it is," Hart said, with impressive seriousness in the circumstances, and brought the insects level. "Very well, drop the handkerchief."

"Ready. Steady. Go."

Hart released the beetles. The left-hand one set off at a stately pace, making Robin realise its size might not be an advantage. The right-hand one scurried forward.

"Damn it, Lefty!"

"Ha! Come on, you beauty!"

Hart's beetle made a sudden bolt sideways. Hart put out a finger to demarcate the lie of the track and stop it fleeing off the table. It veered off the other way, apparently unaware of what was required of it.

"Your horse is doctored," Robin said. "Ho, Lefty!" He crowed as his beetle—less nimble, but steadier—made its way past the finishing post. "Victory! I think that could catch on."

"Propose it in your club," Hart suggested.

"I've got more important propositions to make. Because, as you will have noted, I won. Which means, I believe, that I can ask what I want of you for the night."

"And have it. Whatever it may be."

Hart's voice had that delicious rasp again. Robin's chest felt tight with love and lust. "In that case, come here and kiss me while I decide what that is."

Hart did so, with sufficient focused determination that Robin found himself half-lying on the little table—he hoped his noble beetle had got out of the way—with Hart's thigh between his, blood pulsing like a mill-hammer, and a strong urge to beg for satisfaction.

Which was wrong. He could demand it.

"What I want," he said, looking up into those summer-blue eyes. "I want you to understand that I love you—you,

271

Hart, the most desirable, wonderful man in the world. I want you to take me to Aston Clinton and teach me to brew beer and grow roses. I want you to tell me you love me."

"I love you, Robin Loxleigh. My fortune hunter, and my greatest fortune."

Robin had to kiss him for that. "Excellent. And since we've cleared that up, and you are at my disposal…" He sat up and dragged a hand over his breeches-front, rough and unsubtle, watching Hart's eyes follow the movement. "Let's see where your imagination takes you, my Hart. Pleasure me."

EPILOGUE

The skies were the blissful clear blue that English summers received so much poetical praise for, yet so rarely delivered. The late roses were a riot of colour around them, their dizzying scent underpinned by the hum of bees and the shrill scraping of grasshoppers. Robin was absorbed in a letter from Marianne, his face lit with pleasure as he read. Hart was ignoring a newspaper in favour of watching him.

Marianne and Alice had safely arrived in Heidelberg, with Dr. Trelawney in tow plus a sturdy footman. Edwina had faced her temporary bereavement womanfully, and arranged several trips around the country in order to get used to life without her daughter. That meant Hart would be looking after young George for a few weeks when he returned from a visit to friends. He was looking forward to time with his nephew, and suspected Robin would be good with the boy.

"What news?" he asked.

"Alice is throwing herself into her studies, and her tutor may be able to arrange for her to attend university lectures with the men. Marianne is very proud of her accomplishments with the language, which you can tell because about a quarter of this is in German. They have made friends, seen the sights. Nothing about Verney, in case you're wondering."

Giles Verney had come to see Hart a day or so after the Aylesbury ball with the words, "I have had a great deal to think about." He'd apologised for a number of things that Hart had never particularly considered wrongs, then gone to Marianne to beg her forgiveness, and been sent off with a spectacular flea in his ear. He'd made his feelings perfectly clear, she informed him; she had no patience with chopping and changing; she was going to Heidelberg and would not be reneging on that for anything so trivial as himself.

Giles had accepted his schooling, but he hadn't given up, and when he'd told Marianne that he had asked for a posting to Frankfurt and begged her blessing to take it, she hadn't consigned him to perdition. Maybe he would regain her affections, maybe not. Robin said the process would be good for them both, whatever the outcome, and Hart had no doubt he was right.

He wasn't quite sure what had passed between Robin and Giles. Robin was never rude to or about him in Hart's hearing, but Giles had skirted him very warily indeed before his departure. He'd decided to let that play out as it would. If Marianne chose Giles in due course, he had no doubt that Robin would accept it.

"There's a full page of description of the city," Robin went on. "They seem to be enjoying themselves wonderfully. She sends her love."

"Return her mine when you next write."

Hart had taken a little time to fully grasp that Marianne knew all about her brother's affairs; that she had gone into battle for his sake as well as for her own. It still felt like a tiny miracle to be acknowledged as Robin's by someone else. Marianne approved; Evangeline Wintour had laughed raucously for some time at the news, then told him to bring Robin over, and got out the good brandy. And, possibly, there was James.

Robin had spent a fortnight staying with James Alphonso, receiving an intensive education in the mysteries of the brewing trade. They had got on like a house on fire, and Robin had charmed Theodora too, but when James had sent him back it was with a note to Hart saying how much he'd enjoyed getting to know his *dear friend*, underlined.

Dear friend—cher ami? Hart wasn't going to press for more, but the thought that James knew and liked Robin warmed his thoughts like sunshine. And Robin had done superbly. He was taking to the trade like a duck to water, absorbing information with his usual quick wit, befriending within weeks men who had been nothing but colleagues to Hart for a decade.

Robin gave a snort of amusement at something in the letter. Hart watched him, his newspaper forgotten on his lap. His lover was framed with flowers, his hair lit to honey-gold by the afternoon sun, his lips curved in a smile at the letter that Hart might have envied if he didn't have so many of Robin's smiles for himself.

Robin looked up, as though sensing his gaze. "Mmm?"

"I was just thinking how well roses suit you," Hart said. "As if you were born to be here, in my rose garden. You look like summer."

Robin put the letter down. "Do you know, Alice once told me you were incapable of giving such trivial things as pretty compliments or flowers, and she's usually right. And yet you've put me here amid an entire garden in bloom, and now you say something like that. You've been hiding your light under a bushel."

"You've taught me well," Hart said. "Or possibly I was

275

always capable of paying compliments, but I didn't know anyone who deserved them. Most people don't."

"That's my Hart."

Robin grinned at him. Hart smiled back, relaxed in his chair, and let himself smell the roses.

Thank you for reading! For more Regency shenanigans by KJ Charles...

Band Sinister

Sir Philip Rookwood is the disgrace of the county. He's a rake and an atheist, and the rumours about his hellfire club, the Murder, can only be spoken in whispers. (Orgies. It's orgies.)

Guy Frisby and his sister Amanda live in rural seclusion after a family scandal. But when Amanda breaks her leg in a riding accident, she's forced to recuperate at Rookwood Hall, where Sir Philip is hosting the Murder.

Guy rushes to protect her, but the Murder aren't what he expects. They're educated, fascinating people, and the notorious Sir Philip turns out to be charming, kind—and dangerously attractive.

In this private space where anything goes, the longings Guy has stifled all his life are impossible to resist...and so is Philip. But all too soon the rural rumour mill threatens both Guy and Amanda. The innocent country gentleman has lost his heart to the bastard baronet—but does he dare lose his reputation too?

"I have read some great romance books this year, but this rises to the top. Entertaining, intricately peopled, tightly plotted and simply ... perfect."—HEA USA Today

"A wonderfully entertaining read that, for all its light-heartedness, nonetheless manages to convey a number of important ideas about love, friendship, social responsibility and the importance of living according to one's lights. It's a sexy, warm, witty trope-fest." — Caz's Reading Room

The Society of Gentlemen Trilogy

Society of Gentlemen is set at a time of incredible privilege for the few and social turmoil for the many. Regency England is torn by war, poverty and social unrest, ruled by a draconian government. People are starving, rioting, rebelling. But the aristocrats dance on, in their glittering existence of balls, gambling, silks and scandal…

The trilogy covers three couples between autumn 1819 and spring 1820. A young Radical discovers his noble birth and is catapulted into a world of privilege, fashion and murder with a dandy as his guide. A government official and a revolutionary seditionist find common ground in their unconventional desires, under the threat of the gallows. And a lord in love with his valet struggles to find a way across the social abyss that divides them.

Each book is a standalone romance but the plots are linked.

"To truly appreciate the magnificence of this series you need to read the whole lot of them, preferably one after the other. This is because the stories are as intimately entwined as the lovers."–Sinfully

A Fashionable Indulgence

When he learns that he could be the heir to an unexpected fortune, Harry Vane rejects his past as a radical fighting for government reform and sets about wooing his lovely cousin. But his heart is captured instead by the most beautiful, chic man he's ever met: the dandy tasked with instructing him in the manners and style of the *ton*. Harry's new station demands conformity—and yet the one thing he desires is a taste of the wrong pair of lips.

After witnessing firsthand the horrors of Waterloo, Julius Norreys sought refuge behind the luxurious facade of the upper crust. Now he concerns himself exclusively with the cut of his coat and the quality of his boots. And yet his protégé is so unblemished by cynicism that he inspires the first flare of genuine desire Julius has felt in years. He cannot protect Harry from the worst excesses of society. But together they can withstand the high price of passion.

"The writing is superb with a strong feel for time and place, and all the relationships—the friendships as well as the romantic ones —are very strongly written. I will definitely be reading the other books in this series as soon as I can get my hands on them." —All About Romance

A Seditious Affair

Silas Mason has no illusions about himself. He's not lovable, or even likable. He's an overbearing idealist, a radical bookseller and pamphleteer who lives for revolution . . . and for Wednesday nights. Every week he meets anonymously with the same man, in whom Silas has discovered the ideal meld of intellectual companionship and absolute obedience to his sexual commands. But unbeknownst to Silas, his closest friend is also his greatest enemy, with the power to see him hanged—or spare his life.

A loyal, well-born gentleman official, Dominic Frey is torn apart by his affair with Silas. By the light of day, he cannot fathom the intoxicating lust that drives him to meet with the radical week after week. In the bedroom, everything else falls away. Their needs match, and they are united by sympathy for each other's deepest vulnerabilities. But when Silas's politics earn him a death sentence, desire clashes with duty, and Dominic finds himself doing everything he can to save the man who stole his heart.

*KJ Charles writes some of the most inventive historical romances around, and **A Seditious Affair** is one of my favorites. ... The stakes are high and deeply felt, and once you start, there's no way to stop reading this one. —Courtney Milan*

Many congratulations to KJ Charles proving that it can be done. Romance can incorporate meaty socio-economic and political context into the story-telling. And the resulting tale can be riveting and most definitely hot. —Smart Bitches Trashy Books

A Gentleman's Position

Among his eccentric though strictly principled group of friends, Lord Richard Vane is the confidant on whom everyone depends for advice, moral rectitude, and discreet assistance. Yet when Richard has a problem, he turns to his valet, a fixer of unparalleled genius—and the object of Richard's deepest desires. If there is one rule a gentleman must follow, it is never to dally with servants. But when David is close enough to touch, the rules of class collide with the basest sort of animal instinct: overpowering lust.

For David Cyprian, burglary and blackmail are as much in a day's work as bootblacking—anything for the man he's devoted to. But the one thing he wants for himself is the one thing Richard refuses to give: his heart. With the tension between them growing to be unbearable, David's seemingly incorruptible master has left him no choice. Putting his finely honed skills of seduction and manipulation to good use, he will convince Richard to forget all about his well-meaning objections and give in to sweet, sinful temptation.

"The realities of class, societal mores and politics heighten the tension in this emotional, deeply romantic look at the remarkable lengths we will go for love." —*Washington Post*

*"Everything I enjoy in a historical romance can be found in **A Gentleman's Position**. Accurate, confident and luscious, the writing brings Lord Richard Vane and his 'fox', David Cyprian, to glorious life."* —*All About Romance*

For more books by KJ Charles go to
kjcharleswriter.com/books

ABOUT THE AUTHOR

KJ Charles is a RITA®-nominated writer and freelance editor. She lives in London with her husband, two kids, an out-of-control garden, and a cat with murder management issues.

KJ writes mostly historical romance, mostly queer, sometimes with fantasy or horror in there. She is represented by Courtney Miller-Callihan at Handspun Literary.

For all the KJC news and occasional freebies, get my (infrequent) newsletter at kjcharleswriter.com/newsletter.

Pick up free reads on my website at kjcharleswriter.com.

Join my Facebook group, KJ Charles Chat, for book conversation, sneak peeks, and exclusive treats.

facebook.com/kj.charles.9
twitter.com/kj_charles